CHASING CLOUDS
FURTHER STRANGE TALES
FROM THE IVORY CRESCENT

— BOOK II —

Marcus Flacks

Chasing Clouds

FURTHER STRANGE TALES
FROM THE IVORY CRESCENT

— BOOK II —

SYLPH
EDITIONS

Contents

Dramatis personæ

KAI

Judicious and honourable prince of the realm, whose
tortured path leads him to find life and meaning in the
southern hinterlands of the Empire. Exudes a calm yet
regal presence. Has a great fondness for sweet cakes.

The Prince of Twilight,
The Lantern Lighter, Fated Fusion

FENG

Effervescent and elfin 'tomboy' daughter of a village doctor.
Strong-willed and animated, with a cutting tongue. Despite
her reticent femininity, her eyes are of rare beauty and
allure. Likes to tuck her hair behind her ears.

The Prince of Twilight,
The Lantern Lighter, Fated Fusion

LAN, 'THE LANTERN LIGHTER'

Enigmatic, blind servant shrouded in layered robes and
mystery. Appears as if from nowhere to bring light to
Prince Kai's evenings and perhaps his heart.

The Prince of Twilight,
The Lantern Lighter, Fated Fusion

ZEMIN

Large, powerful demon with green-tinged skin. Charged
with rounding up stray souls in the labyrinths of Diyu,
he is singular in the Kingdom of Hell for finding violence
abhorrent. His big heart and inquisitive nature eventually
lead him to risk all for love.

The Human Germ

YING

Poor, abused and partially crippled boy who is finally
thrown out and left for dead by his father and stepmother.
Finds his place in the shadows of a noble mansion, where
he learns to better himself to a point where impossible new
horizons open up for him. Silent, stealthy and shrewd.

The Palace Detective, The Enigmatic Eunuch,
Chasing Clouds

ZHONG KUI

Fearsome and formidable figure whose unfortunate
ugliness led him down a strange and unexpected path.
Now the powerful and mystical 'Demon Queller' charged
with the hunting down of all demons and ghosts on earth.
Has the unusual power of presenting an awe-inspiring first
impression which magically recedes from memory within
a short time.

The Palace Detective, The Demon Queller,
Mad Monk Bo, Chasing Clouds

THE CAPTAIN

Brilliant and loyal strategist and soldier who devotes his
life to his country's murkiest causes with nary a thought
for personal reward. His unwavering commitment is
deeply rooted in tragedy and loss. Tall, strong, handsome
and unnecessarily modest.

Clouded Realms, The Enigmatic Eunuch,
The Bloodied Brush,
The Portrait, Chasing Clouds

POLO

> Exotic, olive-skinned eunuch in charge of the young boys of the Palace. Has an unusual history and a strong personal bond with the Emperor. A kind heart with a mysterious side, but loyal and dependable. Exudes a subtle elegance and allure.
>
> *The Enigmatic Eunuch,*
> *Chasing Clouds*

MAD MONK BO

> Unexceptional man who somehow manages to circumnavigate the rules of reincarnation, thereby unwittingly locking himself into a dreary never-ending cycle. Old, withered, rude and cantankerous, he often resorts to wit as a weapon. Uncommonly flatulent.
>
> *Fated Fusion, Mad Monk Bo,*
> *Chasing Clouds*

CHUNG

> Hapless young soldier unexpectedly drafted to join the royal convoy in a dash to the Capital. Inexperienced and naive, he often becomes the butt of the jokes and pranks of his superiors. When the sole witness to a vile tragedy, he is faced with a great decision.
>
> *Self-righteous Suicide*

OTHER
CHARACTERS

LADY JIU

Aspirational and conniving governor's wife. Determined for her daughter to make it to Court. Her ambition seems to know no bounds. A fine-looking woman with crisp, sharp features.

The Prince of Twilight,
The Lantern Lighter, Fated Fusion

LORD JIU

Powerful, ambitious and treacherous governor of a southern province. Skims profits off military and economic funds designated for protecting the border from the province's barbarian neighbours. A small man with a character to match.

The Prince of Twilight, Fated Fusion

JIU FEI

Lord and Lady Jiu's effete and entitled daughter. Has a certain charm, but is used to having every aspect of her life orchestrated by her ruthlessly ambitious mother. A tragic waste of youth and beauty.

The Prince of Twilight,
The Lantern Lighter, Fated Fusion

THE EMPEROR HUI

Ageing and weary patriarch of China and father to Kai. Wise old head who manages to paper over the cracks of an ailing Empire. Forms an unusually strong bond with Polo, the eunuch in charge of the Palace boys. Has unusually elegant hands and long fingers.

The Prince of Twilight

THE EMPEROR YU

The Emperor's loyal and steadfast brother, uncle to Kai and his two brothers. Fearless, brilliant general who is the right arm of his ageing brother. When crisis hits, he steps up to take the reins of the Empire to halt a bloody succession battle. Has two sons who fall under the influence of the powerful Wu clan.

The Prince of Twilight

WENLING

Shepherdess trapped in a bucolic prison by her powerful, absent husband. Finds true love, family and tragedy when two worlds unexpectedly collide. Fastidiously clean and always well put together.

The Human Germ

DUKE OF WU

Treacherous, devious and powerful leader of the Wu clan who manages by foul means to ascend to the position of Emperor of China. Generations of his descendants continue on his dark path in search of ultimate power.

The Human Germ,
The Demon Queller

THE GREAT YAMA

Awe-inspiring King of Kings of Diyu, the underworld. For ever struggling with the complexities and pitfalls of running a vast bureaucracy and often forced to wield his immense power to maintain his domain's delicate equilibrium. A thoughtful, complex character, immeasurably powerful and diffident at the same time. Has a penchant for true quality and artistry.

The Human Germ,
The Demon Queller,
The Lantern Lighter,

CHU LAI

Infallible servant of the Empire from his position as Minister of War. Sagacious and politic, he is also not afraid to operate in the grey areas of running a country. A powerful and loyal friend.

The Prince of Twilight, The Palace
Detective, The Enigmatic Eunuch,
The Bloodied Brush, Chasing Clouds

FAN

Tragic ex-wrestler, soldier, local militiaman and drunkard who loses his child, his wife and his way. Finds love again but ends up abandoning another child. Powerful and large-framed, he cuts a formidable figure.

The Palace Detective

STEPMOTHER

Buxom cook and housekeeper at the mansion of a prominent nobleman. Finds love in the arms of a broken man, but has no compassion for his wretched son. A woman of great energy with an eye for a deal and a flexible approach to morality.

The Palace Detective

THE MARQUIS

Powerful noble with even more powerful friends. Hosts the Empire's top brass at his impressive mansion. In league with a potent, clandestine cabal. Elegant man with chiselled features.

The Palace Detective

LORD WU

Influential and scheming current leader of the Wu clan. Orchestrates every strategic action of his large and powerful family, with one eye always on absolute power. Has a crescent-shaped birthmark on his neck.

The Palace Detective

THE MAGISTRATE

Accomplished, pragmatic and respected scholar who manoeuvres in the complex political world with brilliant subtlety and sterling results. Approaching retirement, he proves an extraordinary teacher and mentor. A man of innate elegance and disarming charisma.

The Palace Detective

QUEEN HONG

Extraordinary queen of the Kun. Sharp, witty and kind, her attention is always on the well-being of her subjects. Supremely capable in the arts of governing and negotiation, she is often called upon by neighbouring kingdoms to mediate in order to avoid armed conflicts. Allergic to bee stings.

Clouded Realms,
The Bloodied Brush

KING OF KUN

Benevolent and artistic joint ruler of the most benign and consummate kingdom on earth. More at ease with organizing festivities and nurturing artistic talent than with statecraft. Particularly fond of purple robes.

Clouded Realms

BAI

Amazonian, Nordic beauty who is captured by the cruel An kingdom and enslaved. Her journey leads her from the darkest depths to the highest peaks. Has near-white hair that flows down the length of her back.

Clouded Realms

MOTHER TIGER

Mythical and majestic creature at the heart of the An origin story who returns to bring about an ancient prophecy. Has snow-white fur striated with pale grey.

Clouded Realms

DU PING

Zhong Kui's handsome and popular childhood friend, who stands by him to the bitter end and beyond.

The Demon Queller

HAI

Zhong Kui's sister. Slender, demure and quiet, but with a sharp intellect and dry wit.

The Demon Queller

SHAO XU

Jovial chief of the Palace police who enjoys the company of young boys. A polite and clever man who maintains good relations with all. Particularly fond of Polo. Has an insatiable sweet tooth.

The Enigmatic Eunuch

THE CHIEF EUNUCH

Venerable chief administrator of the Palace household. A charming and kindly man, of high moral standards and great empathy, who develops an unfortunate compulsion towards gambling in his dotage, which leaves him open to unforeseen problems.

The Enigmatic Eunuch

MADAME YAO

Tall, elegant owner of the most prestigious and respectable pleasure house in the Capital. Thoughtful and empathetic, she would do anything for a friend, colleague or employee. Has seen much sadness in her life.

The Enigmatic Eunuch

DU YUN

Highly knowledgeable and skilled connoisseur who rises to be the keeper of the Imperial Collection. A loyal and valued friend and colleague of Chu Lai who becomes a member of his unconventional group.

The Enigmatic Eunuch,
The Bloodied Brush, Chasing Clouds

WEN NA

Talented artist from a respected southern family. A woman of effortless charm yet feisty character. Moved to the Capital to apprentice under a celebrated master before becoming a sought-after artist in her own right.

The Bloodied Brush, The Portrait

OLD LADY MENG

Kindly matron of Diyu who administers her famous 'Tea of Forgetfulness' to souls before they are reincarnated.

The Lantern Lighter,
Mad Monk Bo

GENERAL WU

Young, ambitious general who has risen through the ranks on the back of his family's connections, influence and shadowy strategies. Nonetheless a strong leader who commands fear in his men.

The Prince of Twilight,
Self-righteous Suicide

PRINCE AND HEIR TO THE THRONE

Capable and highly educated eldest son of the Emperor and brother to Prince Kai. Strong military leader and diplomat ready to take over the reins of leadership when a fateful and dastardly act changes everything.

The Prince of Twilight,
Self-righteous Suicide

SHY

Enigmatic spy at ease in the company of Chinese, Mongols and nomads alike. Feels he owes a debt of honour to China and to the Captain's family in particular.

Chasing Clouds

JI REN

Fascinating demon with a host of powers that he can only call on instinctively. A master of hunting and evasion in the service of a sinister brotherhood. Tired and jaded with more to live for than the dangerous errands he is forced to run. Strangely handsome.

Chasing Clouds

THE OBJECTS

LINGBI SCHOLAR'S STONE

Dramatically shaped stone on an old *tieli* wood stand. Charged with vital *qi* energy, it has a mesmerizing effect on its owners. Beguiling.

Proem

DAYBED-SHAPED TABLE STAND

Very rare scholar's table stand made to resemble a fine daybed. The *huanghuali* frame is beautifully offset against a *huamu* (burr) central panel that recalls the soft, inviting nature of a woven cane seat. Unusual feet add to the piece's mystique.

Proem

OVAL BRASS CENSER WITH CHILONG DRAGONS

Of highly unusual oval form, this elegant censer can easily double as a handwarmer on chilly winter evenings in the studio. The lively coiled *chilong* dragon in the opening dances freely in the billowing clouds of incense when the censer is in use. Mesmerizing.

Proem

SMALL GILT BRONZE STRIDING DRAGON

Evocative figure of a sauntering dragon in a lithe, almost feline pose. Delicate and refined but with a distinct sense of power.

The Prince of Twilight, Fated Fusion

HUANGHUALI INCENSE HOLDER STAFF

Extremely rare and unusual wooden shaft carved with a
dragon at the handle and a bronze phoenix head at the
end. Used to hold an incense sphere on a chain.

The Prince of Twilight,
The Lantern Lighter, Fated Fusion

SLENDER ZITAN DOCUMENT BOX

Exquisitely conceived and crafted box with deeply rounded
edges and brilliantly integrated white brass metalwork.
The solid pieces of timber used are dark and lustrous
like jade.

The Palace Detective

HUANGHUALI MITRE-JOIN TABLE
WITH SWORD-SHAPED LEGS

Extraordinary feat of design and craftsmanship with crisp,
refined beadings, complex joinery and deeply curvaceous
lines. A piece of profound archaic resonance.

The Palace Detective

SET OF BOXWOOD DESK IMPLEMENTS

Superbly crafted brush rest and seal paste box both
carved with the motif of the *lingzhi* fungus, a powerful
symbol of longevity. Faithful travel companions for an
elegant scholar.

The Palace Detective

BRUSH CARVED WITH DRAGONS

Impressive and oversized calligraphy brush crafted
from mellow-toned timber and carved with animated
long-nosed dragons amongst clouds.

Clouded Realms,
The Bloodied Brush, The Portrait

HUANGHUALI THREE FRIENDS OF WINTER CUP

Unusually large wooden cup crisply carved with the 'Three Friends of Winter' – pine, prunus and bamboo – plants revered by scholars for being faithful companions in the barren winter months.

Fated Fusion

HUANGHUALI FOLIATE TRAY

Skilfully crafted tray of evocative shape, emphasized by well-carved beadings. The rich textures of the patinated surface are a testament to its great age.

Fated Fusion

DRUNKEN LORD'S CHAIR

Unusual folding chair with a cane back crafted from *huai* or locust wood. Of antique design, the reclining back and elongated arms are exceptionally comfortable for the weary scholar who wishes to rest, especially after a few flasks of fine wine.

Fated Fusion, Mad Monk Bo,
Chasing Clouds

SMALL IMPERIAL BOX CARVED WITH CLOUDS AND INLAID WITH SILVER

Extraordinary small treasure crafted for imperial pleasure. Body covered with animated, overlapping clouds carved from the *zitan* surface, whilst the central panel is alive with the archaic thunder and lightning motif inlaid in silver wire.

Self-righteous Suicide

IMPERIAL CLOUD PILLOW

Elegantly arched pillow crafted from a single, solid piece of rare *zitan* timber. Surfaces carved all over with graceful, stylized clouds. Only an imperial head could be supported by such a heavenly object.

Chasing Clouds

Proem

wherein the curtain is raised, revealing
a happy man overcome by an uncanny
dolour, whose circling thoughts are
interrupted by a rather unusual
interlocutor who proceeds to take him
on a journey to the primordial oceans,
the bustle of ancient marketplaces,
the boudoirs and kitchen cabinets of
improbable past personages, and ends by
dispelling the gloomy cast over his mind.

A MAN CAN STAND ON A THRESHOLD or on the edge of a precipice, but unless he knows what is on the other side, he does not know which one it might be. So it was for Victor, a middle-aged man of reasonable success, decent intelligence and high tastes. Life had been good to him, especially in his adulthood: beautiful wife, two fine children, prestigious address and, above all, a rather fine collection assembled over decades with guile and knowledge as well as passion, a rarity these days. However, of late, he had felt something shift – nothing tangible, no mid-life crisis, no affair either by him or his wife, no illness and no children with dramatic problems. Nonetheless, he had a feeling, something lurking in the back of his mind or hovering over him like a cloud. He felt on the very edge of something, but could not make out if it was bad, good or indifferent. But he knew it was there, he could sense it, he could feel it, a physical presence in his life that he could almost touch.

True, the world was in a mess, changes and uncertainty were everywhere, in every corner of an ever-shrinking globe, but that, it seemed, was not it. True, he was of middle age, more worn, more cynical and yet somehow more romantic and hopeful too, almost as if, when one approaches the final adventures, one wants them to be greater and more meaningful than those that went before. But how could one retain the same passion, the same verve and most of all the same belief, when one has seen and done so much already, been both impressed and disillusioned by people, things and experiences? Don't we lose the joy of knowing and wanting to know? Don't we fade as optimistic forces of nature to mere shadows of our youthful, vibrant selves? Don't we lose the ability, bit by bit, to laugh, love and lust…to live? Perhaps he had just had a hard day, or week or month; but he hadn't. Perhaps it was this lack of either despair or elation that was making him feel like this, floating along, in a not at all unpleasant void of normality, anchored and transient at the same time. He had never believed in heaven or hell, or God for that matter. He believed in the one journey, and that had always seemed like more than enough. He had also believed in people, until little by little they had let him down – and yet, there were always the lifetime companions, ever there and ever dependable, and the bright new stars with all the vivacity and vitality of novelty and the promise that they might prove true. There were also the individuals who surprised in the positive and a whole new generation that he had watched grow.

Above all there were things. The objects and treasures that he felt defined a great part of him; placed him in a position of privilege and prosperity as a collector and aesthete, though they were becoming exceedingly hard to add to and were often superseded in the public psyche by vacuous fashion and untethered commercialism. 'Sounds to me like you are getting to be an old fart!' he would say to himself. So, on this particular evening, with his wife already retired for the night and his second or third, 'last' glass of wine in his hand, he found himself standing in the centre of his study, barefoot, actively seeking out, with his toes, the very edge of this imaginary precipice or threshold, whichever it may be. Amused by his childish imagination, he walked over to his favourite table and drew up a chair. Here he sat and took stock of the old friends on the table.

To his left, a complex *lingbi* scholar's stone, a wave, a splash, a mountain; he was never able to decide which, but its raw elemental power had always moved him. To his right, a table stand in the form of a platform or daybed; its monumentality, for such a small thing, always struck a chord, its refined details and juxtaposition of timbers ever engaging his fickle eyes. Upon this stand, an unusually shaped incense tool vase, impossibly linear and curvaceous at the same time, and also a bronze, oval covered censer, its lid adorned with a pierced *chilong* dragon that glistened with antiquity. He had prised the latter from a famed collector who would always be twice or thrice the connoisseur, scholar and enthusiast than he might hope to become.

Deciding to commit to the moment, he went to the kitchen seeking some incense to burn. Opening the drawer where he remembered it being, all he could find was a single, unfamiliar cone. 'Bloody kids must be into incense now too,' he chuckled to himself, remembering how they mocked him for burning that awful-smelling stuff when they were small. Returning to the table, he placed the cone inside the oval censer, lit it and replaced the lid, the *chilong* apparently pleased. It had been a long time. His eyes took in the warm, intimate scene as his nostrils inhaled the incense and his ears enjoyed the silence, broken only by the occasional car passing outside.

Enveloped by this quilt of artistry, antiquity and ritual, he was suddenly overwhelmed by a small avalanche of emotion. He placed his crossed arms on the table and buried his head in the folds, hoping for a small pocket of comfort that he feared he hardly deserved. As the emotion welled up inside him, he tried to breathe and resist, to bend his mind and body to his will, in the firm knowledge that all was well and that he had a wonderful life. But his body, or soul, was not to be denied this night and he began to weep, first just a few rolling tears, then a torrent, punctuated by sobs and near convulsions. The liberation was almost palpable, and he totally ceded to the demands of his capricious psyche.

'Why do you weep?' he heard a deep, mellow voice ask.

Surprised and embarrassed, he sat up bolt upright and turned to the doorway to see where the voice had come from. His wife? His son? His daughter? The ignominy of it, caught weeping into one's sleeve alone at night for no good reason. But to his surprise there was no one at the door, which remained firmly closed, nor in the room, as a quick scan soon confirmed.

'Over here,' the voice said again, 'to your left.' Staring, somewhat disconcerted, toward the left corner of the room, he could see nothing.

'Here,' repeated the voice, 'right by your side.'

Now slightly concerned, he elected, given the absurdity of the situation, to cede again and reply in kind.

'May I ask', he began tentatively, 'whom I have the pleasure to be speaking to?'

'It is me, your favourite *lingbi* stone. You know – the one that you sit staring at occasionally. The one whose calcite vein you sometimes fantasize about skiing down.'

Staring incredulously toward the fine stone on the table, he traced its contours and crevices with his eyes. It looked as it normally did, but its surfaces seemed somehow effervescent, almost alive with energy. The light? The incense? Probably the wine.

'Tell me,' it continued, 'why do you weep?'

Now genuinely unsettled, but not knowing where to turn, he answered simply and in all honesty.

'I don't know.'

'Perhaps I do. I hope you don't mind. You are only the second of my custodians that I have been able to converse with.'

'Not at all,' he replied, feeling rather silly. 'Please, go ahead.'

'I believe you have allowed yourself to become trapped in the Dusty World.'

'The Dusty World?' he enquired. 'That's the humdrum world of the ancient Chinese scholar official. How can I be trapped in that world?'

The stone sighed in seeming impatience. 'The Dusty World is the human world, a human creation, made up of human desires, concerns, obligations and most of all man's temporal clock. The Dusty World can be a magnificent world, as it can be a terrifying and awful one. Its joys and pleasures are equalled only by its horrors and injustices. But there is an ever-growing problem.'

'What do you mean?' he asked, now genuinely engaged.

'Whilst many have become adept, and some even expert, at navigating this world, they forget that it is simply their creation, with rules and values they have dreamt up themselves. To appreciate fully the wonders of life one has to escape from time to time.'

Suddenly regaining a certain amount of cynical lucidity, he felt a rush of heat course through him, perhaps anger, perhaps fear. Probably both.

'I am not sure I understand. Or care to, for that matter. Who are you, anyway? Show yourself, explain yourself!'

'Yes, perhaps I have overstepped. Please forgive me. Let me first tell you about myself. Would that be alright?'

Calm returning, despite the abnormality of the situation, he nodded his consent.

'For a long, long time,' the stone began, 'I was not. I was a part or millions of parts of a single whole flowing in a vast sea. Over aeons, sediments of many types began to meld as other layers formed above. Through pressure and the concentrated influx of *qi*, a solid was born, deep in the mud beneath the sea. More aeons, and my world heaved and lurched, grinding plates, eruptions of molten energy. Masses rising above the waters. This was a time of physical chaos and disruption, followed by a settling, peaceful slumber. Now buried not far from the earth's surface, I lay in blissful tranquillity as the subterranean waters flowed over my surfaces at will, slowly shaping my contours. The waters were my constant companion, connecting me to the greater whole. As were the mud, the minerals, the organisms and other stones like me.'

The stone seemed to pause and after a brief silence Victor felt compelled to interject. 'Please continue.'

'Yes, of course. Those were times of balance and serenity. But then came the cold, and the waters stopped visiting; stillness and silence reigned, and I was alone, isolated in a cold grave. It was a never-ending epoch of void, with the flow of *qi* barely perceptible.'

'Then what?' Victor interjected.

'Ah, then warmth returned, and slowly the waters returned to caress my bruised and lacerated surfaces, healing and soothing them with their constant flow. The *qi* coursed strongly once again, and richness and diversity filled my world. And then...' Again, the stone paused.

'And then?' he questioned.

'And then my world was shattered, and my existence was transformed for ever.'

'How? By what?' he implored.

'By the Dusty World,' the stone replied. 'First, I heard the thudding and scraping nearby, and slowly but steadily it grew louder and closer. Then one day I felt a movement in the earth around me. Sharp objects thrust into my nest, disrupting the waters and striking my surfaces. Then in an instant I was wrenched from my underground paradise and heaved up to the surface. Stunned and terrified, I feared that this was some sort of end, perhaps the end of the world. But as I was hauled out of the trench, through the clinging mud that had for so long been my blanket and companion, I was bathed in something of untold warmth and intensity. This was my first encounter with sunlight, you see. It felt like raw *qi* searing into my core. I was then washed and had a small protrusion chiselled off, then placed on some soft grass. That night – a concept that was new to me – my now naked surfaces were bathed in a different light. Cooler, more mysterious, but no less majestic. And I lay there under this cycle of lights for what would be months to you, but felt like an instant to me.'

'Then what happened?' Victor asked, unable to mask his eagerness.

'I was taken on a cart to a village, where this fine stand was fashioned for me out of *tieli* timber. Then I was taken to a city and passed from person to person, amongst much noise and enthusiasm, until I found my first custodian. Or rather, he found me, in the shop of a renowned dealer in objects of beauty and antiquity. He was a young man with an exceptional eye, called Du Yun. He had the unusual job of looking for treasures that might befit the Imperial Palace.'

'And did you end up in the Palace?'

'Goodness, no!' chuckled the stone. 'I was far too complicated and cumbersome to be of imperial taste. No, my path took an altogether different direction.'

'And did you speak to your custodian Du Yun as you do me?'

'Not at that time. He did not hold onto me for long and soon gifted me, albeit reluctantly, to his mentor, the magistrate Yang.'

'That is some gift,' mused Victor, inadvertently out loud.

'Indeed, but not for Du Yun, because to him Yang was like a father figure. Unfortunately, for one with such a sharp eye, Du Yun was never able to see the true measure of this man. I could feel his ignobility almost at once.'

'How is that?'

'Well, when I was first gifted to Magistrate Yang, there was much delighting about my rarity and quality. Yang thanked Du Yun profusely as he examined me and pawed my skin, seeing and feeling nothing. Then he struck me with a brass chopstick, and I emitted a most sonorous tone. It was the first time I sang. I had no idea such pure notes lived inside me. But after just a few days, he consigned me to a dark, cold corner under a table. In the end, he discarded his friendship with Du Yun too, in a most cruel and treacherous way.'

'What happened to you then?'

'I remained there, gathering dust, for many years, until I was accidentally discovered by his young son, Dan.'

'And did he keep you and cherish you?'

'No, unfortunately, he was to leave the household shortly after finding me. For one so young, he was a child of extraordinary perception and the *qi* coursed

through him with great power. Only later did I discover that he was born of a Fox Queen.'

'A Fox Queen? Really?' enquired Victor sceptically.

'There is much you don't know about your world, custodian, and even less of other ones. Yes, the Fox Queen Wei was his mother, and a magnificent beast she was too.'

'And what happened to you next?'

'Well, the fact that I had been cast under a table led people to believe I must be of little or no worth. So, the Magistrate's family gifted me to the family housekeeper, a Miss Yeoh.'

'And did Miss Yeoh cherish and appreciate you? Did you commune with her?'

'Miss Yeoh was a kindly person, but simple. She did not have the time nor the inclination to contemplate a scholar's stone. She kept me in the bottom of a linen cupboard until a travelling merchant passed through town and she sold me, or rather undersold me. I changed hands several times in a short while, as merchant sold to dealer and so on, until the price on my head had reached a fair approximation of my value.'

'And?' Victor questioned.

'Well, when an object is under-priced there are always many people ready to purchase it with the idea of turning a quick profit. But when an object, however fine, reaches a price that reflects its true worth, one has to wait for a true collector.'

'And did this collector come?'

'Well, you might not believe it, but yes, and it was quite a surprise.'

Victor looked bemused and waited for the stone to continue.

'One day, as I sat in a merchant's shop covered by a velvet, for full dramatic effect, a man and a boy came in looking for interesting treasures. After the usual build-up, I was revealed, and you won't believe who I saw sitting opposite me.'

'Who?'

'None other than Du Yun, the man who had owned me for a brief while, and Dan, the boy who had bumped into me in that dark corner under evil Yang's table! I could not believe it. There they were together.'

'And what happened?' asked Victor.

'Well, of course they were not going to leave without me, so they bought me! And they had to pay a pretty hefty price for me too, as my merchant owner was no fool and knew what he had.'

'And did you commune with them?'

'With Du Yun, some time later, but perhaps that is a story for another time. Suffice it to say that I changed hands several times after my rebirth. Eventually, I did return to Du Yun. By then, he was finally ready for me. After that, most of my custodians kept me until they passed on, and on one occasion I remained in the same family for three generations. But we will have plenty of time to discuss that...perhaps this would be a good time to return to discussing your Dusty World?'

Victor nodded, though less than enthused by the abrupt change of subject as he was greatly enjoying the history of this most unusual stone.

'I was aeons in the making and millennia at one with the ebbs and flows of the natural order of things. The *qi*, or life force as you like to call it, was strong within me. Then came the cold void, a feeling like I had been abandoned by the universe. Normality returned and, like with most things, one is far more appreciative of them once one has lost them and finally gotten them back. But' – here the stone paused, perhaps unsure how to proceed – 'but fortune saw to it that I was reborn into another dimension, above the surface, kissed by the lights of both ethereal circles. Moreover, I became an individual thing, a revered object in a world that moved at a million miles an hour, where changes come almost as fast as the cycle of light and darkness or the seasons. And I have been exhilarated by my short moments in this new world, but have also seen a tragic flaw develop day by day, year by year and decade by decade.'

'A flaw? What flaw?' Victor asked forcefully.

'The flaw in humankind is its dwindling ability to escape the prison of its own making: your Dusty World.' The stone's tone was far more sombre now. 'As you stride with ever-increasing pace to fulfil the duties and goals you have created over time, you forget to escape from time to time and reconnect with a larger truth. Many of my owners loved me for the compliments they would receive about their fine taste, but they rarely pondered my surfaces or lost

themselves in my ridges and valleys. My purchase alone seemed to placate their desires and they forgot why people began to commune with stones such as me in the first place. I have not communed with a human for almost two centuries. Not because this requires a magical power or a special bond, but simply because they had forgotten their part in the process. Their participation required a desire to commune, a commitment to stop, breathe, and take a step away from their world and attempt to glimpse into mine.'

A little humbled by this discourse, Victor took a deep breath and sheepishly said: 'So how come you communed with me? As you said, I have become trapped in the Dusty World, without even contemplating escaping from it.'

'Because, my dear custodian,' the stone continued with a tone that washed over him like a warm ray, 'although your mind and intellect, refined as it has become, never considered such a communion, your natural body has been yearning for it for many years.'

Victor was struck by the idea that his body or soul might have been yearning for something that his intellect seemed totally ignorant of. Almost at once, he understood, without fully understanding, the damage that such an inner conflict might cause within a person. He stared at the stone, his teacher, and smiled. How arrogant and stupid he had become to consider that he alone could determine the parameters of happiness. How soulless a life if one believes one has all the answers. As his fingers inadvertently caressed the seductive curves of his favourite table, he felt himself taking a step over the threshold that had been perturbing him of late.

'It is just a first step on a long path,' whispered the stone, 'but I hope we will have more opportunities to discuss this…after all, there are so many old friends in this room that you have not yet properly met.'

Suddenly overcome with a deep weariness, Victor could feel slumber closing in around him like a warm, inviting blanket. He was awakened by the dawn chorus of birds chirping in the trees outside his window. Rising gingerly, he walked over to the curtains and drew then open. He was met by a spectacle of natural beauty the likes of which he had rarely seen. The light, dancing between night and day, was casting its magic on the naked branches. The dew on the grass glistened as if winking at him. He stood mesmerized for some time. Then, regaining his composure, he turned to go upstairs, catching a glimpse of his favourite *lingbi* stone sitting proudly on his favourite *huanghuali* table. A smile crept across his face as he turned and headed toward the door.

Whilst he knew, in his heart, what he had experienced to be true, he could not help himself.

'Crazy dream!' he murmured out loud.

Chasing Clouds

Further Strange Tales
from the Ivory Crescent

The Prince of Twilight

wherein the germ of love is planted under rosy-fingered skies; wherein threats are overlooked and thwarted; wherein a man aged by trial, though not bereft of hope, returns to a tarnished haven.

Chasing Clouds

FURTHER STRANGE TALES
FROM THE IVORY CRESCENT

Twilight

IT HAD ALWAYS been Kai's favourite time of the day. Each day when the sun began to sink in the sky, he could be found on his habitual perch on the high terrace to watch its final yellow rays illuminate the horizon. Before his eyes, the sky would transform itself slowly, almost imperceptibly, into a pantheon of colours, punctuated here and there by lazy meandering clouds. A sudden freshness would rise in the air, borne along by an animated breeze. As he sat there in quiet contemplation, he would turn over in his hands the small figure of a gilded dragon that he was never without. He often imagined it soaring across the burning sky. And then came his very favourite moment of all, a moment he dared not miss: the lighting of the lanterns. As the shadows lengthened, threatening his elegant estate with darkness, so the lanterns were systematically lit, welcoming the evening and bathing the house and garden in the mellow hues of a hundred dancing oil lamps. The ritual was captivating, breathing a new life and energy into the rooms, corridors and walkways as the glow of the lanterns revealed them one by one. But most of all, there was the ethereal elegance of the lantern lighter.

Apparently she had arrived at the estate a few weeks before his return, seeking employment as a lantern lighter. The head of the household was somewhat bemused, given that she was a woman, draped head to toe in strange, multi-layered pale green robes and, most surprisingly, because she was blind and had her eyes covered by a silk scarf of the same pale green. Thinking how he might send her politely on her way, he watched as she withdrew from her robes a strange-looking wooden shaft and glided into the next room, the main reception hall. After a moment's hesitation, he followed her, resigned to throwing her out for her insolence if nothing else. However, on reaching the main hall, he was astonished to find that all the lanterns were lit and burning bright. He had no idea how she could have lit more than twelve lanterns, hanging up high, so quickly, but by then he had ceased to care. She was hired on the spot.

Kai first spotted her about a week after his arrival, when he had finally been able to shake off some of the strain of his final tumultuous weeks at Court, the anxieties of his escape and his interminable journey down to the

southernmost borders of the Empire. For these had been the most testing months of his life. But perhaps we should start at the beginning.

Southern tour

Kai was the middle son of the Emperor of China. He was given his name, which means 'triumph' or 'victory', in the hope that he would grow into a proud leader in the imperial forces. This was not an unusual aspiration to apply to a prince of the realm, especially a second son, who traditionally often became a military commander. However, in this case, it was a particularly unsuitable name. Not because Kai's career was lacking in victories over China's enemies, but rather because his personality was the complete opposite of the stereotype of the triumphant leader.

From very early on it was clear that Kai was a studious and conscientious young man who tended to excel at most things. However, he was not one who enjoyed the spotlight, praise or fame. His natural inclination was to help others – his father when he had to hide a mistress, his brothers when they locked horns, his country when it needed protection, even his uncle when he needed his wayward sons rescued. All this and more he did with sterling results. But then he would deflect the praise onto those he helped, and fade again into the background.

As a teen, Kai had been sent on a grand tour of the southern provinces by his father. This was quite customary, as a second son was always more likely to serve on the peripheries of the Empire rather than at Court where his elder brother and his heirs would wield power and influence. Before he left, his father gave him a special gift. It was a small gilt bronze figure of a striding dragon and was said to be a thousand years old. 'You may not be the biggest dragon in the kingdom,' his father said, 'but you are a golden dragon to me.'

His trip was long and trying, but fascinating. Of the endless stream of impressions and experiences, it was his stay at a large estate near the border to the southern barbarian state that remained most deeply etched into his memory. The estate was owned by the governor of the province, Lord Jiu, a man of great power and ambition. It was near a small village and about five miles from a large border town made vastly prosperous by trade with its exotic neighbours. News of Kai's impending sojourn had sent all of the local gentry into a delirium as they all began to vie to meet such an important dignitary. Such a visit would have been an event in a town in a province neighbouring the Capital; imagine the furore it caused in one of the farthest outposts of the Empire. All the great and the good prepared banquets and festivals that they hoped would entice the prince's presence. They were also particularly eager to display their daughters in the hope that one might capture the prince's heart and propel the entire family into the highest echelons of nobility.

Of course, everyone understood that it was Jiu's young daughter Fei who stood the greatest chance, both because of the unbroken proximity she would enjoy to the prince and because of her secret weapon: her mother. Fei's father Lord Jiu was a skilful manoeuvrer, able to navigate even the most treacherous political waters and still come out on top. However, even his notable talent for back-room dealings paled in comparison to the brilliance of Fei's mother, Lady Jiu. Using every skill in her formidable arsenal, from flattery and manipulation to intimidation and outright sadistic violence, she would stop at nothing to promote the rise of her family. Fei herself had received the most extensive education and training in everything that might be required to ensnare a powerful mate and thrive in the most genteel and demanding of courts. She was also very beautiful and exceptionally shapely for one her age.

From the evening of his arrival Kai found himself at the centre of a seemingly endless progression of banquets, fêtes, carnivals, hunts, dinners and parties. And night after night, he found that he had been seated yet again between Fei and her mother. Kai, however, was a shy soul and in certain ways still quite naive. He was ill at ease with all the attention, but also blissfully unaware of the intricate machinations going on around him. His respite was twilight. At this time, as all and sundry were busy preparing for the evening festivities, he was left alone to sit on the high terrace and delight in the smells, glows and colours of the vista. As darkness fell, a procession of servants would appear to light the great number of lanterns that lined every walkway and illuminated every room. Somehow, in this exotic landscape warmed by the balmy air, filled with the perfumes of rare plants and bathed in the fading southern light, he found this ceremony profoundly magical.

On the fourth and penultimate day of his visit, he asked to visit the local village. His father had always minded him to learn about a place from the ordinary people who lived there. Of course, no one of any import was interested in joining this lowly expedition, so Kai and his faithful manservant were accompanied only by a small retinue of his personal guards and a very earnest local scholar. The walk to the village was almost entirely through the grounds of the estate. At its boundary was a wooden gate, unmanned, that joined the main path to the village. He was introduced to, amongst others, the local monk, carpenter, blacksmith and town policeman. He took time to talk to each of them, hard as it was for him to overcome his shyness, and he slowly relaxed into the visit.

The physician's daughter

The final stop was a house on the edge of the village that stood in the shade of a giant *wutong* tree. This was the house of the local apothecary and physician. A person of such importance would normally have resided in the larger nearby town, but his proximity to the Jiu estate was seen as necessary, especially given the many eminent visitors they entertained.

As they approached, the physician was standing in front of his house with his wife, young son and daughter, who was about Kai's age. Kai attention was drawn to the daughter, solely because he noticed her begin to pull away from the group before her mother grabbed her arm. She was tall and slender, with a physique more like a young boy, perhaps emphasized by her short hair. She was, apart from her clear desire not to be there, wholly unremarkable. Yet, as he approached, smiling at each of them in turn, he caught a glimpse of her eyes as she raised them briefly from her default sulking downward stare. Her eyes were quite exceptional, piercing and welcoming at the same time. Their aqua colour was made up of an indecipherable melange of blues and greens shot through with fiery streaks of orange. They were unlike anything he had ever seen.

The physician stepped forward, bowed deeply in greeting and introduced first his son, who followed suit, then his wife, an exotic-looking woman clearly from a neighbouring kingdom. As she stepped forward to pay her respects, she released the girl's arm. In a flash, moving with all the speed, dexterity and elegance of a panther, the girl turned, ran and climbed up the *wutong* tree, not stopping until she had reached the highest branches.

'Feng!' the physician and his wife screamed in unison. 'Come down here at once!' But to no avail.

After a rather embarrassing and prolonged series of apologies, the party were invited in for tea. Their hosts had obviously gone to a great deal of trouble, with an impressive spread of rare fresh fruits and pastries, as well as some truly excellent tea. The visit was however fraught with tension for the hosts, as a result of the unruly and unforgivable behaviour of their daughter, and they must have been greatly relieved when the party bade them goodbye. There was no further sign of their daughter, presumably still hiding away high up in her tree.

That evening a simple banquet was prepared, with just the Jiu family and a dozen or so other local dignitaries in attendance. Again, Kai was seated between Fei and her mother. Almost immediately, they both began to interrogate him about his day.

'Was it horribly dull?' asked Fei.

'Yes, not much to see there,' agreed Lady Jiu. 'Especially for someone like you.'

Embarrassed and discomfited by their words, Kai nonetheless began to recount his day. Though they feigned the bare minimum of interest, they could clearly not have cared less about the people he had met and only perked up somewhat at the mention of the physician.

'Oh, yes!' said Lady Liu. 'He is a very fine person. He has been most helpful to us over the years. He has known Fei since she was born.'

'Yes, and I almost met their daughter, Feng, except she fled and climbed up a tree!'

'What!' shrieked Fei.

'Oh, awful child. Part barbarian, you know. I never understood why such a fine man could not find a suitable Chinese wife.' Lady Jiu's condemnation left no room for misunderstanding.

'Well, I thought his wife was very beautiful,' Kai ventured tentatively, wanting to defend them but also not wanting to cause offence. 'I can certainly see where Feng got her extraordinary eyes!'

'Her eyes?' questioned Lady Jiu.

'What was so extraordinary about them?' Fei quizzed with an accusatory tone.

Kai was saved by one of the local dignitaries rising and proposing a toast to the prince. As they drained their cups, Kai was sure he heard Lady Jiu mutter, 'Her eyes indeed!' under her breath.

The day before Kai's proposed departure to begin the long journey back to the Capital, a messenger arrived with important news from the borders of the province. Heavy storms had caused flash floods and the river had broken its banks. The torrents had greatly damaged the bridge that was the only major crossing for over a hundred miles. Rather than embark on a journey that might be hazardous and many weeks longer, Prince Kai's entourage, at the invitation of their host, settled on staying where they were until repairs to the bridge could be made. In the end, their sojourn was extended by six weeks. With little planned and Lord Jiu often away on various 'essential' trips, Kai was often left to his own devices. Having quickly exhausted all the nearby sights, he took to strolling through the estate, admiring the unfamiliar plants and birds, then continuing into the village, where he was always greeted warmly and soon with far less formality and pomp. Soon these leisurely, unaccompanied strolls became an almost daily occurrence.

On the first of these walks, passing the physician's house, he spotted Feng, who upon seeing him dashed inside. The next time, he strolled past whilst she was helping her mother with the laundry. Not able to escape so easily, she simply looked down at the ground, but as he passed, he glanced back and his eyes found hers for an instant. They were truly extraordinary. Over the course of a week, he made sure to pass the house every day and by the end of it was greeting them with a wave which was cheerily reciprocated by all except Feng, who was too embarrassed, but did afford him a half-smile.

The next day, Kai said he was just going for a stroll in the grounds and would perhaps try to meditate or compose some poetry; either way, he would appreciate solitude. This greatly put out Fei, who overheard this as she was on her way to invite him for a stroll herself.

Kai meandered through the grounds for a while. Once he was out of sight, he set a direct course for the village and the physician's house. However, when he got there he was distraught to find that the house and grounds looked deserted. Disappointed and not sure what to do next, he performed a couple of comic about-turns. Finally, when he had resigned himself to returning to the estate, he heard a voice from high up in the *wutong* tree:

'No one is here, they've all gone to town.'

Taken aback, but also exhilarated, he replied as best he could.

'Oh, I see. Well, never mind.' Then drawing up all his courage he ventured: 'And may I ask who you might be? High up in that tree. A monkey, perhaps.'

'A monkey? Certainly not! I am a majestic phoenix perched high in my *wutong* tree!' the voice replied.

'A phoenix?' said Kai. 'That's certainly impressive. I live in a palace and I have never seen a phoenix in the flesh.' And then again pushing his nerve to its limits he asked, 'I would very much like to see such a rare bird. Might that be possible?'

Silence.

Then after a few seconds the voice replied:

'Well, I don't see why not. You seem to be a polite enough chap. But you will have to come up here if you really want to see me.'

A previously unknown energy coursed through his blood. Luckily, when it came to physical challenges, Kai was both fearless and very well trained and although it took him some time, he finally made it to a large branch near the top of the tree, where he perched somewhat awkwardly. Here he was greeted by the sight he had hoped for. Sitting on a branch about four feet away from him was Feng, the physician's daughter, peering at him with those captivating eyes. After a tense attempt at polite conversation, they found they could break the ice with a series of jibes and jokes about magnificent phoenixes and tree-climbing princes. And so they stayed up in that tree for over two hours until Feng spotted her family coming back down the path, about two hundred feet away. Jolted out of her affable mood, she panicked

and bolted down the tree with almost impossible skill and elegance. Kai followed, far more slowly, and as she was about to dash into her house, he shouted, 'I may come by again tomorrow, lady phoenix!' It was the bold and instinctive move of one who did not wish this moment to end. And Kai regretted it almost immediately, until, almost through the door, she turned and shot him a smile that almost made him lose his balance.

Kai had no recollection of walking home that afternoon. He felt like he had been floating on clouds. The following day Kai returned to visit Feng and every day after that. They spent many hours together, joking, walking, throwing stones, climbing and talking. She was the first real friend he had ever had. To her, he was not a prince, because she had no real concept of what that meant. To her he was just an awkward boy; to him, she was all he was not and could never be: fearless, reckless and fun-loving, with no pretensions and no desire to be anything else. One day, he invited her to walk through the estate with him. At first she was hesitant, but when he told her that the entire family was away on a short trip to visit relatives, she agreed. When evening came, he persuaded her to stay for his favourite moment, twilight. Together, in silence, they imbibed the spectacle, occasionally glancing knowing smiles at each other. Then, when the lantern-lighters began their tour, he instinctively grabbed her hand and pointed for her to look.

That night, Kai could hardly sleep. He could not remember a more perfect day.

The next day brought the return of the Jiu clan and some very unwelcome news. Whilst on their trip, they had made a detour to the damaged bridge to inspect the progress of the repairs and they were happy to report that it was now strong enough to allow horses to pass. It would be another month or less before heavy carts could pass. The prince's entourage resolved that they had imposed on their hosts' hospitality for far too long already and would make arrangements for the long journey home. Kai felt a knot deep in the pit of his stomach. As uncomfortable as staying with the Jiu clan had been, with their constant entertainments and pretensions, not to mention their transparent machinations, Kai realized one thing above all else...the very last thing he wanted was to leave this place. Still, he had some time.

Over the next week, he tried to see Feng as much as he could. The Jiu family, however, were intensifying their arrangements involving him, probably hoping to milk every last drop of benefit from their illustrious guest. Only Lady Jiu seemed a little different. A little colder, more diffident and quick-tempered with him. In preparation for their impending departure, Kai decided to write a letter to his father to let him know of the new plans. With the express postal system, it would arrive long before him. He gave a brief description of his sojourn with the Jiu family and of their hospitality. 'I think they would like me to marry their daughter,' he joked. Then he proceeded to tell him all about Feng, that she had been an amazing friend and had made his time here so much more enjoyable. 'You would like her,' he wrote. 'She is more boy than girl, can climb trees like no other…oh, and she has extraordinary eyes.' Kai sealed the letter as he had done so many others and handed it to one of Lady Jiu's servants to take care of.

Late one afternoon, about a week before their departure, he claimed to be feeling unwell and excused himself from another dull expedition to town to show him off. Instead, with the aid of his manservant, he snuck out and headed off to meet Feng. They walked to a vantage spot that overlooked the neighbouring kingdom, with its expanse of rice field terraces making a wonderful sight. Feng had brought a picnic and they sat on a log, eating and laughing and joking.

'Why were you called Kai?' she asked him.

'Oh, I suppose all princes have to be given names that predict great achievements. Mine are apparently victories and triumphs. Although that seems unlikely!'

'You never know,' she said kindly. 'I am sure you could be whatever you put your mind to.'

'And you…how come you were named Feng? Was it because you have a nose like a beak?' he joked and she threw a twig at him.

'No, actually…Feng is not my given name. I had, and have' – she chuckled – 'a habit of hiding in our *wutong* tree when I was upset. So my parents nicknamed me Feng, after a phoenix, which traditionally lives in a *wutong* tree.'

'I see. So what is your real name?' he asked.

'Oh, that I will never tell you. Never ever...it's so embarrassing.'

'Surely it can't be that bad.'

'Oh, but it is. It's a stupid pretty girly name,' she huffed.

'How about a clue?' he prodded. She shook her head. 'Just a little clue?'

'Very well, it's a stupid flower...and that's all you're getting.' And she threw another twig at him.

'Well, if you aren't going to tell me I shall have to give you a name. Perhaps one fit for a young lady.' She frowned. 'I know...how about Fei? That's a lovely name,' he said with a wry smile.

She shot him a fierce scowl, then picked up a large leaf and hid her face behind it as if it was a fan. Giggling and fluttering her eyelids, she began her parody.

'Oh, my. I am beautiful, rich, talented and did I say beautiful Fei! I am so wonderful that I am sure I will become a princess one day. All I need is a handsome prince to marry!' She intensified her pouting and fluttering. 'I would be perfect for a life at Court!'

They both roared with laughter. Then he said half-jokingly, 'Perhaps one day you might come and visit the Capital?'

'Oh...I am not sure Court is the most appropriate place for a bumpkin like me.' Seeing his disappointment, she added, 'But perhaps you will be able to visit again.'

Her tone was optimistic, but she could see a sadness glazing over his eyes. So, she stood up, pushed him over and ran to the nearest tree, shouting, 'You'll never catch me, your Highness!' in an affectionately mocking tone. Kai gave chase, temporarily forgetting his melancholy. As he chased her up the tree, straining his every sinew to keep up, he realized that this was the happiest he had ever been. He also realized that this may be one of the last times he would be able to see Feng. His departure was approaching fast.

As it happened, the following day he was engaged with some farewell festivities arranged by the Jiu family. At the evening banquet Fei, again sitting next to Kai, was trying to play her final cards.

'So, tell me,' she began, 'what will you tell the Court was the highlight of this prolonged stay in our humble province?'

Slightly embarrassed, Kai replied with all the tact he could muster: 'Why, this wonderful estate, of course, your family's exceptional hospitality, the balmy breezes and of course your spectacular twilights.'

Fei smiled. Then, gently placing her hand on his, she cooed: 'Anything else? Anyone else…a young girl, perhaps?'

And here, looking back on this moment all those years later, he saw that his naivety had got the better of him.

Impetuously, he replied: 'Well, yes, of course, Feng, my best friend!' Even as the words came out, he knew it was a mistake.

'What?' Fei protested. 'The scrawny tomboy from the village?'

Kai saw red and almost lost his composure as he noticed Lady Jiu eavesdropping. 'Yes,' he said, 'that's the one. She is great fun.' Fearing that he had not defended her enough, he impoliticly added: 'And she has extraordinary eyes, don't forget!'

That night Kai berated himself for allowing himself to be goaded into such an unsophisticated retort. The next morning, as the final plans were being made for the departure, he wondered if he might be able to sneak off to the village for a final farewell. However, overhearing a conversation at breakfast between the head servant and Lord Jiu, he leapt to his feet, excused himself as elegantly as he could and started running toward the village. Apparently, there had been a serious fire in one of the houses. They had been able to stop it from spreading, but the one house was totally destroyed, and all the inhabitants feared dead. The head servant had not mentioned which house it was, but as he sprinted, his lungs exploding with pain, Kai had a dark premonition. The first thing he spotted when he approached the physician's house was the scorched trunk of the giant *wutong* tree. As he drew closer, he saw that all that remained of the house itself was a pile of still smouldering beams and debris. Dropping to his knees, he wept uncontrollably into his hands. How he got back to the estate, or indeed much of the journey home, was still a blur to him.

A painful return

Over the years, during the many meetings at Court he attended about the state of the Empire, he would always enquire about that distant southerly province that had once been his temporary home. With time, the tone of the reports shifted. Apparently, the southern neighbours had become far more bothersome and audacious, mounting numerous raids on the rich trading towns on the border. Governor Jiu had repeatedly asked for and obtained ever greater sums of financial support from the Court in order to raise and maintain a large standing army to defend the Empire from this growing threat.

At Court, Kai had grown into his position of power and was a great support to his ageing father as well as his older brother, the heir to the throne. He also had to act as a calming influence on his two brothers, who were often at odds with each other on matters of policy and strategy. Kai's younger brother, unlike him, was extremely ambitious and had his sights set on ever greater power. Meanwhile, his uncle, a highly decorated general, had been away on a successful campaign against China's enemies in the north-west, so the Court could not count on his stabilizing influence. Instead, the Court witnessed the emerging influence of his two sons, the younger of whom, during his posting in Mongolia, had come under the influence of the powerful Wu clan. Kai was thus called upon to spend much of his energy and time putting out fires and soothing egos amongst the many different cliques vying for power.

One person whom Kai could always rely on was one of his father and brother's closest confidants, Chu Lai, a trustworthy and very gifted minister. So, Kai was hardly surprised when Chu Lai came to visit him late one night. What surprised him more was Chu Lai's flustered state and the news he brought. After the formal greetings and a calming drink of tea, Chu Lai explained that he had come straight from briefing the Emperor. The southern province governed by Lord Jiu had been attacked by the neigh-bouring kingdom and was under threat of being totally overrun. When Kai asked how it was that the large standing army there had been unable to defend the border, Chu Lai told him what he had just heard from a returning

spy he had sent. Lord Jiu had apparently been keeping most of the monies sent to finance the standing army for his own family. Meanwhile he had been tasking mercenary nomadic soldiers from near Tibet with the defence of the border. This scheme seemed to have worked for several years, until the mercenaries started raiding and looting local towns on both sides. The king of the powerful southern kingdom that bordered the province got wind of Lord Jiu's arrangement and, using the raids as an excuse and Lord Jiu's weakness as an opportunity, invaded first the border towns, then a large chunk of the whole province.

Of course, an army would have to be sent to repel this invasion, and, together with the Emperor, Chu Lai had thought that Kai might be the perfect man to lead such an expedition.

First, he had some experience with the territory. Secondly, he had an excellent military record and was both well liked and respected within the army. Thirdly, sending one of the Emperor's own sons would send a clear message that should dissuade China's other neighbours from any similar ideas. But, Chu Lai explained, it was too risky a mission to entrust to Kai's exuberant younger brother; after all, after repelling the invasion there was still a lasting peace to be negotiated. It would also be unwise to send his elder brother, the heir to the throne. His presence was needed in the Capital. Fully understanding the situation and not at all unhappy at the prospect of being away from the intrigues at Court, Kai agreed and said he would make arrangements to leave as soon as possible.

The campaign was far more straightforward than anyone could have imagined. The enemy, perhaps lulled into complacency by the decades of dwindling Chinese defences, was no match for the imperial crack corps. There was no need even for Prince Kai to delve into his impressive tactical arsenal. Once the invaders had been driven to the border, Kai made the decision to push on with a smaller force whilst the bulk of the army set up suitable defences and prepared to back up the advance forces if needed. As it happened, within a week, the Chinese forces were besieging the enemy's capital. This was exactly what Kai had hoped for. Whilst he had no interest in a drawn-out siege, he was now in an excellent bargaining position. Others might have tried to enforce a greatly punitive peace, with loss of territory and vast tributes to be paid to China, but Kai took the negotiations in a different direction. Acknowledging Lord Jiu's part in this debacle and thus, by association, China's part, he crafted a peace in which the long-term safety of the borders was secure and, more importantly, the safety, promotion and expansion of trade routes was agreed upon as a joint venture, with each country benefitting.

The negotiations concluded, the Chinese forces retreated to the border towns and set up temporary garrisons there. Kai had thought that he might make a quick return to the Capital, with a small force, leaving the province in the hands of one of his generals. His job was done, and he was keen to return home. Before leaving, he decided to visit the estate of Lord Jiu, who had disappeared with his family after the invasion, their whereabouts unknown. Arriving at the main house, he was delighted to find that it was largely untouched, the invaders having used it as a base after finding it abandoned. He also found, to his surprise, that many of the former staff had returned to the estate and resumed their tasks, despite the fact that nobody was paying them.

The head of the household explained that they had resumed their duties more out of loyalty to the estate than their disgraced former employer. Besides, one of Lord Jiu's hidden stashes of coin had escaped the invaders' plunder. He thought they had enough to see out the year, by which time perhaps a new owner might be found.

Late that afternoon, Kai took up his usual position on the high terrace, ready to enjoy once more, for old times' sake, the spectacle of the twilight. As he sat there sipping his tea, he thought of how much had happened since he was last here. He had been just a teenager then, innocent and free. Now he was a battle-hardened, highly experienced and pragmatic man. He had never had much time for emotions in his later life. His position and tasks at Court were far easier to perform if he limited himself to largely superficial relationships. But as the wind picked up, bringing with it a rich bouquet of familiar smells, and the light began to change, he felt himself suddenly overcome by emotion. In that moment, on that terrace, he sat watching and feeling again as he had not done for a decade. And he wept. Tears of joy for what now seemed like yesterday and tears of grief for what had been lost. He realized that in his maturity he had coerced his mind to suppress all the instincts and feelings that had made that summer so extraordinary. But now, with his senses once more unlocked, his soul felt like it had just been jolted back into life.

The following day, he summoned the head of the household and all of the staff. He suggested to them that if they were in agreement he would become the new owner of the estate and keep them all on for as long as they were happy to stay. He would stay for a month to oversee some minor refurbishments and changes. After that, he could not be sure when he might return, but they were to keep up the estate as if he were living there. Visibly delighted, they agreed. There was much rejoicing and a makeshift feast was arranged that evening. The following morning, he asked if he could be taken to the village by cart. Arriving at the spot where the physician's house had once stood, now barren and overgrown in the shade of the charred remains of Feng's magnificent *wutong* tree, he dropped to his knees and wept again, as he had done all those years before. Regaining his composure as best he could, he instructed the servants that the site was to be cleared and maintained. They were also to dig up three cartloads of earth from there and transport them back to the estate.

Over the following weeks, Kai directed some minor changes to the house and garden. The earth from the charred site had been placed in a mound in full view of his favourite terrace. He instructed the head gardener that the following spring a mature *wutong* tree, as large as he could find, was to be planted on top of the mound, which was then to be covered in high grasses. Feng and her family would at last have a suitable resting place. Although he could think of them as a family, he could not yet allow his thoughts to rest on Feng. That was a wound he knew would never heal and right now it was as raw as that cursed day.

In the end, he stayed at the estate for just over a month, enjoying his twilight ritual and feeling somehow reborn. But he knew it was only a matter of time and the day soon came when he had to bid this haven goodbye once more.

Empire in turmoil

Prince Kai's return journey to the Capital, with his small retinue of horsemen, was far quicker than the march down. In under a month he was back at Court and being briefed on the darkening skies by his friend, the minister Chu Lai. Taking advantage of the army's expedition south, China's north-western neighbours, now unified under a single khan, started making regular raids on the border. The general in charge of the Chinese defences, the Emperor's brother and Kai's uncle, had been wounded and was on his way back to the Capital. The Emperor had decided to deal the barbarians a decisive blow and ordered for a huge Chinese army to be raised. The Emperor's firstborn and heir was to lead the expedition. Kai immediately offered to accompany him despite having just returned, but his offer was turned down. He, together with Chu Lai and other trusted ministers, was to help the Emperor keep the Court and its rivalling cliques in check.

That autumn, the largest Chinese army in a century set off for the north-western provinces. By mid-October they had arrived and began engaging the enemy immediately in an attempt to avoid a drawn-out winter campaign. The strategic master plan drawn up by Kai's convalescing uncle, now back in the Capital, was to try and draw the barbarian army out into open battle whilst a further Chinese army from Mongolia, led by General Wu, would come up and attack the enemy's unprotected rear. Faced with the already vast first army, the enemy would never suspect that a further force had been mobilized against them. Secret messengers kept the two Chinese armies in constant contact. By early November, General Wu's cavalry was close to being in position to deal the final blow.

However, on a cold and blustery night just days before the assault was to begin, a storm began to brew over the Capital. Despite the crashing rain, many came out to watch the violent, almost continuous flashes of lightning, interrupted only by deafening claps of thunder. As the skies began to clear, a comet was seen shooting across the night sky, chased by a cloud distinctly shaped like a dragon. Improbable a sight as it may have been, hundreds claimed to have seen it. This inauspicious portent was followed the next day with the news that the Emperor had died of sudden heart failure that night.

With events moving at breakneck speed, General Wu's army inexplicably turned around and headed back to the Mongolian border. Kai's brother immediately began his return journey to the Capital to take up his father's mantle and be declared emperor. However, during his trip back, rumblings about the loss of the mandate of heaven began getting louder at Court. These fires of discontent were fanned by a continuous stream of rumours and disinformation emanating in the main from the powerful Wu clan.

With a swift victory in the north-west now impossible, the large Chinese army would have to bed down for winter. As the heir to the throne made his way swiftly across the northern provinces, the situation at Court was deteriorating. Things went from bad to worse. When he was about three days from the Capital, the heir apparent set up camp in a small valley to rest his men and horses before the final push. Whilst they slept, a force of highly skilled assassins entered the camp, slaughtering every man. When news of this massacre reached the Capital the following day, the Court became a frenzy of activity. Fearing a coup, possibly by the Wu clan, Kai's uncle, perhaps the only man in China with the requisite authority and support from both the military and the Court, declared himself emperor and was enthroned as the Emperor Yu, after an emperor of the mythical Xia dynasty of antiquity. Within a few weeks full order was restored. The new Emperor had been able to avert further disaster, but his actions were not welcomed by all.

Kai was one of the first to lend his support, which was gratefully received by his uncle. However, Kai's deceased brother's son and Kai's own younger brother, having seen their lines of succession to the throne all but destroyed, were furious and out for revenge. For the next three months Prince Kai, Chu Lai and many of the most senior ministers at Court worked tirelessly to appease discontent and shore up the new Emperor's political power. In mid-March, an attempt was made on the Emperor's person, but he narrowly escaped. Anyone who stood to gain in any way from his death was seemingly under suspicion from some quarter or other. Soon enough, fingers began pointing at the previous Emperor's surviving sons, Prince Kai and his younger brother. Within days, a plot allegedly hatched by Kai's younger brother was brought to the Emperor by a leading eunuch. He was arrested in the early hours of the morning and imprisoned without trial.

That very same morning, Chu Lai visited Prince Kai extremely early, before news of the plot or arrest were made public. Chu Lai explained that the Emperor had no doubt of Kai's loyalty, but that the situation at Court had reached such an incendiary pitch that Kai's position was no longer tenable. Kai protested in the most vigorous terms, in disbelief that anyone would call his loyalty to his Emperor into question. Chu Lai however said that the Emperor insisted, as he could no longer guarantee Kai's safety.

'I am afraid he is right,' said Chu Lai. 'I fear that the Wu clan have been behind this whole thing, from murdering your older brother to framing your younger one. It doesn't take a genius to work out who is next.'

Kai couldn't argue with Chu Lai's dark foretelling and reluctantly agreed to leave the Capital without delay.

'The Emperor has suggested you return to your new estate down south,' said Chu Lai. 'There you will be appointed governor and, at least, can keep one border safe from threat.'

Return to the sanctuary of twilight

And so it was that Kai found himself once again sitting on his favourite terrace, awaiting the arrival of his favourite time of day. He was well into the fourth month there and slowly the toxic residues of his final days at Court and his perilous journey south were being washed away by the seemingly imperturbable tranquillity of this sanctuary from the dusty world. The works he had ordered had all been carried out in exemplary fashion and from his vantage point he had a perfect view of the majestic *wutong* tree that had been planted earlier that year. Already it had shown its first flowers, by next year it would be in full bloom. And so, as he sat, reclined, with a cup of wine in his hand, feeling fresh streaks of cool air begin to intermingle with the fading heat of the day, an inadvertent smile spread across his face. For soon the shadows would lengthen and the estate begin to glimmer in the intoxicating glow of the lanterns and finally, she would appear.

The lantern lighter would step quietly onto the terrace, almost totally hidden beneath her flowing robes. Only her mouth and nose were visible. Her movements were silent and impossibly lithe. And though she inexplicably managed to light the hundred lanterns that illuminated the estate in a fraction of the time that would have seemed possible, here, on the highest terrace, her tempo slowed to an elegant saunter as she performed her captivating dance. One of her conditions on taking up her position was that no one could be present whilst she worked. However, knowing that this could hardly apply to the master of the house, here, on his favourite terrace, she resorted to an artful and deliberate ceremony that he found it impossible to look away from. Working at this pace, it would have taken her most of a day to light all the estate's lanterns.

As she moved from lantern to lantern, the lantern lighter would rise on her stepladder and deftly hook each lantern on her short, exquisite hanging staff whilst she kindled the flame. When she was done, she would give a small bow, her only acknowledgment of his presence, and head off down the garden in the direction of the *wutong* tree before disappearing from sight. Kai would heave a deep sigh that both bemoaned the end of his twilight reverie and began his anticipation of the next day's ritual.

One evening, as she was tending to the lantern nearest him, the ceremony almost complete, he was seized by an almost desperate sense that this moment should not yet end. As it happened, serendipity lent a hand and she accidentally dropped part of an oil lamp onto the floor. Seizing the moment, he leapt from his seat to retrieve the fallen object. She took it back and thanked him, though he could hardly make out the words. Now totally unsure how to proceed, he surprised himself.

'I am sorry to have startled you,' he said tentatively. 'I was just thinking that you come here every day and perform your task in such an exemplary manner and…' He paused. Had this been a mistake? 'Well, I really just wondered what your name was?'

'My name is Lan, my lord. After the orchid flower,' she replied, her voice betraying a trace of agitation.

'That is a very pretty and graceful name…very…feminine,' he answered awkwardly. What a fool, he thought to himself. Were those tensing creases around her mouth betraying a sense of displeasure? Had he offended her or simply made a fool of himself, or both?

But then she seemed to relax and smiled, with a warmth that dazzled him, but long before he could even catch his breath she was halfway down the garden. That night when he shut his eyes he could still see that smile bearing down on him from above and he drifted off into a deep sleep the likes of which he had not experienced in decades. The next morning, he awoke with a renewed energy and sense of purpose. He set about his day with a vigour and enthusiasm that he had not had since he was much younger. All day he rode this wave of unexpected *qi*, in animated anticipation, for each day was sure to end with twilight…and the lantern lighter.

—II—

The Human Germ

wherein a creature most atypical, though sound of heart and mind, finds the exit to his sunken lair & becomes enamoured of the sylvan hills beyond; its poise disturbed, his former home, a dark realm, begins to roil with wrath and mutiny.

Chasing Clouds

FURTHER STRANGE TALES FROM THE IVORY CRESCENT

Diyu

THE UNDERWORLD, or the Kingdom of Diyu, is perhaps the most labyrinthine place ever created. In physical size, it mirrors the earth above it. Its capital, Youdu, is a city as large and bustling as any above ground, with palaces and temples, administrative buildings and city walls, roads, trails and stairways. There are jagged mountains and raging rivers, leafless forests and frozen seas, lightning storms and hurricanes. What there is little of is light. In Diyu darkness reigns; darkness and cold. Freezing, shadowy, lonely cold – except for those places cursed with raging fires, molten liquid and infernal heat.

However, this is not only a place of judgement and purgatory. For some, this dark, inhospitable place, this ruined landscape of anguish and penance, is home. Who are the wretched creatures cursed to live out their existence here? Well, they are many and they are varied.

Whilst Diyu's transient inhabitants are made up of the souls of the dead, there are more than just souls in Diyu. To deal with the mere logistics of this constantly changing population of human souls awaiting judgement, purification and rebirth, there is an entire army of kings, judges, officials, bureaucrats and guards. These beings range from celestial spirits to industrious administrators, from permanent human souls to mythical creatures. And then, of course, there are the demons. But perhaps first we should look briefly at how Diyu actually works.

Infinite cycle

Upon arrival in Diyu, a soul is escorted by guards, many half-man, half-beast, to a dark lofty chamber to hear its judgement. Originally, it was the reigning King of Hell, the Great Yama himself, who would sit in judgement over these souls, directing them to their ghastly destiny. However, it soon became evident that for all his ominous power, the Great Yama had a very unusual character fault: empathy. Before long, the other lords of the ten Courts of Hell were challenging him on judgements they felt were too lenient. Though he privately found the idea that anyone could best his judgments ridiculous, Yama was nevertheless aware, from long experience, that his underlings were only too eager to pounce on any sign of weakness. After a brief deliberation, he therefore announced a new protocol. The duties of judging souls would now be undertaken by the lord of the first Court of Hell, his closest ally, Qinguang Wang. The Great Yama's mind, he declared, was too vast and complex to undertake such a straightforward and linear task. He was required to deal with far greater issues, issues that the other lords of Hell could not possibly begin to comprehend. In one elegant move, he had both extricated himself from an onerous and unpleasant task and strengthened his hold on his kingdom.

In the first Court of Hell, a newly arrived soul is placed in front of a magic mirror that replays all of its mortal sins. Nothing escapes the mirror, although it is unclear if the sins replayed are the most serious committed or the ones that torment the soul the most. On the rare occasion that a soul is blemish-free, it is sent to Paradise, where it resides for a time before returning to earth or sometimes remains as a deity. The condemned soul, however, is invited to visit the appropriate one of the remaining Courts, depending on its sins. To get there, it has to wander through the cold and dark mazes of Diyu, then present itself to the lord of its particular Court. The punishments administered by the Court are designed to fit the crime. These include the Pool of Filth and the Hell of Ice for conmen and robbers, gamblers and thieves. Perpetrators of murder by stabbing are forced to climb a mountain of daggers. Drug addicts and tomb robbers are grilled. Tax dodgers and rent avoiders are pounded with large stone mallets. Gossips have their tongues ripped out and exam cheats are disembowelled. This is just a taste of the major punishments, as they are endless in variety and sometimes unique.

Once a soul has been purified, having been tortured in all of the appropriate ways, it is escorted to the tenth and final Court, where a final judgement is passed. But the obstacles do not stop there. The soul must pass through the Wheel of Reincarnation to determine, based on its past life, if it should return to earth as a human or animal. To a life of comfort and joy or sorrow and suffering. Finally, in order to erase the soul's memory of its previous life, Old Lady Meng gives it a cup of the Tea of Forgetfulness before it is sent back

to earth as a pure slate. It is then reborn and lives its life, only to die and return to Diyu once more to be judged, tortured, purified and returned. It is a simple system and fool-proof, except if one considers the sheer number of souls that need to be processed in a never-ending cycle. The bureaucracy, the paperwork, the logistics that go into shuttling millions of souls from one Court to another are easily overlooked by the outsider. With the population on earth growing ever faster, the strains and stresses on this archaic machine increase daily, weekly, monthly and yearly. So, it is hardly surprising that the odd mistake happens.

Demons and functionaries

The apparatus at the centre of the daily running of Diyu is made up of two main groups: functionaries and demons. Now, functionaries are a strange lot. Some are formerly mortal souls, others celestial beings. Others still are strange half-breeds that are often of human form with animal heads. Like humans on earth, functionaries come in all shapes and sizes. They also come in every shade of virtue, from the brightest white to the deepest black, though most are an undecipherable grey. Also like humans, they are vulnerable to the lure of ambition, jealousy, rivalry, greed and every other petty shortcoming you can imagine. As there is no money in Diyu, the going currency is dependent on the passions and predilections of the parties involved. Some crave fine or exotic foods from the surface, others wine and tea. Many are prone to a strong desire for one of Diyu's rarest commodities: sunlight. There are of course many other, rather more idiosyncratic cravings, but in the end, the major currency of Diyu is power. Every functionary in the vast bureaucratic apparatus spends his days jockeying for position and influence, constantly primed to leapfrog a colleague or bring down a superior. Most of the time, they are not even sure why they do this, what their final objective might be, but they toil toward it no less fervently every day, by foul means or fair.

Demons, on the other hand, are a far purer sort of breed. Their job in Diyu is to administer the punishments determined by the judges of the ten Courts, so that the souls in question might be purified prior to reincarnation.

Demons were created expressly for this purpose and are exceptionally good at their jobs, aided by certain special attributes and powers – size, strength, fire-breath, venomous fangs and razor-sharp claws, to name but a few. They too have simple desires – chiefly for food, blood and, oddly, sleep – but as long as these are satisfied, they are usually happy enough to go about their work, taking pride if not outright pleasure in the heinous acts of torture they inflict. By and large they have no great ambition and pose no great threat to anyone but to the souls they torture. That is, unless they are somehow placed in unfamiliar surroundings. Here, without their familiar boundaries and schedules, they can get disorientated. Even in the corridors and tunnels of Diyu, it is not safe to let demons roam free. So, with the systems in place to keep them segregated and content, all had been well for millennia – until, that is, something rather unexpected occurred.

Black sheep

Demons were created long before man. How they came into being has always been somewhat of a mystery, but legend has it that they sprung from fragments of rock that fell to earth when the great goddess Nua repaired the broken sky with the five coloured stones. It is said that this is what gives demons their strangely tinted skin and special powers. Once they were freed from their stones, they were found to be the perfect tools for the purification of souls in Diyu. As already mentioned, the demons took to their new task with great zeal and efficiency. One cannot help but imagine what other purposes might have been found for them.

Amongst demons, there is great variety. No two are the same. There was one, however, who was perhaps the most singular of them all. His name was Zemin. Even his name was most unusual for a demon, as it meant 'kindness'. At first glance, he was actually fairly typical: large, fast and powerful, with green-tinged skin and an excellent sense of smell. The problem was that for some reason Zemin abhorred all forms of torture and violence. Even the Great Yama could not understand what was wrong with him. In Diyu, a 'kind', gentle demon is not much use at all. It was only after several centuries that the perfect job was found for him. The corridors and tunnels of Diyu are dark and twisting, and the souls of the dead often lose themselves for days, months and sometimes years whilst trying to find their appropriate Court. Zemin was found to be particularly adept at rounding up these lost souls and taking them to their destination. In time he became known as the 'shepherd' demon and was even given a large staff as a joke by a mocking official. In his duties, he became the only demon to have free access to every part of Diyu. Soon, he knew every corner of this dark kingdom as well as he knew his own two feet, which were large and covered in calluses.

One day, about the time he should have been turning in for the night, Zemin found himself in one of the distant extremities of Diyu. This was a most inhospitable labyrinth of rocky tunnels and crooked paths that he had rarely visited before, mostly because the trek there was on a steep incline and humans, in death as in life, were inherently lazy. However, he thought he had picked up an unusual scent and had absent-mindedly been following its trail for much of the day. Climbing through a tunnel of jagged rocks, he was now following a faint sound as well as the scent. It was a muffled cry, short bursts, but repetitive. 'How on earth could one of those wretched things have got this lost?' he thought. The sound was getting louder, so Zemin persisted, even though the tunnel was getting very tight for his large frame and he often had to pause to smash a larger opening in the rocks to fit through. Finally, he reached a large, damp cave. In a corner, he saw a strange small creature that appeared to have got its hind leg stuck in a sharp crevice. Unable to free itself, all it could do was bleat. Zemin had never seen such a beast. It had four legs, a long snout and was covered in soft black fur. It looked up at Zemin with a most plaintive expression, bleating pitifully.

Zemin set about freeing the small beast and as soon as he had done so, it shot off. Instinct took hold of Zemin and he set off in pursuit. This creature was not as fast as him, but nimble. However, it was ultimately no match for the demon's prowess and after a prolonged chase, Zemin had it safely in his grasp. As he rose with the beast in his arms, his eyes met something he had never seen before. At the end of the cave was a large, jagged arc of pure light. Intrigued, Zemin walked toward it and was soon at the mouth of the cave,

staring out at a vast spectacle of undulating grassland dotted with at least a hundred creatures like the one he was holding, but all pale, casually roaming.

Zemin was dumbfounded and enchanted. He could never have imagined such a place: the light, the colours, the gently floating clouds. The air he was breathing was so sweet it was making him giddy. The soft damp grass was tickling his large feet. He strolled aimlessly for a few minutes, taking in this remarkable sight, until his gaze fell on something far more extraordinary; something that would change his life for ever.

The shepherdess

She was unlike anything he had ever seen. Whilst he was of course accustomed to humans – after all, their souls were more or less identically shaped – he had never laid eyes on one so vibrant and radiant. He had never encountered anything in his age-long existence that made his chest feel like it was about to explode, but somehow in a warm and exhilarating way. Unable to control himself, he slowly approached this beguiling vison until he was but a few feet away from her. When she saw Zemin, she seemed taken aback – he did, after all, cut quite a fearsome figure – but the sight of her black lamb was such a relief that tears welled up in her eyes. She grabbed it and kissed it, like one would a child, and thanked him profusely.

Her name was Wenling and she lived alone in a cabin overlooking the vast grassy plain at the base of Mount Tai. She had been born into a highly respected family of landowners, and her parents had been able to arrange her marriage to one of the most powerful and ambitious men in the kingdom, a dark soul, the Duke of Wu, a man obsessed by power and status. If in public life he was a feared and imposing personage, behind closed doors he was nothing short of a beast. Wenling's first years of marriage were harsh and lonely, but her inability to bear him a child probably saved her from a lifetime of torment. The Duke of Wu soon took a younger bride and had no more use for Wenling, but his ego would not allow anyone else to enjoy his property. Thus, she was banished to this remote wilderness, its solitary idyll tarnished only by the threat that one day, if he was passing, he might return.

Over the next year, Zemin made secret visits to see Wenling almost daily. He helped with the work around the farm and she made him delicious meals, the like of which he had never tasted. Whilst she had initially been shocked by his appearance, his kindness and selflessness allowed her to quickly overcome her reservations. Soon they were deeply in love. They would sit on a strange pair of round stools in her house and talk for hours about anything and everything, eagerly exploring one another with innocent desire. Wenling had known such horrors first-hand that she simply saw Zemin's innate goodness. She was totally accepting when he first told her he was from Diyu, but of course had a multitude of questions. And Zemin felt he could confide in her completely.

For years, Zemin kept up this double life. He was happier than he had ever thought possible. Together, they had four children, who grew up in a bubble of love and nurturing. Zemin went about his work in Diyu with renewed gusto, finding lost souls, guiding them to their eventual salvation.

Return of the Duke

One balmy summer evening Zemin was strolling happily through the secret cave, out into the rich glow of the fading sun. He was rounding a small hillock when he realized something was wrong. He could smell horses and men, sweat and danger. Running to his family home, he was met by a horrifying sight. The house was surrounded by a small army of soldiers in black uniforms, brandishing swords, pikes and bows. In front of the house he saw Wenling being held by the back of her neck by a sinister-looking cloaked figure. The children, to his horror, were crammed into a wooden cage.

Zemin saw red and charged. The first soldiers he encountered were dispatched with such effortlessness that their comrades retreated to where the hostages were being held. Tips of daggers were thrust at necks, just shy of drawing blood. His children's shrill screams stopped the enraged demon in his tracks. Despite all of his great strength, his foe had easily found his weakness.

What had happened was this: the Duke of Wu was en route to raiding a neighbouring town when he decided, on a whim, to take a small detour to visit his wife, now just one of many, taking a retinue with him. On arrival, he was quite surprised to find her flourishing and in the company of four rather striking children. Now, the Duke of Wu was a seasoned rogue, so it did not take him long to get Wenling to recount her unusual story in all its details. Fascinated, the Duke immediately saw the potential benefits of this strange tale. So, he decided to wait for her devoted demon to return.

It did not take long for the Duke to impress upon Zemin the gravity of his situation. Seated on Zemin's favoured round stool, which looked even more bulbous under the Duke's thin frame, he explained that he would keep his retinue here to build a small garrison of trusted men. They would be charged with keeping Wenling and the children prisoner. Zemin would be allowed to visit them in return for doing whatever the Duke asked of him. As added insurance, Zemin's eldest son would travel with the Duke at all times. Any attempt to free his family, harm the Duke's men or refuse to do his duty would result in the deaths of Wenling and the children.

First, the Duke demanded information. Details about Diyu, its mechanisms and particularly its demons. He took detailed notes in a small leather-bound book. He also set Zemin some more physical tasks. Attacking an imperial tax cavalcade, breaching the walls of a fortified town – violent, martial tasks to which, the Duke noted, grinning, he was after all so well suited. The Duke was very careful to keep Zemin a secret. Only his most trusted men knew his true nature. For his missions, he was simply dressed in a black cloak, with a specially made helmet. Zemin could only stomach such violence knowing that by committing it he was keeping his family safe. Soon, however, the Duke became more ambitious. With access to this new, extraordinary resource, he felt that he could almost certainly mount a serious challenge to the throne itself. One dark, overcast night, the Duke handed Zemin a list of names, all of them demons. Zemin was to round them up and lead them to the surface, where they would help the Duke overrun the province and begin his campaign for the ultimate prize: the Empire.

Although horrified, Zemin was powerless and did as he was told. The Duke made clever use of his new demon force and was able to greatly expand his territories, ruling through fear and violence. The demons made perfect

soldiers, obedient, totally lacking in ambition, freakishly powerful. So pleased was the Duke with their sterling service that he wished to reward them. But how to reward hellish demons? Drawing on his own evil predilections, the Duke proceeded to introduce them to the joys of rape, alcohol and drugs, power, pillage and the delights of human flesh, roasted at first but soon taken straight from the living victim. After each task or campaign, Zemin would lead the demons back through the secret cave to Diyu until they were required again.

Inspired as the Duke's plan was, it did not foresee a catastrophic consequence. Demons had for centuries been simple, isolated creatures. Now, they had been infected with something totally alien to their nature. Something exclusively human.

For all of their sophistication, brilliant innovation and dominance of the planet, humans also carry something that is not found in other creatures. It is almost impossible to pin down, but it is as devastating as it is enriching. It may be a virus, a power or simply an accident of evolution. Some call it free will. Others believe it is given by heaven. Suffice it to say that this 'germ', be it physical or mental, is not only highly dangerous, but also highly infectious. It can lead to the slaughter of an entire race as it can lead to the discovery of a cure for a plague or disease. It can make a man take pleasure in inflicting misery as it can cause another to save a stranger. Murder, rape and oppression can be traced to its source, but so can poetry, music and love. Humans had been struggling with this 'germ' from the beginning of time. Now, it had infected demons.

Rebellion

Over the years, their extended periods on the surface began to affect the demons' behaviour in Diyu. Jealousy and ambition crept into their daily lives, as did laziness and dissatisfaction. Perhaps the mere awareness of an alternative was too great a lure for them ever to be content again. There were arguments and fights. Cliques and factions began to form. There were demands made of the functionaries: 'we want human flesh', 'we demand freedom of movement throughout Diyu' and so on. The Great Yama and the other lords of Hell were bewildered. What was happening? How could a centuries-old system be crumbling so quickly? Meanwhile, as the Duke of Wu's campaign against the Emperor was gaining momentum, he had greater and greater need for his demons and was recruiting more at a dizzying pace.

Finally, at the behest of Wenling, Zemin was forced to reveal to the Great Yama the awful extent of his initially small transgression. Yama's fury was terrible. A sacred threshold had been breached, throwing the delicate balance of the entire world into discord. In a tone that chilled Zemin's blood in his veins, Yama spat that he would deal with him later. For now, his kingdom required all his power and wrath.

Yama descended to the depths of Diyu to challenge the rebel demons. He stood in front of his subjects in his most awe-inspiring manifestation. There could be no question of the dire severity of this matter and his unshakeable resolve to quash any dissent. However, Yama's terrifying presence and the threat of his fury had long ceased to have any effect on those within whom the infection had taken root most deeply. They refused to stand down. The Great Yama yielded to no one; it was imperative that he be an absolute in this precariously balanced world. As he towered over the masses of rebel demons gathered before him, it became clear that the time for discourse had passed. Raising himself up to his most majestic self, Yama unleashed his brutal power on his wayward subjects below.

Many demon lives were lost that day, a day that would alter hell for ever. Faced with certain defeat, many of the rebelling demons retreated, making their escape to the surface through the hidden tunnels. Zemin chased after them but many eluded him. Reaching the mouth of the cave, he could see plumes of smoke in the distance. He began to run toward them and was immediately confronted with evidence of the carnage the demons had left in their wake. Zemin stopped, turned and retraced his steps to the mouth of the cave. He sent a last glance out over the smouldering landscape, toward the house in which he had spent his happiest years. Racked with guilt at the devastation his actions had wrought on not just one world but two, he began to rain a series of mighty blows on the walls of the cave. As his frenzy grew, so did the power and speed of his blows. Cracks began coursing through the walls, debris falling, but Zemin continued unabated. Soon, he had brought down a giant façade of mighty Mount Tai on himself and the cave, sealing it for all eternity. Zemin, who had inadvertently acquired free choice, made, in his mind, the most honourable one he could.

—III—

The Palace Detective

wherein an uncertain boy, bruised and bedevilled by his father, grows into a young man of skill and promise, aided by a gruff, square-headed stranger, a wise teacher and an uncanny gift for dwelling in the interstices; the long shadows cast by men of blood and power.

Chasing Clouds

FURTHER STRANGE TALES
FROM THE IVORY CRESCENT

Original sin

YING WAS BORN AN UNFORTUNATE infant, small, weak and with one misshapen leg. His mother loved him nonetheless, as he was her first-born and as such was a gift from up high. His father, Fan, was a different matter. Fan was a strong, physical man who had been a champion wrestler in the region and had joined the army, where he was rising up the ranks, in large part owing to his physical prowess. However, after being badly wounded in a border skirmish, he was forced to resign his commission. At first, he worked for the local magistrate as an enforcer or type of policeman. His mere stature was usually enough to dissuade or persuade as each case required. To his credit, Fan tried to be a good father. As Ying grew up, he tried to teach him physical skills and worked on improving his strength and speed. He also tried to love his son, but whenever he gazed upon him all he could see was the weakness and debility that had halted his own career, reducing him to a crude and clumsy oaf. Although Ying cherished this attention from his father, he was constantly aware that in his father's heart, he was a malediction.

When Ying was about ten, his mother fell pregnant once more. However, the baby, another boy, was born with far worse disabilities than Ying and only survived a few weeks. Ying's mother fell into a dark depression and his father became convinced that he had been cursed. He began to ignore Ying and began to drink more and more, and with the drinking came the beatings. To survive, Ying became highly skilled at avoiding his father and hiding, often making himself practically invisible just by standing motionless for long periods in a darkened corner. Soon, Fan's drinking led him to lose his job, heaping even greater strain on a difficult situation.

Ying would steal as much time as he could with his mother, as much to console and look after her as to be loved. As soon as his father was home, though, he became a shadow. One particularly harsh winter, Ying's mother become seriously ill. In truth, she had never recovered from the loss of her second child. The severity of his wife's illness forced Fan into some form of sobriety. For all of his faults, he had always truly loved her. After a few months, Ying's mother died. Devastated, Ying recoiled even more into himself. His father went straight back to the bottle.

Then one day everything changed. Fan, who was now performing sporadic odd jobs, was called to the summer mansion of a local marquis. A large stone was being delivered for the garden and muscle was required. It was at the mansion, a large house with extensive gardens and woods, that he caught the eye of the housekeeper, a buxom widow with a crooked smile. Fan was not the man he used to be, but he still cut an impressive figure. The two soon started an affair and she was able to get Fan a permanent job at the mansion. They were married later that year. For a while, all was fairly calm. Fan and his new wife were happy together and she doted on him, having missed company and having someone to look after. She did not mind Ying as by this time he had become a veritable master of remaining unnoticed, his very existence often barely perceptible.

House of shadows

In order to stay out of the way as well as to occupy himself, Ying spent many hours of the day exploring the grounds of the mansion. He worked on his physical skills, which were slowly improving with time, although his deformity still seemed to define him. At the mansion, he also honed his already keen eye for spotting things and remembering details, learning to recognize almost all of the plants and flowers as well as which birds and insects preferred to visit which and when. Ying took no notes, but simply stored all of these facts and observations in the seemingly infinite library of his mind.

One day, as he was carefully studying a hummingbird, he was disturbed by the sound of a gate opening in the wall that surrounded the main house. A servant entered, looked around nervously to see if anyone was about, and shut the gate again. Ying thought it odd and decided to continue observing. He sat there for several hours, waiting to see what else would happen. Night had begun to fall when he finally noticed a cloaked man approaching the gate, carefully pushing it open and slipping inside. What had troubled Ying before was simply the servant's furtive demeanour while opening the gate; now he saw that he had left it unbolted. Ying was so intrigued that it did not take much for him to overcome his initial fear and follow the mysterious man through the gate and into the house.

Inside, the house was sombre and dark. Lanterns had not yet been lit in this area and there were a multitude of dark shadows, nooks and crannies for Ying to manoeuvre in as he kept pace with his target. The man was making his way, as quietly as he could, through the house toward the kitchen area, with Ying imperceptibly on his heels. Arrived at the entrance to the kitchen, Ying found himself a perfect vantage point from which to observe what was happening within whilst remaining unnoticed. Inside, the man joined two other figures, a man and a woman, whose silhouette was unmistakable to Ying as his stepmother. Some transaction took place and a small purse of coins was exchanged for a bundle wrapped in a heavy cloth. The business concluded, the man cheekily squeezed his stepmother's buttock and was off. Ying, concerned that he might get stuck in the house, followed him out and returned home.

Over the following months, Ying was able to gain entrance to the house most days in one way or another. He explored all of the outer pavilions, studying the layout of all the different spaces, their styles and uses. He also observed all of the comings and goings of the various servants, gardeners and labourers, making a mental note of the idiosyncrasies of their movements and characters as well as how they interacted with the other staff. There was no purpose for this and no goal, but it was a mental exercise that filled his hours and that he found both calming and exhilarating at the same time.

Soon he had identified multiple ways to gain access to the central compound of the house and here he repeated the exercises that he had performed with the outer buildings. Exploration, observation and study, all committed to memory. All this was only possible because of his ever improving stealth and uncanny ability to disappear, made somewhat easier by the multitude of shadowy corners and niches from which he could do his work. The house was magnificent in its own worn and sombre way. Ying began to feel so at home there that he could sense even the smallest change in the household and even in the mood of its members. This became his kingdom, which he experienced, observed and studied from the comfort of his innumerable anonymous vantage points. Throughout these intriguing months, Ying's father and stepmother were continuing to enjoy the excitement of their new relationship. Ying was no burden as he was rarely seen and as such they were both very well disposed toward him when they did happen to cross paths. Whilst this was hardly a conventional and happy family life filled with warmth and love, it was a calm co-existence that all three found comforting. But once more, change was on the horizon.

Birth of discord

It was early autumn when Ying's stepmother told Fan that she was carrying their child. Overjoyed, he shared the news with Ying, telling him that he was soon to be a brother. Ying was delighted. His father deserved this happiness despite his harshness toward him. Now Fan would truly believe that he was not cursed and could live out his days in security and happiness, and have a second chance at being a good father. For his part, Ying made an extra effort to be helpful around the house, despite spending most of his time at the mansion. Ying's little brother was born in spring. He was unusually large, like his father. Seeing him develop in his early months into a strong and healthy infant brought Fan an immense feeling of happiness. His wife doted on him but was happy to share her time with Fan too. Ying kept himself to himself as always, interacting with his baby brother when the rest of the household was busy or asleep.

As the child grew and became a toddler, problems started to emerge. He was strong and curious and was thus a handful for his mother, who was anxious for his safety. Ying was often called upon to look after his brother, a responsibility he relished. Even so, with the extra hours she was putting in at the mansion to support the newly expanded family, his stepmother would reach the end of each day exhausted. This meant she had little time or energy for Fan, who began to resent this and turned once again to drinking. In a short time, the entire atmosphere of the household had changed. A sense of menace began to creep back into the air. Ying helped where he could but otherwise tried to make himself scarce. His stepmother began to resent the time Ying got to spend with his brother. His mere presence began to irritate her. However, she also disliked his not being there every time she needed him;

she would call but he would not answer, ensconced as he was in the mansion. Fan in turn began to resent Ying for being another irritant in his wife's life and thus another obstacle to regaining his previous happiness. In this tinderbox of unspoken tension, even the smallest spark could ignite an inferno.

That spark came in the depth of winter. Fan had come home drunk from the tavern and was in a vile mood. Ying had offered to entertain his young brother so that his stepmother might get some rest. Entering the small house, Fan's eyes fell upon his sons, playing happily together in a corner. Drunk as he was, all he could see was the two artifices of his misery. Ying, the weak and pathetic son who had destroyed his previous life, and his innocent infant brother, the pilferer of all of his wife's love and attention. Ying's ever sharp instincts read the situation immediately and he rose, both to placate his father by inviting him to sit down by the fire, where he might bring him some food and more wine, and to carefully place his meagre frame between the menacing bulk of his father and his young sibling. But Fan was having none of it. He had to do little more than raise his massive arm to send Ying crashing across the floor. Turning his sights on his infant son, he strode toward him only to be halted by a jug flying across the room, smashing on the wall next to him. Fan turned on Ying and began to administer a severe beating. At one point, seeing Ying's deformed leg trapped by his hold, he brought his boot down with all the force he could muster, shattering the bone. Vengeance on an innocent limb blamed for his cursed life. Amid all the din, Ying's stepmother appeared, furious at having been woken up and by the mess. Fan explained that he had caught Ying trying to harm his brother and was beating him as punishment - a lie that had the advantage both of getting him off the hook and prompting his wife to join in the attack.

Ying awoke in a deep patch of thicket, a freezing storm whirling around above. Every fibre of his body was aching and the wounds he had sustained were tightening agonizingly in the icy air. He was frozen and burning at the same time. Slowly, he was able to rise to his knees and begin to crawl out of his thorny prison. He struggled, crawling along the edge of he path until he had no more strength and collapsed. His final thoughts were of the rich, textured walls of the mansion. Its shadows, its corners, its warm fires. Its

glowing lanterns that created an early gloominess that was his home and his sanctuary. Would he ever be able to return there? To observe the ebbs and flows and delicate balances of its daily life? In that moment, he realized that more than any other place this had been his happiest home, even if its inhabitants, from the Marquis to the lowliest servant, were all ignorant of his existence. Darkness overcame him; he was floating in a void. His body felt light as the pain of his injuries faded away. Blackness. Nothing.

Nascent sleuth

Ying was first aware of warmth on his face, then the amber glow of a nearby fire. Next he felt the brush of a warm, heavy fur as he gingerly stirred an arm. His wounds were still raw, but he was aware that his malformed leg was bandaged up with a stiff splint of wood. Squinting across the fire, he could make out a large figure on the other side, carefully roasting some meat over the open flames. As his eyes began to focus, the figure aquired a face – a familiar one, large and square, with round, bulging eyes. To say that the man was unattractive would be very kind. Slowly regaining his faculties, Ying was able to recall that the man had been a regular at the mansion over the past week. He remembered that he was a skilled artisan who had been called in to freshen up some of the painted murals in the west wing. The lady of the house had recently given birth and a thorough programme of redecoration and repair had been undertaken in celebration. Ying had noticed that this artisan kept himself to himself and spent much of his free time reading or wandering around the house seemingly lost, but clearly not so.

'Ah, you're awake, boy?' The voice was deep but kindly. 'Lucky I found you when I did. I doubt you would have survived the night.'

Ying nodded, not yet trusting himself to speak.

'I set your leg straight, put a little something on it and bound it with a splint,' said the man. 'Could have been done years ago. Although you would have needed someone like me.'

Ying instinctively touched his bound leg. 'You're the painter?' he croaked, his voice weak and hesitant. 'From the house. I've seen you there.'

'Really? I haven't seen you around,' said the man. Ying remained silent. 'So!' he continued, 'can I assume that you are the presence that lurks in the shadowy corners of that house?'

Surprised and disappointed in himself, Ying replied, 'So you did see me?'

'Not at all,' replied the artisan. 'But you don't always have to see something to know it is there.'

Ying stared at him, somewhat bemused. His saviour, seeing the confusion in his eyes, elaborated.

'I am not only an artisan. Amongst other things, I am a hunter, and hunters learn to hone all of their senses...sight, hearing, smell...even hunches.' He laughed.

Ying remained silent. Suddenly the large figure rose and took a few steps toward Ying, holding out his hand either in greeting or to help Ying sit up.

'My name is Zhong Kui,' he said gently, heaving Ying into a seated position. 'And you', he added, proffering a steaming skewer of roasted meat as he spoke, 'need to eat.'

'Like the Demon Queller?' Ying asked, immediately regretting how stupid he sounded.

'Sure, something like that,' Zhong Kui replied, smiling. The smile sat awkwardly on his unusual face.

They sat mostly in silence as Ying managed to force some food down, his mouth and lips lacerated by the onslaught of familial blows.

'Have you noticed any new additions to the household lately?' Zhong Kui suddenly asked.

What a strange question, thought Ying. Why would he want to know something like that? As if he were able to read Ying's mind, or at the very least his expression, Zhong Kui went on.

'I'll tell you why, boy,' he said. 'As well as being an artisan, as I said I am also a hunter and at the moment I am hunting something that I fear might be a danger for the Marquis' new-born.'

Ying cottoned on immediately, his mind now working at its normal levels. Is he a bounty hunter, he wondered.

'Sure, something like that,' Zhong Kui replied.

Ying recoiled. Had he just asked that question aloud? He thought he had just asked it in his head. Ying was at once troubled and enlivened by this stranger. Was he simply a figment of his imagination? Had Ying actually died?

Strangely emboldened by this uncertainty, he felt a freedom to engage him further.

'What are you after, a kidnapper? An assassin?' Ying asked, a tone of excitement in his voice.

'Let's just say I can't say right now. So, have you noticed anyone new?'

Ying mentally scrolled through his recent days at the mansion.

'Well,' he ventured, 'there is the physician who delivered the child and has come to check in on mother and child regularly.'

'No. He is fine!' snapped the stranger, leaving little room for doubt.

'I suppose there is the wet nurse?' Ying suggested, racking his brain. 'She has been there a few weeks now.'

'A wet nurse...' mused Zhong Kui. 'Now that is clever.'

As if he could now read Zhong Kui's thoughts, Ying, mind now racing, said, 'But it's not her.'

'How do you know,' Zhong Kui demanded, seeming a little irked at the interruption of his thought process.

'I've watched her with the child, and she is a natural. I watched my stepmother handle my brother when he was tiny, and she was loving but tentative. This woman has handled many, many infants. She has a gift.'

Zhong Kui leaned back, bemused. Then he abruptly leaned forward. 'Then tell me, boy. If you had to guess. Is there anyone there that you get a strange feeling from?'

Ying was hugely flattered that this peculiar stranger was actually asking for his opinion. It was perhaps the first time in his life that he had been treated as being of value or as an equal. So, he redoubled his efforts of recollection.

'There was a new gardener...no, he left last week,' he mused. 'A cousin visited, but she seemed totally genuine.'

He continued ruminating out loud until he finally had to admit defeat.

'No, sorry, no one,' he said dejectedly. 'There is just one odd new thing in that household, but it's not that.'

'What?' asked Zhong Kui, his eyes suddenly burning bright. Probably a reflection from the fire.

'Nothing, I was just being stupid.' Ying desperately hoped he would drop it, so infantile was his thought.

'What is it, boy? In this world, nothing is ever too stupid,' Zhong Kui insisted.

Ying hesitated. He did not want to make a fool of himself, but looking up he could see his companion's eyes demanding an answer.

'Well...as I said, this is stupid,' he began, 'but the Marquis is very close to the Emperor and about ten days ago, the family received a gift of two small lion dogs.'

Before he could go on, Zhong Kui interjected. 'That's strange...those are almost never allowed outside of the Palace. The Marquis must be very close to the Court.'

Encouraged that his information did not seem to strike Zhong Kui as totally useless, Ying continued. 'One of the dogs is adorable. Playful, cheerful...er, dog-like,' he said, not able to finish his thought more elegantly. 'But there is something strange about the other one. I have observed it roaming aimlessly whilst the other puppy plays or gets treats. I don't really know, but there is something...' Losing confidence, he broke off.

'A dog!' Zhong Kui mused, rubbing his large protruding chin. 'Crafty swine. I would never have thought of that...but from the Palace? How did he manage that?'

Not wanting to push his luck, Ying decided not to question his host's sanity at suspecting a small dog. So he changed tack.

'Can you tell me what this person wants with the baby?' he asked.

Zhong Kui fixed Ying with a fearsome stare and replied, 'What we are dealing with here is a nasty creature that has an appetite for infants, the more high-born the better.' Then, looking up at Ying's eager face, he swiftly put an end to any further questions. 'That is all I can say, boy. We should sleep.' This sounded like an order more than anything. Ying lay obediently

back under his furs, exhausted now in body and mind. He was about to drift off when Zhong Kui unexpectedly spoke again.

'Boy,' he said. 'Listen carefully, no need to speak. When I found you, you had been left for dead. I suggest you never return home or next time they won't be so careless. Go back to the mansion. Stay there. You know it well and will be safe there.' He paused. 'There is something about you, child. A spark behind the darkness. You may have a bright future yet, but much of that will be up to you,' he said in a tone that did not invite further conversation. 'Now sleep.'

House of learning

Ying did not see the stranger again. When he woke the next morning the stranger had packed up his things and left. Ying noticed a bundle wrapped in rough cloth next to the fire and started to unwrap it. Inside he found an exceptional document box. Fashioned from two solid pieces of rare *zitan* timber, it had rounded edges and elegant curved white brass mounts. It was, without doubt, the most valuable thing Ying had ever held in his hands. Had the stranger forgotten it? Inside the box, however, together with some coin, he found a note.

> Boy – This is a gift for you. Thank you for your help.
> I couldn't have done it without you. Keep this box near
> you. We will meet again, I am sure.

By the time Ying was well enough to resume his usual routines of observation, the dogs were long gone. Ying's wounds had healed well and in fact his leg was straight, although weak and stiff. Ying had taken the stranger's advice and not returned home, moving permanently, if secretly, into his adopted home. It was so large, and he so adept at hiding, that it was never a problem. It was warm and comfortable, with plenty of food. Sometimes at night, unable to sleep, he was warmed by the recollection of his young brother's innocent smile. But this warmth was short-lived, dark memories following close on its heels. Perhaps he also felt guilt at having left his brother? At having been the cause of his own anguish?

However, he had decided to make this place his home and his home it became. He continued to observe and keep tabs on everyone and everything. Sometimes he would overhear his stepmother moaning about his father's drinking and would momentarily be hauled back to his past life. Just as he was beginning to tire of nothing exceptional happening, a stranger arrived at the house. He was tall and slender and wore the robes and hat of a *jìnshì* scholar. It transpired that he had been employed by the Marquis to tutor his two older children, one of Ying's age and the other three years older. Now Ying had a new pastime. Hiding in the upper compartment of a huge compound cabinet, he was able to observe and listen to all of the lessons the tutor prepared for the children.

At night, whilst everyone else slept, he would often creep back into the room to practise his calligraphy. Mimicking the rituals he had observed that day, he would start by preparing the ink on the inkstone. Adding small amounts of water from the simple water pot, he slowly ground the ink cake in a hypnotic circular motion until the ink was of the correct consistency. Then, placing some thin paper over the tutor's own work, he would trace each character over and over, trying to achieve the naturally fluid movements he had committed to memory through his observation. Whilst his earliest attempts were crude, the more he observed and the more he practised, the more he could feel the movements becoming ingrained and almost natural. These were the times he was at his happiest and most fulfilled. Finally, albeit by proxy, he was getting the education his mind had always cried out for.

For a full five years, Ying was able to live in the mansion secretly and comfortably, eavesdropping on every form of lesson, from poetry to strategy, calligraphy to agrarian practices. And his mind being as it was, once the information was absorbed, it was there for good. When he was not secretly observing lessons, Ying made himself busy observing everything else. Gardeners, cooks, servants; he saw and noted every detail, from the way they carried out their duties to their speech. At night, when all was quiet, he would re-enact what he had studied, mimicking his subjects with ever greater accuracy.

One day, he was lurking near the back gate when he witnessed the delivery of assorted new uniforms. This led to great excitement within the household, which was soon to host a large gathering and hunt. Numerous exalted guests were invited, some even from the Capital. The house would be awash with new servants brought by the visitors and others employed temporarily to help with the great increase in numbers and tasks for that special week. All this gave Ying a mischievous idea. But could he pull it off? That night he snuck into the supply closet and picked out a nice new uniform for himself. The stage was set.

Playing a role

The day the guests were due to arrive, the mansion was a veritable pandemonium of activity. As Ying had expected, the yard was awash with servants, both familiar and newly employed, waiting to be assigned their most valuable charges. Ying positioned himself at the back of this mass, dressed in his new servant's uniform. In all this commotion, no one would ever notice one extra servant. He patiently observed the arriving guests and waited for an opportunity to present itself. There were local dignitaries, noblemen and rich merchants. Each was appointed a servant and shown to their quarters. Those that arrived with their own servants were given a liaison to make sure they received everything they might need. A particularly fine carriage soon pulled up, the occupant apparently the patriarch of the famous Wu clan, a family with a vast land-owning fortune and political influence to match. Next, Ying noticed an austere figure dressed in official robes and overheard a servant say that he was the Minister of War, arrived all the way from the Imperial City. He had a servant with him, but trailing them was also another scholar dressed far more humbly and carrying several bags. Ying thought this might be his chance and strode confidently up to the man, offering to help with his bags. The minister was appointed an extra servant and they all set off for the quarters that had been set aside for the pair. After the minister was shown his rooms, Ying followed the younger official into his.

'My name is Ying, sir,' he said, 'and I am here to help you in any way I can. Please do not hesitate to ask me for anything.' He bowed deeply. Had he overdone it? The scholar thanked him and replied that all was fine and

that he just wanted to wash and rest. Ying left the room and hurried to the kitchens, where he fetched him some hot water for washing and some fresh tea and dates. He delivered these with little fuss and bade his charge goodnight. He was now a bona fide servant, and no one was any the wiser.

The scholar's name was Chu Lai and, whilst he was a junior official in the Ministry of War, he had become the minister's favourite and was the rising star of the department. He had a sharp mind and keen eye and Ying felt an immediate affinity for him. They seemed to notice the same things. Chu Lai was not very talkative, preferring to stand back and observe the more illustrious guests. After a few days, he began to open up a little and Ying was able to keep him up to date with any interesting bits of gossip from around the mansion, which he greatly appreciated. It struck Ying that this man placed great importance on information and was ready to reward it with coin as well as with a greater propensity for chat. He was clearly highly talented, but still cautious and insecure. Little did he know that in a few short years he would himself be Minister of War and have the ear of the Emperor.

One evening, Chu Lai summoned Ying to his room. He was clearly about to write a letter or notes as he had laid out a very elegant set of objects on the table. They must have been designed for travelling as they were all smaller than one might usually find. There was a small brush rest in the form of *lingzhi* mushrooms, a tiny seal paste box also carved with the fortuitous fungi and a free-form washer. All were fashioned from boxwood, whose aged surfaces and amber tonalities made an impression on Ying. There was even a small scholar's rock, the size of a small pear, but resembling a vast mountain. Chu Lai was in need of some ink as he had forgotten to pack his ink cake. Ying scurried off and returned with a fresh ink stick. As Chu Lai began slowly preparing the ink, they chatted about the day, the hunt and the other guests. Not wanting to overstay his welcome, Ying was about to leave when Chu Lai asked him to wait a few minutes so he could deliver this letter for him. This was hardly abnormal; Ying, like many other servants, had been delivering notes and letters amongst the guests and for farther dispatch all week. After all, these were important political people. However, when he had finished and sealed the folded sheet Chu Lai handed it to Ying and asked for it to be delivered to a man who would be waiting outside the west gate. Chu Lai's young career had relied heavily on his instincts and he clearly had a strong feeling about his young servant. Surprised, Ying agreed and thanked him.

As he walked toward the west entrance, his mind was buzzing with excitement. What intrigue. His curiosity was eating away at his 'servant's' integrity. Passing a lit lantern that had not been hung yet, he could not resist and, using the flame and his knife, he gently prised open the seal on the letter, which had not had time to fully harden. He felt a pang of guilt for betraying Chu Lai's trust, but the draw was too tantalizing to resist. As it happened, he could have saved himself the bother as most of what he read was gibberish to him. 'Shady Lotus...Northern Bird...Green Ox.' There were no sentences, just random jottings. Most likely a code. He carefully resealed the note and proceeded swiftly to his destination. Once there, he stopped short of the gate, which was manned by two watchmen. Embracing the intrigue perhaps a little too much, he used all of his highly honed skills of stealth and distraction to slip out unnoticed. Just in case Chu Lai wants the passing of this note kept secret, he thought. Outside, he could see no one. Using the undergrowth as cover he moved to the other side of the gate to see if he could find his target.

He was crouched on the edge of a thick cluster of bamboo when a large hand from within the tall plants was placed, without menace, on his shoulder.

'Boy,' a hushed voice said, 'this way.'

He followed the dark form through the bamboo for several hundred feet until they emerged into a clearing where a makeshift camp was dimly lit by a partially covered oil lamp. Instinctively, Ying took out the note and handed it to the very stranger who had saved him years before.

'What does it say?' asked the man teasingly.

'Didn't understand a bit of it,' Ying replied, a tone of whimsy in his voice.

'Good,' said the man, 'our codes work. But you will have to learn to break such cyphers.'

Ying was both delighted and confused. The large man read the note, then lit it with the flame from the lamp. Lifting it up, he used its glow to illuminate

Ying's face. 'You have grown well,' he said, a touching paternal tone in his voice. Then he put his hand on Ying's shoulder and gave it a firm squeeze that was joined by the traces of a smile. 'Until next time,' he said.

Suddenly there was a noise from behind Ying. He turned and instinctively crouched low, scanning the area for the intruder. A shaft of moonlight broke through the clouds, throwing light on a small patch of bushes. There, a white rabbit with strikingly luminous fur was busy enjoying a night-time feast. Smiling to himself, Ying turned to share the joke with his companion, only to find him gone. No stranger, no camp, no trace.

Clandestine council

The week had been a great success and Ying was delighted with his adventures. It was the last day before most of the guests were due to leave and he was busy making sure that his charge had everything he needed for the long journey home. When evening came, Chu Lai thanked him for his service and handed him an envelope. It was heavy with coin. Ying thanked him and turned to leave, ecstatic that he had pulled it all off, when Chu Lai spoke again.

'There is something about you, young Ying, and whilst I can't quite make it out, I have a good feeling about you.'

Ying turned, not knowing what to say.

'You are quick and sharp and observe things in uncommon detail. Perhaps you should not limit yourself to a life of service.'

Embarrassed and at a loss for words, Ying thanked him again, turned and left the room.

That night, raw excitement still coursing through his veins, Ying knew that he would be unable to sleep. He decided to go for a walk. As he turned into the courtyard that led to the kitchens he saw the shady tradesman he had first seen all those years ago. He was engaged in a passionate embrace with a maid. Poor girl, he thought, he must have one in every kitchen! But as he looked again they shifted in their passion and Ying could clearly make out the face of his stepmother. A wave of anger and dismay swept over him. His instinct was to run, so he ran. Thoughts were swirling in his head in a chaotic frenzy. He just kept running. By the time he stopped to catch his breath, he was on a steep, narrow path beyond the borders of the mansion. He was taking some deep breaths to clear his head when he was alerted to something odd. Instinctively, he pressed himself against the trunk of a nearby tree. As he scanned the area he realized it was a smell that had stopped him short. Burning wood.

He crept carefully around the trunk. In the middle distance, the faint outline of a hut was just visible. His eyes had always been excellent at night and as he focused, he could make out slivers of light sneaking through the cracks and edges of the doors and windows. He could tell that this was no ordinary hunter's lodge. Despite its simplicity, the quality of the building and materials was of the highest order. It was inconceivable that this was not built as part of the estate. He decided to take a closer look. Moving with all the stealth of a hunting panther, he was soon crouched beneath one of the windows. The muffled sound of men's voices filtered out, but he couldn't see anything. He needed a better vantage point. In seconds he had climbed the facade and was on the roof, crawling along its overhang in search of something that might help him. Suddenly, it was there, a gap between the roof and rafters. Now perched atop the supports of a beam, he had a clear view of the inside.

The room was not large and lit by hanging lanterns that had presumably been used to illuminate the walk there. Five cloaked men sat at a large table in the centre of the room. He could clearly see the dignified figure of the Marquis seated next to Lord Wu, whose imperious but somehow slippery demeanour had stood out to Ying all week. He could not properly see the two men with their backs to him. At the end of the table, at a slight remove, with his hood still up, was a large figure seated mostly in the shadows. The only thing Ying could see clearly was his hand on the table, curled around a striking string of beads. He noted that his skin appeared to have an unusual green tinge. Probably a reflection from the lanterns. In front of the other four were half-empty cups and what looked like small toggles, in different woods, finely carved in the form of lotus heads.

The Marquis, as host, appeared to be leading the meeting, which, judging by the empty wine flasks, had probably lasted for some time already.

'What of the Tibetans?' one of the men with his back to Ying asked.

'Lord Jiu is advising the king there and is doing an excellent job. We are well placed,' the Marquis replied.

'And the An?' another asked.

A worried crease crept across the Marquis' brow. 'A strange people. We still know so little. It's as if they appeared from nowhere.'

Gazes shifted momentarily to the hooded figure, but he shook his head vigorously.

'At least they took care of those meddlesome Kun, so they may be of some use,' said the Marquis. 'But we must keep a close eye.'

They all nodded.

'And the Eagle Boy?' the first speaker asked.

This time it was Lord Wu who replied, his tone firm and matter of fact. 'He commands about two hundred warriors to date. Mostly from two mountain tribes. He cuts quite a formidable figure with that beast. We are confident that with our resources and support he can go far. Perhaps all the way to a khanate! In any case, he will be a most useful ally.'

There were mumbles of agreement.

Having obviously come to the end of their business, the Marquis refilled all of their glasses with a fresh flask that he had on the floor next to him.

'Now perhaps we can move on to some more pleasurable business,' he said. They all sat up attentively. 'Tell us, Niu,' he asked the hooded man. 'What news of fine treasures to add to our collections?'

The hooded man cleared his throat with a sound reminiscent of distant thunder. Sitting upright, hands in sleeves, he began his report.

'There is a shipment of fine wares, freshly fired at the imperial kilns at Jingdezhen. As usual, my associates will intercept it and the finest pieces will be offered to you.'

There was a nodding of heads.

'The governor of Yunnan is apparently in the possession of a very fine horse painting of great age. I have dispatched my agents. He will either sell it cheaply or lose it for nothing.'

This news was greeted with mumbled approval and wry smiles.

'Finally,' he went on, 'there has been talk again of the remarkable table with sword-shaped legs.' All four leant forward eagerly. 'As you know, it was apparently made by a lame craftsman in the valley of carpenters. It was sold to a wealthy merchant who moved several times. The last we heard is that it changed hands several times. I have not found it, but it is certainly somewhere in the Capital.'

Again there was a murmur of approval, until the Marquis proposed a toast.

'The brotherhood!' he cried, raising his cup.

'The brotherhood!' they all chorused.

The Magistrate

Ying climbed down from the roof and scurried silently back to the mansion. In his refuge in the tall cupboard, he lit a lamp and faithfully recorded everything he had seen and heard. Whilst he was sure he would remember it all, it somehow felt like what he should do. Having finished, he placed the sheet inside his *zitan* document box where he kept his few most valued things. Summer was ending and soon the Marquis and his family would move back to their town residence. Whilst in previous years Ying had been content to stay behind and study the servants, labourers and other members of staff, this year, especially after the past few exciting weeks, he was yearning for more. Moreover, after what he had witnessed in the kitchen courtyard, he wanted to get as much distance as possible between himself and his estranged family. He also felt an uneasiness about the Marquis and his secretive conference.

One of the last formal visitors to the mansion that season was a magistrate of some renown. Although he lived and worked in a fairly small town, it was a busy trading crossroads, so there was always plenty of work for him. He had also gained quite a reputation for his skill in investigating frauds and other crimes, recovering stolen goods and often bringing the perpetrators to justice. As such, he was on occasion called to larger cities and once even to the Capital when his particular skills or even a fresh pair of eyes were needed. On this occasion, however, the Magistrate's visit was purely social. It had become tradition for the Marquis to invite him at the end of summer and subtly interrogate him on his more interesting cases. Ying, with the insight he had gained at the hut that night, could imagine just how keenly news of stolen or recovered treasures might interest the Marquis.

So, Ying found a perfect spot in the banquet hall from which he could see and hear everything. This time, it was under the large altar table, which had been dressed with heavy cloths and velvets for the occasion. Through the gaps in the cloth, Ying watched as the party entered the hall. The Marquis was flanked by his eldest son, who had just passed the national exams, and a tall, slender man in dark official robes whom he assumed to be the Magistrate. Although in his mid-seventies, he was a striking man of angular features, with piercing eyes. His movements and speech were slow and considered, but not inelegant. Over dinner, little of great interest was discussed. General gossip, most of which Ying had heard before. Ying learned that the Marquis' son was headed for the Capital in the autumn. The Magistrate, perhaps out of politeness, expressed his dismay at this news, claiming that he wished he might reconsider and come and join his practice instead.

'It is not quite the Capital, of course,' he said, 'but it is good training and I could most certainly use the help of a talented mind.'

After the meal, wine and fruits were brought out, and little by little the ladies and the other guests excused themselves. Soon only the Marquis and the Magistrate remained, and it struck Ying that this was exactly what both of them had been waiting for. The conversation, though still vague and convivial, took on a different tone. The Marquis was clearly fishing for information on subjects of his particular interest.

'Have you heard the strange rumours of recent thefts involving fine artworks?' he asked.

'That's right, I had forgotten, you are quite the collector,' replied the Magistrate. 'Remind me to show you a wonderful brushpot I found on my last trip down south.'

'What kind of brushpot?' the Marquis replied, his curiosity clearly piqued. 'Carved? With dragons? Oh, I would be very interested to see it.'

The Magistrate simply smiled. The moment passed and the Marquis resumed his prodding.

'And how is your old friend the governor of Yunnan?' he asked. 'I had heard he recently acquired quite the treasure.'

'Please!' the Magistrate exclaimed. 'Don't get me started on Yunnan. We have just employed a new cook from the province, on the governor's recommendation, and my stomach is bearing the brunt of her exceptionally spicy cooking.'

Ying was amazed at the skill with which the Magistrate said nothing of value whilst sounding like he was sharing intimate knowledge. In amongst these defensive parries, he managed to subtly drop in subjects or people that he clearly wished to know more about.

'Is Lord Wu concerned about the consolidation of power of the northern tribes?' the Magistrate would ask, or, 'How did you find the Minister of War? Last time I saw him he appeared to have aged.' As he asked these questions, he hardly listened to the answers, instead watching every subtle and unconscious change in the Marquis' face at the mention of certain names or subjects. The interrogator was being interrogated without suspecting a thing.

It was a masterful display and Ying was mesmerized. That night, lying in his makeshift crib, Ying decided he would attempt the most audacious ruse of his life so far. His only problem was that it would require all the coin he had accumulated thus far. If he failed, he would have nothing once again. Undeterred, the following morning he packed up his few possessions and began to make his way to the town where the Magistrate lived, some twenty miles away. He arrived in the mid-afternoon and took a few hours to acquaint himself with the general layout of the busy town. He found both the Magistrate's house and the courthouse from which he ran his practice. Ying also identified his future lodgings, a large house on the edge of town, boarded up for the winter, its owners presumably seasonal residents. He then found a tailor where he was able to purchase the sombre and dignified gowns that he required. With the little money he had left, he purchased brushes, ink and some basic stationery tools. Nothing approaching the quality of Chu Lai's delicate set, but functional and inexpensive. He also purchased a bamboo seal that he had carved with his own, newly designed, insignia. The next morning he hand-delivered a letter to the Magistrate's office asking for an audience at his earliest convenience.

The Magistrate's assistant

It was several days before he received a reply. He had given a local inn as the return address, having slipped the owner a tip for receiving any correspondence for him. The letter, clearly written and signed by the Magistrate's clerk, simply stated a date and time. On the appointed day, he presented himself at the courthouse and was shown into the Magistrate's private studio. It was a refined and elegant room, well appointed but sparse. It had clearly been designed as a sanctuary from the hectic comings and goings of the courthouse. He was invited to sit and offered tea, which he gratefully accepted. The Magistrate asked how he could help and Ying, opting for a direct approach, launched into his plea for employment.

'I am young, bright and hard-working. Although I have no references, I am an excellent calligrapher and reader. I have good numeric skills and am very hard-working…' Nerves getting the better of him, he was beginning to repeat himself. 'I am also extremely observant and sensitive to any detail, however small…' Now he was waffling. The Magistrate waited until Ying paused for breath and politely stopped him.

'Young man,' he began, 'it takes a lot of courage to come into a magistrate's office asking for work.' He paused. 'Although such an approach is quite irregular, I am impressed by your boldness and candour.'

Ying was anticipating a 'but' and did not have to wait long. The Magistrate explained, very calmly, that he was inundated by applications from suitable, degreed candidates every month. He already employed two more clerks than he needed. He said that he was in need of help, given his advancing years, but that the work was highly specialized and unusual. Ying's hopes sunk to the pit of his stomach. He could hardly have been surprised. He had dreamt and reached far higher than his station. The Magistrate had paused. He appeared to be closely scrutinizing Ying, his face, his expression, his demeanour.

'Would you mind playing a little game with me?' he asked.

Taken aback, Ying simply nodded.

'Close your eyes, please.' Ying did as he was told. 'Now can you list for me all of the things in this room?'

Confused, Ying simply nodded again and after a short pause began.

'You are seated at a fine painting table, architectural style, with fine beadings, hardwood, *tieli* perhaps...there is a burn mark on the top, partially covered by your teacup, almost certainly from an oil lamp...'

He was just getting warmed up when the Magistrate stopped him short.

'Very good,' he said. 'But, keeping your eyes closed, can you tell me what is in the room behind you? If you had a chance to glance there when you entered.'

Again, Ying reeled off a list of things he had only caught a glimpse of but had instinctively committed to memory.

Impressed, the Magistrate rubbed his chin, trying to conceive of a more challenging task. Then he said in a challenging tone: 'Now I will close my eyes and you must move or remove something from my table. I will be trying to sense your every movement. You have 20 seconds.'

The Magistrate closed his eyes and was just beginning to count down when Ying politely interrupted. 'I am done, your honour.'

Amazed and slightly vexed, the Magistrate began to examine his table. He had heard nothing and felt nothing, so he assumed Ying had done something on the periphery of the table. However, try as he might, he could not see any change. For a full ten minutes, in total silence and demonstrating no regard for Ying's presence, he studied his tabletop, occasionally placing a finger on a possible piece and slowly retracting it.

Eventually, and with the grace and elegance that only experience and lack of vanity can bring, he gave up.

'Tell me,' he asked. 'Please.'

'I drank your tea!' Ying replied merrily.

The Magistrate was shocked and seized his cup to see that it had indeed been drained. Here, he thought, was a unique mind. Whilst the obvious thing would have been to target something nearest to him, Ying had gone for the thing that was farthest and most difficult. Then, he had avoided the Magistrate's second trap. Moving a piece would appear to have been the most logical and least risky thing to do, but in fact it would have been the easiest to detect. Thirdly, he had chosen to remove something that was only ever there temporarily, in the cup, waiting to be removed by being drunk anyway. The Magistrate, already impressed, creased his brow. Suddenly, it struck him that perhaps Ying had not drunk his tea at all, that he himself had drained the cup and Ying had just noticed this and claimed to have drunk it. But the truth did not really matter; what the young man had done was outwit him in the most unexpected and intriguing way. This was a mind he could happily work with.

The Magistrate's decision was made, but, for protocol's sake, he had Ying do a few more such tests before agreeing to take him on as his apprentice. Overjoyed, Ying said that he would happily work for free, provided he were fed. The Magistrate frowned.

'Absolutely not!' he hissed. 'Unpaid work is slavery and slavery has no place on earth, in heaven or hell! Every man has his worth and you would do well to learn and value yours.'

The golden apprenticeship

Ying started work the next day, on a salary he could only ever have dreamed of. His role was to help the Magistrate in his investigations, visiting scenes of a crime, gathering evidence, talking to witnesses. This was legwork, but the thrill of the chase, the solving of the puzzle, was exhilarating. At first, the Magistrate would simply send him on short fact-finding missions. 'Go to this tavern at such a time. Pay attention to who is there and what happens and report back.' Of course, Ying followed instructions, but as time passed and his confidence grew, he would sometimes ask 'why?' This would be met with total silence. Or 'what am I looking for?' More silence. Perhaps it was none of his business. However, he soon discovered that if he asked a specific question after his surveillance, this would be met with a sincere and transparent conversation.

'If I tell you why, you will go in with a prejudice,' the Magistrate would say. 'And if I tell you what to look for, you may miss something truly important.'

It turned out that apart from being a brilliant mind, the Magistrate was also a most gifted teacher.

And Ying proved himself to be a most gifted pupil. Quick-witted, with a razor-sharp eye for detail, he undertook all of the challenges he was set with great enthusiasm and growing confidence. His reports were exacting and thorough and on several occasions where Ying was sent to observe a particular subject, a random detail from his report cast light on another case that the Magistrate was working on. Soon, the Magistrate came to rely very heavily on his young protégé and was always generous with his praise.

'Excellent work Ying,' he would say, a tone of genuine admiration in his voice. 'Soon enough, you will not be needing my guidance anymore.' And together they would laugh, though the Magistrate knew his words carried an undeniable truth.

Ying was more than content with his new life, he was actually happy. At last, he had found a way of putting his unusual gifts to work. He was learning new skills every day. Moreover, although he did not know it, his soul had found balance because he had finally found a mentor in whom he trusted. Over the next two years, as they worked more and more closely together on cases, the Magistrate would take Ying into his confidence about all manner of things. For his part, Ying, for the first time in his life, had a father figure and a confidant. These were days of hard work and rich reward, but perhaps it was inevitable that they would come to an end.

One evening while they were out in the tavern celebrating the successful conclusion of a case, the Magistrate surprised Ying with some news. Citing his advancing years as well as a growing concern about his sister's health, the Magistrate said that he had been toying with the idea of retiring and moving back to his home town to be closer to his remaining family. Ying was taken aback. Having at last found the stability and friendship he had craved all his life, could this really be taken from him overnight?

'I will go with you,' countered Ying when he had recovered from the first shock. 'We can continue our work in your home town. I am sure it is a wonderful place.'

'Yes, it is,' the Magistrate replied. 'And we could. But…' There was a long pause and in that moment Ying understood that this chapter of his life, this rich, warm, wonderful chapter, was drawing to a close. 'But, my dear boy,' the Magistrate continued, 'I fear I have taught you all I can.' Ying thought he could detect a gloss in his mentor's eyes. 'Furthermore, I am convinced that you have outgrown both me and this town.'

Ying objected, argued and even pleaded, but in his heart he knew there was no escaping the inevitability of the situation. Whether in a month, a year or a decade, Ying would at some point move on. The Magistrate had realized this for some time, but Ying's deep contentment with his current life had blinded him to this destiny.

Returning ghosts

The Magistrate and Ying continued to work as before. The days were growing shorter and the Magistrate would certainly not make any definite changes until spring. Now fully aware of the finite nature of his current life, Ying was even more grateful and appreciative of how fortune had favoured him. He was aware that he would need to make a plan for his future, just as he was aware that he could still count on his mentor to help guide him in the right direction. Surely, together, with Ying's skills and experience and the Magistrate's multitude of contacts, they would find a solution. Then, as so often happens, when Ying was least expecting it, in the depth of winter, destiny provided the path.

It was a blustery winter night and Ying was in a deep but troubled sleep. It was a dream that recurred, not often, but often enough. He was at home playing with his brother when his father burst into the room. He was drunk and blind with fury, brandishing his hoe, which was kept by the door, in the direction of the defenceless boys. But now Ying was watching the scene from the doorway behind his father. He was at once participant and observer. As his father came closer, eyes burning red with rage, Ying placed himself in front of his brother to protect him. As his father loomed over them, poised to deliver a great blow, memories of pain and fear overwhelmed the observing Ying. It was at this point that he would wake up in a cold sweat. But not on this night. Tonight, just as his father was about to launch his second assault, a large hand seized his arm from behind and with effortless ease tossed him out through the open door. Participant and observer were one again and Ying found himself briefly gazing into familiar eyes. He awoke, heart pounding. Zhong Kui.

The next morning, retracing the events of his traumatic dream in his mind, Ying felt a compulsion to commune with his saviour. That mysterious figure who had rescued him from death and somehow partially healed his deformed leg, whom he had encountered again that night in the woods when he delivered that unintelligible letter. Thinking of this man, Ying inadvertently found himself holding the fine *zitan* box he had been gifted. He opened it to reveal the notes he had taken the night he had stumbled across the shadowy meeting in the hut. He had not thought of that night for a long time. Then, next to these notes, another piece of paper caught Ying's eye. Picking it up, he immediately recognized the seal as the same one that had been on the letter he had delivered to Zhong Kui from Chu Lai. The letter was brief, direct and totally unexpected.

Honourable Ying,

I learned of the passing of our esteemed friend with great sadness. The Magistrate often spoke of your great progress. It is with satisfaction that I inform you that you are required to present yourself to the Ministry of War in the Capital forthwith. I have use for your particular talents. You will be working, very discreetly, directly under me. Inform no one of this.

I look forward to welcoming you to your new role as Palace Detective.

Chu Lai
Minister of War to his Imperial Majesty

—IV—

Clouded Realms

wherein a wary tribe withdraws behind a wall of ice to guard a secret, raising in its sunless lee a hideous hierarchy and a grasping appetite for war; wherein an ancient legend stirs to life, and a lone, blood-stained memento escapes the fray.

Chasing Clouds

FURTHER **STRANGE TALES**
FROM THE IVORY CRESCENT

Virtuous realm

IN THE FAR WEST, just beyond the farthest frontier of the Empire, high up in the Kunlun Mountains, was an extraordinary kingdom ruled for generations by descendants of a wise old family. The Kingdom of Kun was situated on the eastern face of a wide mountain peak which descended into a fertile plateau. Whilst the summit of this majestic mountain was perpetually encased in ice and snow, it had a vast, deep terrace below that provided natural shelter from the harsh elements.

It was in this unusual natural recess that the kingdom's magnificent capital was built using stone hewn from the mountain, as well as fine timber imported from its neighbours. By necessity, all of the dwellings and buildings of this city faced east; large windows were designed so that each morning all its residents might awaken to the majesty of the sun rising and the prospect of a luminous new day. At the very rear of the great terrace, piercing the peak, were two vast natural openings, hundreds of feet wide, that looked over the dark, narrow valley below to the great expanse of the Kunlun mountain range beyond. These large natural windows often gave rise to a quite spectacular effect, of which the architects of the city had taken full advantage.

On clear evenings, these apertures flooded the entire city with the glowing light of sunset, bathing it in an ever-changing spectacle of rich, warm hues. There was a further opening in the mountain on its right-hand side which had once been a busy thoroughfare to the valley on the other side. However, this had frozen over in the Great Cold several centuries earlier. In the very centre of the highest peak, beneath the almost boundless expanse of snow, was a third, much smaller aperture. Practically inaccessible, this was a revered and special place, visible for miles and miles from both sides of the peak.

Although it was a remote place, sometimes isolated during the worst winter storms, its proximity to the age-old silk road meant that the influence of this small but remarkable people was felt far into the Chinese Empire. Whilst the natives of this kingdom had originally descended from a single mountain tribe, their peaceful and welcoming nature had made them an obvious place of refuge for individuals and small groups escaping persecution and trying to start a new life. They were a cerebral people, known for their diplomacy, humanity and deep spirituality. They were also famous for their highly refined skills in the arts, on display especially in their complex and richly detailed paintings.

For centuries, this kingdom had been a vassal state of the Chinese Empire. It had no army. Being so hard to reach had its strategic advantages. Moreover, as its wealth lay predominantly in the skills and high culture of its people, it was hardly an obvious target for invasion. For the rest, being skilled diplomats and kindly, thoughtful people, the Kun were always on good terms with neighbouring states. It was not uncommon for them to be called upon to act as arbitrators in disputes between families, clans, provinces and even countries, such was their reputation for considered impartiality. In their entire history, they had never been involved in a war or border dispute. In trade, they were keen promoters of multi-generational symbiotic relation-ships, at times paying above market price for goods when they could see their trade partners suffering as a result of war, famine or bad weather. However, the kingdom did have one sworn enemy, and they were, geographically at least, their closest neighbours.

Ruling house

The rulers of the Kun were historically benevolent and thoughtful, always at pains to ensure the well-being of their subjects as well as to maintain stability in the empire to which they were attached. However, the current queen and king were exceptional even by Kun standards. Childhood sweethearts, the couple projected a sense of unity and warmth that was infectious for the entire population. The queen of Kun was a highly skilled administrator and strategist. She was immensely beloved by her people, not least because she spent nearly as much time amongst them as in her palace. She would throw lavish feasts during festival days, inviting the whole population into the citadel. Queen Hong had been named after a rainbow and never ceased to delight in the colours that so often played across the venerable stone surfaces of her kingdom. Her only regret was that she and her beloved had been unable to have children. This was the one void in her life, even though succession would not be a problem as the couple would be able to choose from any number of suitable heirs from other families and be sure to leave their paradise in good hands. However, in the end, unforeseen events made it so that no such decision was necessary.

The king of Kun was no less impressive. He was a fine calligrapher who specialized in large-scale lettering of a highly expressive nature. On the occasion of the Chinese Emperor becoming a grandfather, he sent as a gift such a wonderful example, which simply contained the characters for 'legacy', that it almost moved the Emperor to tears. A gift of such simplicity and genuineness was a rare thing for an emperor to receive; moreover, it spoke to the Emperor's ageing. In return, the Emperor sent the king a magnificent brush carved with dragons. The note that accompanied the gift, in the Emperor's own hand, simply read: 'Emperor to King...Dragon to Dragon.' The king was overwhelmed by this gesture and his wife would recollect years later that he from then on refused to use any other brush. Even if its size was not fit for purpose, he would rather adapt his style and technique than swap it for another.

Some years later, the new Emperor, brother of the one now deceased, called on the Kun to act as an intermediary in a summit with China's neighbours in Tibet. The Tibetan kingdom had been rapidly growing in economic and military strength and now presented a serious threat to China's western border. Provocatively, the Tibetan king had engaged a former Chinese governor as political and military advisor. The Tibetans had started to employ a far more aggressive strategy with regard to their neighbours. Border raids had become quite common. However, under the skilled guidance of the queen and king of Kun, an agreement was reached and a treaty signed, preserving peace and promoting the growth of both nations, which should have lasted a hundred years. As it happened, though, only a few short years would pass before this accord would be tested in an utterly bewildering manner.

Dominion of darkness

On the other side of this majestic mountain was a very different world indeed. Shrouded in almost perpetual darkness was a narrow valley. On this side, the wondrous mountain was almost a sheer wall. Narrow crevices and fissures in the rock face were packed with ice and snow, creating a striated façade of black and white. At the base of the mountain was a deep recessed cave. Where once a natural tunnel had provided access to the other side, the Kingdom of Kun, the plateau and the silk road beyond, this had frozen shut several centuries prior. As such, this side was accessible only by treacherous mountain paths and passes on the facing peak, which turned into even more perilous, barely navigable trails clinging to the near vertical mountain wall on the other side. Only the most skilled and hardy were able to traverse these trails, leaving this one of the most remote and isolated places on the entire continent. It was in this place, this dark, cold, foreboding place, that the people of An resided.

The state of An was not a kingdom, but rather a domain ruled by an elite of religious priests and monks. Once part of the same prosperous mountain tribe as the Kun, the An were the descendants of one clan who had refused to move when the Great Cold had threatened to totally isolate the valley centuries earlier. The elders of the tribe had pleaded with them in vain to leave and join them on the other side of the mountain, explaining that they were risking the lives and futures of their families, but were consistently rebuffed. In fact, the clansmen had not only refused to move, but had actively forced anyone not in their clan to leave the valley. The reasons for their refusal were kept a closely guarded secret, well after the tunnel had frozen over. In the end the explanation was simple: greed.

Several years before the unexpected change in climate had begun to threaten access to the valley, members of the An clan who lived at its farthest end had discovered something quite by chance. They were hunters by trade, but also scavengers, as one often had to be living in such a hostile place. One day, scavenging for anything that might be tradable in the outside world, they stumbled on a deep cave whose high narrow opening could only be reached by rope and hook. The first thing they discovered was the lair of a rare white tiger. Thankfully for them, the tiger was out hunting for food for her two newborn cubs. These the clan members took and slaughtered, making a feast from their meat and gloves from their virgin fur.

Returning to her cave, the mother tiger, a magnificent, sapient beast, saw the raging fire of the invaders and smelled the sickening stench of her cubs' roasting flesh. Her instinct was to exact vengeance there and then, but she knew she would almost certainly die. Somehow she found the resolve to turn and flee, but she vowed to haunt and torment these people for as long as she lived. Meanwhile, the scavengers explored the cave, going deeper and deeper as the months went by. At first, they found some residues of stones and powders that were valuable for the making of pigments; these they traded secretly without revealing their source. One day, now deep into the cave, whose narrow passages they had begun to widen with the help of hammers and picks, they made an extraordinary find. Silver.

Silver, at this time, was the most important material in the Chinese Empire, the basis for its entire financial system. The clansmen saw that they could make themselves rich beyond their wildest imaginations. They would be able to buy whatever they desired, build palaces and mansions and live like kings. In fact, there was enough silver to be mined to make every member of their tribe wealthy and more. The entire tribe could become a rich and powerful kingdom, with their clan at the helm. But this was not enough for them. They did not want to share a single ounce of silver, but knew that they were too few to protect it once word got out. So they simply kept it a secret, with only their clan benefitting from the silver they mined and sold on. Even when the Great Cold began and they were threatened with impending isolation and probable death, they refused to divulge their secret. So they stayed, hoping that their isolation would be short-lived and that they could soon return to enjoying the fruits of their seemingly endless bounty.

The Great Cold came and went, but the tunnel remained frozen and the An trapped. In the early years, fellow tribesmen of the An who had settled on the other side of the mountain petitioned their leaders to try to reconnect the two valleys once more. A plan was devised by which, raising taxes from their citizens and borrowing silver from the Chinese, they aimed to employ men and digging contraptions to unblock the tunnel and rescue the An. These plans were communicated to the An through the use of trained messenger birds. Once again, fearing for the loss of their silver, the An refused, threatening to disrupt and destroy any such attempts as well as kill anyone trying to enter their domain. Their would-be rescuers were flabbergasted but could not find a way to change their minds. So, the two peoples, once one tribe, embarked on very different paths indeed.

The development of the An people was, not surprisingly, a bleak and tortured path. The An still had their mountains of silver, but they had no way of spending it. Hunting and scavenging remained their only real means of survival. Life in the caves was desolate. By pure luck, whilst mining, the An had discovered a rich supply of coal, so they were able to heat their cave dwellings to fend off the worst of the elements. This however also had the effect of covering almost everything with a fine dark dust from the coal and smoke. They were eventually able to find a route to the outside world over the opposite peak and across a frozen plateau. This was a treacherous journey that cost many lives, but it did enable the strongest amongst them to open up a trade route and a way for them to cash in on their silver. They were able to return with much-needed goods and foods. They also brought back slaves, who were exclusively young and male, as they were the only ones believed capable of surviving the journey. It was over a hundred years before they were able to improve this route, to make it safer and allow pack donkeys.

As such, the An bred amongst themselves and as often happens in such cases, the very worst of their characteristics, both physical and behavioural, were passed down and amplified from generation to generation. The harshness of their lives meant that only the strongest survived, leading to each generation becoming more resilient, and even more ruthless. They developed deep-set eyes and tough skin to cope with the endless storms and punishing winds. To rule themselves, the An, a highly diffident and superstitious people, developed a quasi-religious hierarchy with high priests at the top, monks who acted as warriors and enforcers, and a growing underclass of serfs and slaves. Imported slaves were considered the most lowly.

Once the trade route had been expanded, the slave population grew dramatically and began to include both men and women. Very soon, the slave population outnumbered the ethnic An, who were now all elevated to a higher status, provided they were of pure blood. Relations between an An man and a slave were encouraged, both to entertain the men and to continue to grow the slave population. Relations between an An woman and a foreigner were punishable by the death of the entire slave family. The division between An and slaves was sharpened further by the building of higher-level caves for the An, whilst the slaves remained huddled in the deep recesses of the vast central cave. The new An dwellings were heated by large pipes funnelling the heat from the coal burned below and heating cavities in the hollow brick walls and floors. The result was that whilst the growing population of slaves and half-bloods was blackened, their skin and clothing perpetually stained with soot, the An were clean-skinned and wore lighter-coloured garments.

As generations came and went, the An developed a serious problem that threatened their very survival: a lack of women. By the time eighty years had passed since the start of their isolation, the female population had more than halved; the harshness of conditions and the dangers of childbirth had decimated their numbers. Soon the problem was so great that the high priests saw fit to create a new set of laws regarding women. Over time, the lives of An men and women became totally bifurcated. As children, girls were taken by the priests, their physical well-being considered vital. Once a girl had achieved maturity, she was expected to lie with only the high priests in rotation until she became pregnant.

If she bore a girl, she was elevated to a revered status as supplier of a vessel to further the clan. She was looked after and pampered and the cycle would be repeated amongst a restricted group of priests who had previously sired girls. If a woman gave birth to three consecutive girls, she was sent, via a massive winch, to the Frozen Eye, a hole in the uppermost part of the mountain that was frozen solid. Here, she would live in a hut for a week to commune with the spirits. If she survived, she was brought back down and could live as a princess amongst the clan, permitted to choose her partners on her own terms. If she died, she would be killed once again, in pantomime,

in a ritualistic sacrifice in front of the whole population. Her flesh would then be consumed by the priests and clansmen. Eating her flesh, the men believed, would not only enhance their ability to sire girls but was also the only way for her spirit to atone for its failure to survive.

If, on the other hand, a woman gave birth to a son, she stayed at the same level as before. If a woman, even one who had previously had a girl, gave birth to two consecutive or a total of three boys, she was considered tainted. Now she was demoted to be the mere sexual object of any man of the clan. She would be used and abused at will until such a time as she was no longer desired, at which point she would be cast down into the slave class.

Over time, with the expansion of the western trade route, more and more slaves were brought in to service the structures and needs of this strange and ruthless society. Occasionally, girls of exceptional beauty were brought to the high priests for evaluation. If the priests, or even a particular one, took a shining to such a girl, she too would enter the cycle. This became another crucial supply route for this rare and sought-after commodity. If these elevated slave girls ever had a son, even after having had daughters, they were immediately passed down to the general clansmen. Their inability to bear a daughter was seen as a great insult to the honour bestowed upon them by the priests and they were often raped and abused until they simply perished.

Tiger tiger

The An had one other problem, which, whilst its casualties were limited, was central to the development of certain aspects of their home-grown religion. Over time, the white tiger, already a much-revered beast in Chinese folklore, came to be the core element of the An canon. She was both demon and deity, bringer of violent death but also benefactor and protector. Patterns modelled after her distinctive markings were central to An decoration; drawings of her made by the original killers of her cubs were amongst the clan's most prized possessions and were often copied and used as totems. It was the white beast who kept outsiders from their valley and their silver. It was also she who regularly preyed on their citizens in vengeful retribution. Their mauled and bloodied corpses were always left where they were highly visible, as if the tiger were taunting them: 'I can strike as you did...only more silent...more deadly.' But I would not stoop to eating your rancid flesh.' The white tiger was the only thing on earth the An truly feared and truly respected. In all their other dealings with the outside world, they perceived themselves as a purer and superior race, their savage power unmatched by their neighbours. A legend grew that whilst the sacred tiger was to be avoided at all costs, one day a great warrior would slay the mythical beast and lead them out of the valley, to conquer whatever lay beyond.

As for the tiger, she was indeed no ordinary beast. She was something created in the mists between heaven and earth. After having witnessed the slaughter of her cubs at the hands of the clan explorers, the tiger withdrew a safe distance to higher ground, near the frozen peak. Here she found a new cave in which to make her lair. Exploring the environs of this high-altitude sanctuary, she soon discovered a track that led over to the other side of the mountain, into the kingdom of the Kun. Navigating it required all of her prodigious agility and balance, but it gave her access to far more fertile hunting grounds on the plateau far below. Yet she always returned to her icy lair. She also ventured to the frozen plateau to find mates and over the years gave birth to a large number of cubs that grew into magnificent creatures that in turn made the area their home and often preyed on men of the An, but never ate of their flesh. At the time our story takes place, Mother Tiger, as she became known, had lived for several centuries and her descendants were more plentiful than ever before.

Fair maiden

It was a fine autumn day, and the priests could hear the drums of their returning warriors in the distance. Soon they would arrive, their bounty in tow, carried by pack donkeys and carts, with the inevitable column of shackled slaves following behind. The return of a convoy was always a time of great excitement. For the priests, it was a time of luxuries and new women. Fresh meat for the hungry. For the clansmen, it was a time to welcome back comrades and partake of the newly acquired goods and the rotation of girls who had been the dominion of the priests. Fresh meat for the hungry. For the slaves, it was a painful reminder of their own arrivals, but also a time of perverse pleasure. The newest arrivals were now at the bottom of the pile, untried, frightened, weak. Fresh meat for the hungry.

In the afternoon, the warriors poured into the caves and there was great cheering and rejoicing. This particular bounty had been rich in both food, luxuries and slaves. But as they passed through the filthy alleys of the lower caves, it was clear to all that there was one very special prize. She was unusually tall for a girl and of athletic build, with subtle, beguiling curves. This alone made her stand out amongst the column of dark scruffy slave girls, but what really made her glow in the icy afternoon sun was her almost white-blond hair and luminously pale complexion. As she passed, all eyes were fixed on her and she cowered down as if trying to disappear. Whilst the other slaves were taken straight to the slave masters, she was immediately taken to the upper citadel where, after being paraded in front of the other clansmen, she was presented to the priests as a potential high breeder. There was little question that she would be elevated, so striking and exotic was this pale maiden. It was more a question of which priest would prevail.

Perhaps inevitably, it was the high priest who claimed her as his prize. This was unprecedented; a high priest had never before tarnished himself by procreating with anyone other than a pure-blooded An girl. Naturally, jealousy and resentments ran high. The high priest gave her the name Bai, meaning white or pure. This angered the other priests and clansmen even further. She was soon with child and, as the day drew nearer, there was a public frenzy about what she would produce. The day came and it was announced that she had given birth to a girl, much to the disappointment of the clansmen eager to savour her rare beauty. At this stage, it would have been expected for the high priest to relinquish her to the other priests, but so jealous was he of his trophy that he refused. The second child she bore was also a girl, unprecedented for a slave girl. The third was also a girl. Would the high priest dare suggest that she be sent to the Frozen Eye? Could he truly conceive of a princess who was of impure blood? He tried, but the resistance from his fellow priests as well as the outraged clansmen was too strong even for him to counter. It was only after she gave birth a fourth time, to twin girls, that he was able to impose his will and declare that she would be sent up to the Frozen Eye, either to perish or return a princess.

News of this decision spread like wildfire through the populace. The An were mostly against such an action, despite accepting that she was a blessed vessel. But amongst the slaves the excitement was palpable. Never had one of their number even dreamed of being elevated in such a way. Soon they had whipped themselves up into a frenzy, singing and chanting for the new princess, their queen. Such dangerous sentiments had rarely presented themselves, such was the iron fist with which the An ruled. There had never been any ambiguity: they were the ruling race and all beneath them were a lowly sub-species lucky to be able to serve them. As the day approached for Bai to be sent up to the Eye, unrest reached fever pitch. The night before, Bai was taken from her chamber and dragged to a room in the citadel. Here priests and clansmen alike took their turn with her. By rights, she should have died, but somehow she survived. The next morning her crumpled body was tossed into the winch's basket. The high priest was furious, but was also aware that her likely death on the frozen peak would undoubtedly be the best outcome, given the problems her story had caused and the importance she was developing amongst the slaves.

She was taken up and dumped in the hut. To make sure she did not return, the food she was left with had been poisoned. Half-conscious, battered and bruised, she watched as the two warriors who had brought her up returned smirking to the winch. Bai collapsed into the pile of blankets on the bed and slept. She dreamed of the northern home from which she was taken, the massacre of her village, the never-ending journey passed from trader to trader until she arrived in this desolate place to endure a hell she could not have conceived in her most harrowing nightmares. She awoke after several days slightly stronger, but resolute. She was resolved to do the only thing she believed would bring her any solace. During her years with the high priest, he had taught her many of the ways and traditions of the An. She learned of the sealing of the valley, of the white tiger, of the Frozen Eye. She also knew what fate awaited her body were she to die on this frozen peak. Thus, mustering all of her strength, she left the hut and began to trudge through the snow, away from the hut. They would not find her corpse waiting obligingly for them so that they could drag her back down to the caves to perform their demonic ritual. She would walk until her final breath, as far away as she could get. They would not venture too far to search for her: this was a dangerous and inhospitable place. She would dig deep inside herself and enact this, her final protest. She would have her small victory.

As the wind picked up, whipping up clouds of freshly fallen snow, she pressed on, every step a small defiance. For over an hour she trudged over craggy frozen ground and through whirlwinds of icy air. When she could feel her feet no more and her strength was waning, she saw a dark aperture in the blank white distance. Instinctively, she headed toward it. This would be her resting place, her frozen sanctuary: a deep dark cave at the border of heaven and earth. They would never find her body, of that she was sure.

Great thaw

Over the years, as was inevitable, the numbers of the An ruling class had been shrinking, whilst the population of slaves was growing both through natural means and through constant additions from the now far more practicable western trade route. The ruling high priests were aware that this situation would not be sustainable for much longer. The events surrounding Bai had clearly demonstrated that the slaves were frustrated and perhaps easily instigated into action given the right cause or leader. The priests knew they had to devise a plan or risk one day losing their grip on the slave population. The answer presented itself in the gradual but steady thawing of the ice that blocked the great tunnel to the kingdom of their neighbours, which had remained frozen shut for many centuries. The time had come. Only by leaving the valley and conquering their neighbours could the An grow and thrive. It was time for war.

For several years, the An prepared for a large-scale campaign. The existing male slaves were elevated to the status of soldiers, which also afforded them

the privilege of citizenship, though they remained inferior in status to their pure-blooded leaders. Many of them had been born into their position. The An were all they knew. Traces of their own heritage were long gone. This new role as warriors for what was now, for better or worse, their own kingdom gave them a sense of pride and belonging. At the same time, the An continued to buy new slaves to service their newly formed army. With this underclass of fresh slaves beneath them, the new soldiers embraced their new identity with zeal. Nothing empowers more than having somebody to tread on. Nothing unites more than having a common enemy. The An used their mountains of silver to purchase weapons, horses and mercenaries. To the outside world, the An were an almost mythical entity, largely unseen, isolated for centuries, ferocious and barbarian. A dark horde was coming, and nobody was prepared. Whilst the army was growing and being trained and armed, secret works began to open up the tunnel. These progressed until there was only the thinnest barrier of ice left between them and their prey. The day was almost upon them.

Uninvited guests

It was just hours before the New Year. The whole Kingdom of Kun was humming with preparations. Bonfires were being lit, feasts prepared, offerings made to any god who might listen for a prosperous new year. Children were scurrying through the streets running last-minute errands for their frantic parents. It was as if every citizen was determined to make this celebration the best one ever. It is a wonderful thing to behold an entire people fermenting with anticipation and preparing for a popular and unbridled explosion of joy. The boisterous energy of the Kun could surely be felt for miles around.

The queen and king were on the royal terrace when the first screams were heard. As the lurid scent of burning flesh wafted up through the crisp air, they dashed to the railings, only to have to watch in helpless terror as a torrent of fierce warriors tore through the streets below. Little resistance was offered by the unsuspecting citizens of Kun, and the ferocity of the early exchanges made it clear that this was ill-advised in any case. They were simply overrun. Shaken to their core, the queen and king went back inside. They decided that it would be best for them to split up in order to lend support to their subjects. The king would go to the ramparts to try and mount some sort of defence. He suggested that she head straight for the main gates to do what she could there. They embraced. It was a moment of unspoken finality. When she reached the gates, she found them near deserted. Her chief guard was standing with a Chinese soldier, introduced simply as 'the Captain'. He informed her that a protocol written by her husband years before entrusted him with her escape and safe delivery to the court of the Emperor of China.

In a moment of horrific realization, the queen tore herself from the officers and rushed frantically back to their studio. There on the floor, surrounded by a vast pool of blood, was her beloved king. He had carefully lacerated all of his major arteries. In his limp hand was his treasured dragon brush. On the white-washed wall, written in his own blood, were two characters, side by side:

HEAVEN TO HELL

Desperate at the loss of her beloved husband and soulmate, Queen Hong closed the door and bolted it, just before the pursuing guards and the Captain could enter. Her destiny was to be for ever with her love and her people.

It did not take the An long to sweep through the Kingdom of Kun. They slaughtered, raped and pillaged. The swift defeat of the Kun was to serve as an example of the An's overwhelming strength and ruthlessness and a warning to neighbouring kingdoms and states. With victory secured, the priests went about organizing their new kingdom. The priests would rule as they had always done, with the pure-blooded An now forming the nobility. The soldier-slaves became the enforcers of the laws whilst the Kun population was subjugated into a semi-servile existence. The new An kingdom quickly began to exert its influence in the region both through the threat of war and the lure of its great trove of freshly mined silver.

Out of nowhere, the name of the An, once shrouded in mystery, was on the lips of anxious leaders for thousands of miles around. Yet despite their new-found power, centuries of isolation had made the An totally ill-equipped for the complexities of statecraft. When the Emperor of China sent a delegation of nobles to negotiate a peaceful co-existence, their heads were returned to him in a silver chest, their eyes gouged out and brains removed. The An were desperate to expand their presence, but diffident of all around them. In the end, lacking a plan or strategy, they resorted to sporadically raiding neighbouring kingdoms, looting and taking slaves, especially female ones, before retreating to the safe confines of their sacred peaks. A new, destabilizing force had been born on the western border, where the Tibetans were already causing concern. The Empire was under threat. In a few short years it had lost its leader to old age and his natural heir in battle. The new Emperor, his predecessor's uncle, who had seized power in order to steady the ship, was not without enemies and his own health was waning.

Mother Tiger

Bai had made it to the mouth of the cave with all of the strength she had left. Dropping to her knees, she crawled further into the cave. They must not find her body. She was aware of a presence. She looked up. A pair of glowing eyes stared back at her from the depths of darkness. The guardian of heaven and hell, she thought to herself. At last, peace. She fell to the floor.

She was awoken by a warm breath on her face, then a moist caress. She tried to open her eyes. Squinting in the darkness, she could just about make out the large silhouette of a head. And those eyes again. As her vision came into focus, she could see that lying next to her, sharing its warmth, was the massive body of a white tiger. Distractedly, as if watching herself from afar, Bai noted that she was not paralysed by fear. Instead, she felt a powerful sense of the benevolence of this magnificent beast. She must already be dead, she thought. She fell back into a deep slumber, the warmth of Mother Tiger's body nourishing her.

Over the next days, months and years, a strong, intimate bond developed between Bai and this great beast. The tiger would go out and hunt, returning with the food Bai needed to recover her strength. Her recovery and convalescence took many months, but soon she was able to leave the cave with her guardian beside her. She gathered wood and made a fire inside the cave, the warmth and rich glow an unimaginable luxury both to her and the tiger. As time went on, they would venture farther afield, Bai observing where she could what was happening in the valley below. Seemingly born of happenstance, this strange union grew more powerful with each passing day and Bai began to recall the stories of the great mythical warrior who would come one day to slay the white tiger and lead the An to freedom.

White tiger

In the valley below, the An continued to mine their silver and work their new slaves. From the old capital of the Kun they ruled, wielding destructive military and economic power in an indiscriminate and often chaotic way. Where their system of rule was once brutally simple and centralized, cliques and clans with desperate goals began to form within the ruling class. The new society was also struggling to assimilate its different peoples – the slaves granted power and freedom with little or no experience in exercising it; the Kun left adrift, with no goal or purpose to which to direct their highly developed talents. This discord was constantly being stoked by the arrival of new slaves and soldiers, rounded up during the regular military forays into foreign lands. These were becoming an increasingly dangerous and unpredictable force whose restlessness, unchecked by a clear outlet or direction, was mounting perceptibly. Once more, it looked like war was what would solve this problem for the An.

It was a dark, dismal day. From the morning, the sky had been bulging with angry black clouds as a storm brewed over the mountains. On the plateau, an army had amassed in the desperate hope of stopping the ever-growing An. It included imperial troops, depleted by the long march, as well as regiments from numerous neighbouring kingdoms and states. Foes who had fought for centuries now stood united. But they had little hope of victory. At the base of the mountain stood the army of the An. Native An warriors lusting for blood were lined up behind a massive force of soldiers, once slaves, and slaves, once free men. All knew that no quarter would be given. The An knew no fear and would not hesitate, would even relish the chance, to slaughter every last warrior who dared oppose them.

As the army began to approach, the An stood their ground. So confident were they in their victory that they mocked and taunted their enemy with chants and songs. Suddenly the wind picked up. A vast streak of lightning struck the plateau. The advancing army halted. The clouds in the distance began to break. A shaft of light flooded through the highest opening of the mountain, the place the An called the Frozen Eye. There was another blinding flash of lightning over the capital that was once the home of the Kun. Then a bone-chilling noise thundered through the whole area. Both armies turned to the source of the cry. There, at the opening of the Frozen Eye, illuminated by a celestial shaft of light, stood salvation. Salvation for the soldiers about to embark, salvation for the Kun people reduced to slaves, salvation for the slaves torn from their homelands. Most of all, salvation for the An, a dark, primitive people whose isolated existence and barbarous traditions had led them to this state.

At the entrance to the Eye, clad in white fur, pale as the snow, holding a simple spear, was Bai. Beside her rose the magnificent figure of the white tiger, her markings exactly as they had been depicted for centuries. It was the very vision the An had recounted for generations to their children. The mythical warrior who would slay the feared beast and lead them to freedom. Only the beast was not slain, and the great warrior was a simple slave girl, long thought dead. Fear and dread began to course through every An warrior and priest. Their day of reckoning was upon them.

Remarkably, there was no blood shed that day. As the opposing armies held their positions, Bai and the white tiger descended to the capital. Entering the great hall of the citadel, she summoned the leaders of the An, the high priests. They entered, ashen-faced and fearing for their lives. Once inside, the sight of Bai, with the fearsome figure of the tiger by her side, was too much for them. Some flung themselves to the ground in an act of desperate supplication. Others simply fainted. The rest stood trembling and expecting the worst. Bai, the young, pale slave girl on whose flesh they had been ready to feast, was now their judge and executioner. The tiger yawned, the sight of her huge mouth and glistening teeth sending a tremor through the assembled An. Then Bai spoke:

'It is not my place to judge your actions. It is not our place to seek vengeance.'

She paused, the An's terrified eyes flitting deliriously between her and the mighty beast by her side.

'However, I find that it is my place to determine how this day ends and how the future unfolds. I do this for the people of Kun and the countless others upon whose lives you have inflicted your dark ways.'

Again she paused, staring down the An with icy composure as she readied to deliver her judgement.

'Your punishment will be of your own making and as such it will be far more painful. There will be no place for your barbaric ways in our new world.'

Bai went on to decree that the An priests and soldiers would return to their valley. The An women could do so too, but only by choice. Any soldiers once slaves would be given the same choice. All slaves would be free to return to their homelands or become free citizens of the new Kun kingdom.

The An, a fierce and barbarian people with deep, dark superstitions, accepted their fate. They slunk back to their valley with the fear of the tiger fresh in their minds. They attempted to return to their ways, but too much had changed. The punishment for the An was a bleak future in their ancient valley. A fierce horde left to feed on each other. With so few women amongst them, they would perish in a few generations. They would be wiped from the face of the earth, soon to be forgotten by history. And yet few of them ever sought to escape or appeal to the Kun for clemency.

And so it was that on that mythical day the Kingdom of Kun was reborn, larger, stronger, richer and more powerful than ever before. On its throne sat a simple slave girl from a distant frozen land, a giant white tiger always by her side. The Kun returned to their former position as defenders of the hunted, arbiters of peace and custodians of spiritual equilibrium. Their mornings were greeted by the majesty of the rising sun. In the evenings the streets of their capital were flooded with the warm hues of sunset. Peace and harmony returned to the western border.

—V—

The Demon Queller

wherein a new personage appears on our stage; deformed of body but agile of mind, he must suffer a cruel rebuff before being clothed in fearsome power, an adjunct to the gloomy Abbadon beneath our feet.

FURTHER STRANGE TALES
FROM THE IVORY CRESCENT

Prelude

THE GREAT YAMA quelled the demon uprising with swift brutality. Order was restored to Diyu and was maintained by a force of specially vetted demons appointed by Yama to ensure that something like this could never happen again. In time, the 'germ' that had infected the demons was controlled, but never fully eradicated. Powerful demons now roamed the earth, acting as their instincts and appetites saw fit. They procreated amongst themselves, with humans as well as with animals, in time creating entirely new and vastly varied beings. Many of these were benign. Many simply used their powers or strength to their own advantage, just as humans did. But some were unable to control the lusts that had been unleashed within them.

Yama and his kings were aware of the great problem that faced them. The sanctity of the division between Earth and Hell had been compromised; they understood that nothing would ever be the same. Although the surface of the earth lay outside their jurisdiction, they knew something had to be done about the dangers that had been released from their hidden domain.

Zhong Kui

Around the time the Duke of Wu had finally achieved his goal of becoming Emperor of China, there lived in a town in the south a young man called Zhong Kui. He was a forlorn figure, having been born with some rather unfortunate physical traits. His head was unusually large, with a bulbous forehead and large bulging eyes. Growing up, he had few friends and was too often the target of the ridicule and pranks so common amongst children. In his loneliness, however, he was at least able to excel in his studies. When he reached adolescence, he befriended a classmate called Du Ping, son of a local scholar and a very popular boy in the town. Du Ping's friends could not understand why he would be friends with the freakish Zhong Kui, but he would explain that Zhong Kui, as well as being kind, had a quite exceptional mind. With an eye to his future, Du Ping nurtured his relationship with his new friend and they often studied together, discussing poetry, music and a host of other subjects on which Zhong Kui was by now expert. When the time came for Du Ping to travel to the Capital to sit the imperial exams, he chose Zhong Kui as his travelling companion. They had become firm friends and this would be a great adventure.

For Zhong Kui, the friendship had been an unexpected and much appreciated respite from the loneliness of his youth. He was aware that Du Ping's decision to befriend him had cost him some popularity and for this he would always be grateful to him. For his part, he had endeavoured to push Du Ping beyond his natural academic abilities. Du Ping was a good student, but not particularly gifted. He had to work hard and benefitted greatly from Zhong Kui's tutelage. Du Ping's wealth, connections and good looks would undoubtedly ensure his success in life, but he strove to reach as high as he could academically, and this was to his great credit. As for Zhong Kui, the imperial examination was his lifeline to a successful career as a magistrate, official or even minister. He was determined to excel.

And excel he did, for after they had both taken the exam, he was convinced that he had scored extremely high marks, possibly the highest of all. At last, he had found a place where his skills would be appreciated and rewarded, where he could carve out a life, where at last he might be afforded some respect if not affection. The ceremony in which most of the candidates received their marks was held in a large courtyard of the academy. The names and scores were read out for all to hear. Du Ping passed with high marks and jumped into his friend's arms upon hearing the news. Zhong Kui's name was not called out; he belonged to the 25 highest-scoring candidates who would take part in a ceremony in the Imperial Palace that would be attended by the Emperor himself. Zhong Kui was delighted, if not surprised, and asked if Du Ping might like to accompany him the next day. Du Ping, already elated from his own success, agreed most enthusiastically.

The ceremony the next day, a most austere affair, was presided over by the Emperor, seated on a raised platform above the head academician who was reading out the names of the remaining candidates and their scores. Each candidate whose name was called would then approach the platform and bow deeply, receiving the Emperor's blessing before being given their diploma. The Emperor was the personification of dignity and elegance, nodding and occasionally uttering a few words of encouragement. They were down to the top ten and still Zhong Kui's name had not been read. Top five and still nothing. Du Ping squeezed his friend's hand. Reaching the top five would make him a celebrity not just in their town, but in the whole province. All but the top three had been announced and still he was in play. In the moments before the second-placed candidate was announced, Zhong Kui could hardly contain his anguish. When the name was called, Zhong Kui realized he had placed first in the entire country.

When Zhong Kui's name was finally announced as the *zhuangyuan*, highest scorer of that year, his heart nearly exploded. He gathered himself with some difficulty and made his way to the platform to receive the Emperor's blessing and his diploma. A world of high government had just opened up, his future was secure, he could finally be happy. He bowed deeply and then stood up straight, as was the custom. But upon catching sight of Zhong Kui's face, unsightly and deformed as it was, the Emperor contorted his features, retched and made a small gesture to beckon over the academician. Zhong Kui was bemused. Stepping away from their cursory conference, the academician delicately cleared his throat and announced to all present that the Emperor had decreed that no creature as ugly as Zhong Kui could ever serve in his government and that for causing the Emperor such distress he was to be stripped of his title. After a brief, shocked silence, the crowd erupted into uproarious laughter. Zhong Kui, mortified, turned and fled.

For over an hour, Du Ping searched every corner of the Palace in an attempt to find and console his friend. After all, he would tell him, even without the title of *zhuangyuan* he was still placed exceptionally high and was on the road to a successful career. He was just approaching the gates of the Palace, having resolved to continue his search in the streets outside, when he noticed a sizeable crowd gathered just beyond the entrance. He pushed his way to the front, only to be greeted by the unmistakable form of his friend, lying face down, his black robes streaked with vermillion blood. He seized the nearest onlooker and demanded to know what had happened. Zhong Kui, he learned, had hurled himself against the Palace gates head first repetitively, howling the words 'deformed' and 'failure' until his head literally cracked

open. Shaking from head to toe, Du Ping took off his gown and laid it gently over his dear friend's corpse. The next day he hired a carriage and driver, loaded up Zhong Kui's body and made his way back home, where he arranged for him to have a hero's funeral. Du Ping observed a year's mourning for his lost friend. He was eventually able to resume his life and begin his career but remained shrouded in a dark cloud. Only following the exceptional circumstances by which he came to marry Zhong Kui's sister did light finally creep back into his world.

Meanwhile, Zhong Kui's soul passed swiftly to Diyu, where judgement awaited. Suicide was a sin from which it was difficult to be purified. However, Zhong Kui's tragic story gave the Great Yama pause. He was suitably impressed by the exceptional mental abilities that had allowed him to be placed first in the entire country. He was also sensitive to the pain and humiliation he had experienced at the hands of the Emperor, the former Duke of Wu and a man whose sinister ways he had witnessed first-hand. Thinking it over for a night, Yama returned the next day with a brilliant idea. He called together all the lords of hell and announced that Zhong Kui was to be granted powers and given a title, the King of Ghosts. His duties would be to keep the discipline amongst all the ghosts and special beings on earth and to hunt down and capture any demons still left on the surface. To aid him in this great task, Zhong Kui was to command an army of eighty thousand trained demons.

The Ghost King returns

New Year was fast approaching and, with only a few hours to go, Du Ping was busy preparing to go to the home of his parents for a simple meal. Given the tragic circumstances of that year, he had preferred to avoid large celebrations. In fact, he had planned to eat alone, but his parents had insisted he join them. It was a pleasant walk from his studio to his parents' estate, through the streets where he had grown up. The night was chilly, with a slight wind that caused the clouds to move swiftly across the sky, creating an ever-changing play of moonlight and shadows on the streets and buildings. For some reason Du Ping was feeling ill at ease, almost like someone was following him. Shaking this thought from his head, he quickened his pace and was soon at the large gate of his parents' estate.

Inside, Du Ping was surprised to hear the sound of numerous voices emanating from the banquet hall. His mother came out to greet him and was met by a scowl.

'Mother,' he said sternly, 'I expressly asked for no one else to be invited. You promised!'

'What are you saying, my child,' she responded, confused. 'They said you invited them. We were very surprised when they showed up.'

Entering the hall, he saw his father chatting to Zhong Kui's widowed mother, younger brother and sister. He had never spent much time with Zhong Kui's brother, who was much younger, but his sister, Hai, was a sight for sore eyes. Du Ping had always had a soft spot for her. She was not only beautiful, but also sharp and quick-witted. Still, he didn't understand why they were all there.

As they sat down for the banquet and the servants began to bring in the food and wines, Du Ping noticed that an extra place had been set. He had just opened his mouth to enquire, with a degree of sullenness, who else was expected, when a blinding flash of lightning, followed by a great crash of thunder, caused him to fall silent. The door to the courtyard blew open and a gust of wind blew out all of the candles and lanterns. Leaping up to close the door, Du Ping froze as another flash of lightning seemed to illuminate, just for a moment, the imposing silhouette of a human figure hovering in the doorway. Du Ping was still rooted to the spot when the servants, having quickly overcome their momentary paralysis, sprang into action relighting the candles and lanterns. With the return of the lights, the storm too seemed to be passing on. Du Ping shook his head and was making to return to his seat when there was a collective gasp. In the doorway, standing proud in his scholarly robes, was none other than Zhong Kui, King of Ghosts and Queller of Demons.

Zhong Kui let out a hearty laugh and within seconds had reached Du Ping, wrapping him in a tight embrace. As he held his dear friend, his gaze was drawn to the others around the table, their faces a mixture of terror, incredulity and delight. He broke off and took a moment to look deeply into his friend's eyes before proceeding to embrace all of the others with similar warmth. After they had all recovered from the shock, Zhong Kui recounted his strange tale, but swore them all to secrecy. That evening they ate, drank and celebrated like it was not just a new year, but a magical moment outside time. As the evening was drawing to a close, Zhong Kui rose to his feet, a little unsteady from the wine.

'Although I am no longer living, I am still a part of this world,' he began, adjusting his hat as he spoke. 'Although I cannot share in your futures, I will always be watching over you. To my brother Du Ping, whose kindness and friendship made my life possible to endure, I want to bestow a gift of thanks. It must be the most precious thing I have to give. So, as head of this family, I would like to offer to you my dear sister's hand in marriage. I can think of no two people who I would rather see happy and in love.'

After an uncomfortable pause during which Du Ping and Hai stared blankly at each other, a huge smile erupted across her face and there was much hugging, shouting, congratulating and, of course, drinking.

The Demon Queller

After Zhong Kui had celebrated with his newly expanded family, he and his army of helpers set about their job with great zeal and continued to do so for centuries to come. Zhong Kui would set out armed with a calligraphic brush, a finely carved object made of coconut shell, in his right hand. He may now be the Demon Queller, but at heart he was still a scholar. Together with his army, he succeeded in capturing scores of ghosts and demons who had taken to terrorizing the people of China. Those for whom there was hope were returned to Diyu to be purified, if possible, and restored to their former selves. Those too far gone were slain, ripped apart limb from limb, their bodies burned, for this was the only way to kill a demon on earth.

Whilst it was impossible to catch them all, especially as time passed and they continued to reproduce, Zhong Kui was able to capture the most troublesome in every generation. After several centuries, the situation was almost totally under control. Zhong Kui persuaded Yama that those descendants of demons and ghosts who had carved out a peaceful existence amongst the humans on earth deserved a chance at peace and happiness. So Zhong Kui disbanded his vast army, preferring to conduct any necessary hunts on his own, perhaps with the use of a few well-placed contacts and allies. Although there were usually no more than a dozen or so cases for him to deal with each year, there remained a group of demons who continued to be a constant menace to humanity. These were descendants of the original group of escapees that had worked for the Duke of Wu, helping him to become Emperor. Over time, with selective breeding, they had become more and more powerful, but also harder to identify and catch. They had learned to blend in seamlessly with humans, rarely drawing attention to themselves, working in the shadows whilst often living in the broad daylight. They continued to serve a small group of ambitious and unscrupulous humans, led by the descendants of the Duke of Wu, determined to exert influence over as much of the Empire as possible. But despite all their sophisticated precautions, their acts were easy to spot if one knew what to look for. And Zhong Kui, of course, specialized in knowing just that.

—VI—

The Lantern Lighter

wherein an innocent love flows strong and supple, attracting the ire of a ruthless saboteur; revenge descends in a sheet of flame, cleaving the lives of the blameless lovers; & a new feeling blooms between apparent strangers.

Chasing Clouds

FURTHER STRANGE TALES
FROM THE IVORY CRESCENT

Wild orchid

LAN WAS BORN IN A SMALL VILLAGE near the southernmost border of the southernmost province of the Empire. Her father was a highly respected physician and apothecary whilst her mother was a great beauty who had escaped a civil war in the neighbouring kingdom and fled to China. When she arrived at the border together with hundreds of others, she was weak and malnourished and suffering from a jungle fever. She was treated by the local physician, who looked in on her regularly during her convalescence. Clearly besotted, it did not take him long to ask her to marry him. The physician had a highly successful practice in the border town until one day he was asked by the governor of the province, a Lord Jiu, if he would move to the village that bordered his great estate. Reluctant as the physician was to leave his town and patients, one simply did not say no to the governor.

So, they moved to a fine house that sat on the edge of the village in the shade of a magnificent *wutong* tree. Soon, two became three and three became four with the births of their daughter Lan, named after the beautiful orchids that grew in their garden, and son Kun, named after the fertile earth that fed them. Their lives were simple but comfortable and the physician was often tending to members of the Jiu family and a string of illustrious visitors that regularly seemed to stay with them at the estate. Kun was a calm, thoughtful child, always happy to play with his peers. Lan, however, was fiery and wilful and from a young age had preferred her own company. Often, when she was at odds with her family, she would climb to the highest branches of their enormous *wutong* tree and happily stay there for several hours. This earned her the nickname of Feng, after the mythical phoenix that was said to reside in a *wutong* tree. She was kind and loving, yet could not have been more different from the delicate, feminine flower for which she was named. On the contrary, she was an extremely active girl with a propensity for physical challenges like climbing, running and swimming. In looks too, she resembled a young boy, always wearing torn and grass-stained clothes and always with her hair kept short or tied up under a cap. However, despite her attempts to hide it, she had inherited great beauty from her mother. She also had remarkable and particularly beautiful large eyes of a greenish blue with unusual streaks of fiery orange.

As she approached maturity, her parents often tried to encourage her to dress and act in a more feminine manner, often citing the fine young ladies from the estate who would occasionally be seen strolling through the village. But Lan, or Feng as she much preferred, had no interest, viewing their giggly, demure and prissy conduct as pretentious and superficial. She had few friends as she had little in common with the local girls and the boys were usually reluctant to play with her despite her physical prowess. Whilst her mother and father worried, they knew there was little they could do. They simply hoped she would grow out of it.

Kindred Spirits

One summer the estate received the most venerable visitor of all, the young son of the Emperor, making a short stop whilst on his great southern tour. The whole province was in a frenzy of excitement, especially the young ladies and their parents, hoping to be the ones to catch the young prince's eye. None more so than the governor's daughter Fei, perhaps the most beautiful and sophisticated girl in the whole area. Feng, on the other hand, had no interest in this visitor, deriding the pomp and fuss that the whole region seemed to be luxuriating in. Feng was not only wilful and stubborn, but also very shy, so she was mortified when she was told that the young prince would be visiting the village the next day and that, being such a prominent family, they would get the chance to meet him. She begged her parents to let her hide in the forest, but they insisted, saying that it was a great and very rare honour. By the time the moment arrived she had worked herself up into such a state of anxiety that her mother had to hold her arm as the prince approached. But Feng was not to be stopped and no sooner had her mother released her grip to bow to the prince than she bolted and dashed with dizzying speed up into the heights of her tree. The prince seemed rather amused, but her family were appalled and feared they may never live down such a humiliation. In actuality, a little time and a broken bridge would help prove the opposite.

The visiting party was preparing to leave when news came that storms and floods had badly damaged the nearby bridge they would need to cross.

As a consequence, they would be forced to extend their stay by over a month, much to the delight of their proud hosts. With a sudden abundance of free time on his hands, the prince began to take regular strolls through the village, always making a point to pass their house. After a while, his efforts were repaid as he and Feng struck up a conversation, then another and another. Over the following weeks, Feng and the young prince, whose name was Kai, struck up a real friendship and became almost inseparable, though they almost always chose to spend their time deep in the forest and out of view of gossiping eyes. Feng's entire disposition seemed to change, and she became more relaxed, more talkative and in general a pleasure to be around. In truth, she was simply happy. Unlikely as it might have been, Prince Kai was perhaps her first true friend. Now that she had tasted the delights of such a bond, she could not imagine a life without it.

On one occasion, when his hosts were called away on a short trip, he even took her to the estate, showing her every corner of the magnificent gardens and house. When the afternoon was drawing to a close, he begged her to stay to watch his favourite spectacle with him. Concerned that her parents might worry or berate her, she hesitated, but she was not ready for this visit to end so she agreed. Together, they sat on the highest terrace and watched the sky turn a thousand different shades as the sun shed its last glorious rays. It was a moment of simplicity and magic that she feared might never be repeated. In that moment, on the terrace with Kai, she was the wind, the chirping birds, the sweet smell of the flowers on the trees. And as she felt at one with nature, she felt at one with her companion in this unlikely adventure. That night, she could not sleep a wink as she replayed the day in her head again and again. Her heart would not settle from its accelerated beating and her whole body and being felt alive, truly alive.

Blind vengeance

The physician and his wife were delighted at Feng's happiness, but somewhat embarrassed about how this unexpected friendship may be viewed by their master and employer, Lord Jiu, let alone his rather formidable wife.

Then, just as the prince and his entourage were preparing to leave, they got their answer.

It was late one night when Feng heard some commotion outside, quickly followed by loud knocking on the front door. Feng ran to her brother's room and grabbed his hand. They tentatively made their way to the main room of the house, where they could now hear raised voices. As they entered the room, the first thing Feng saw was her parents, pinned down in chairs by large, burly guards. Standing in front of them, by the brazier, was the menacing figure of Lady Jiu, with four more thugs behind her.

'Ah, there you are, you scrawny brat!' she hissed 'Did you really think your treacherous behaviour would go unnoticed?'

'Leave her, what could she have done!' she could hear her parents pleading. 'She is only a child!'

Feng felt a large hand on her shoulder as she saw another pair clap firmly on her brother. Overwhelmed by a rush of blood, she broke free and struck her brother's assailant with a blow that almost knocked him off balance. In an instant, hands were upon her and she was unable to move.

'Bring her here,' ordered Lady Jiu, her voice a vicious cocktail of hatred and fury. 'Did you really think that a prince of the realm, the son of an Emperor, would choose you?' she rasped. 'He was probably just intrigued to meet such an uncouth savage, so that when he gets back he can entertain the Court with tales of the primitive creatures that pass as girls in these remote backwaters!' She paused briefly as her anger seemed to be building to a crescendo. 'You have brought disgrace on us, on your village and on the whole province! We shall be the laughing stock of the whole Empire.'

Turning away from Feng, seemingly warming her hands over the glowing embers of the brazier, she gathered herself before continuing in a calmer but somehow far more menacing tone.

'But what can one expect from such breeding. The daughter of a filthy barbarian harlot and a weak-willed degenerate who could not find a proper Chinese wife!'

As the last words left her mouth she flicked some embers in the direction of Feng's parents with an iron that she then returned to the brazier. Turning to the men holding Feng, she yelled, 'Bring her to me! Let me gaze into those eyes that he finds so extraordinary!' She grabbed Feng by the jaw and pulled her face up close. 'I suppose they are quite striking,' she spat.

Feng, her veins coursing with fear and anger, surged forward in an attempt to bite her tormentor's face.

'Animal!' Lady Jiu shrieked, recoiling, and in a fit of rage grabbed the iron from the brazier and drove its blazing tip into Feng's left eye and then her right. 'Not so extraordinary anymore!' she jeered.

An unlikely momentary silence fell over the room as shock prevailed. Only Feng's screams broke the peace as her captor released her in shock and she fell to the ground in agony.

Lady Jiu, her face white, turned to her guards and barked, 'Tie them up and leave them here!' Then she turned and stormed out of the house. After a few moments her brutes joined her outside. Addressing the most senior, she said in a far more controlled voice: 'Burn it down!' She began to head back to her carriage before seemingly remembering something. Stopping and turning again to her man, her composure now fully restored, she said:

'And tomorrow make sure to send for another physician.'

Crossing the threshold

The last thing Feng recalled was searing pain and searing heat, then darkness. No more pain, no more heat, no more screams...just floating in darkness. Time seemed to take on a less linear and predictable form, as if it too were drifting in a void. Minutes seemed like days, but weeks felt like hours. And then voices, distant and muffled at first, then very gradually louder and clearer.

'It was not my fault, my lord – truly! It was an honest mistake!'

A meek and supplicating voice. No response.

'Please, Lord Yama, I am new in this section and I brought her here instinctively. It was such a bloody scene of vengeance, surely her soul needs cleansing? I mean, she must have done something to deserve that level of violence.'

A pause ensued, during which she could hear pacing. Finally, a hauntingly deep voice, imbued with authority and menace in equal measure:

'Do you have any idea the amount of complex and troublesome bureaucracy this will cause? Do you?' The speaker paused, allowing the gravity of the situation to permeate. 'Never presume to be able to judge innocence and guilt!' he boomed. 'You are not here for that! Just follow the protocol!'

Again pacing.

'She should have gone into holding until her case had been reviewed! Thank your lucky stars she has not yet come to!'

Feng was suddenly aware that she had no eyes to open and was thankful she had made no sound. Lying as still as she could in a state of heightened terror, she just listened.

'What should I do with her now, sir?' the quavering voice asked.

'What you should have done in the first place…call Mother Meng and then put her in holding! I will review her case, but from what I can see, she is a pure soul, victim of circumstance and vicious malice. Perhaps I will send her back as a ghost to allow her to seek vengeance on her murderer.'

A ghost, a half-life, thought Feng in shock. The voice was fading somewhat at this point, its owner clearly walking away and talking to himself in the process. 'I am not sure, there may be another way, I will have to review.' She could just about make out these last bits. Then he obviously stopped and shouted something from a distance: 'You see! Work and complications you have made for me! This is why we have protocols!' And he was gone. Feng was concentrating every fibre of her being on not giving away that she was conscious.

After an age of silence, movement. She heard the shuffling of soft shoes on the cold stone floor. Then the smell of a person. Feng was reminded of her grandmother.

'Give her this and wait for Lord Yama,' said an old gravelly voice before shuffling off.

'Yes, yes, of course, of course,' assured the pitiful voice of the terrified bureaucrat. Feng could feel hands on her as he lifted up her head. His fingers invaded her mouth, prying it open as he slid some sweet milky liquid into it.

He tilted her back. 'The Tea of Forgetfulness!' he mumbled. 'That Old Lady Meng is a real alchemist! Sometimes I wish I could have a drink of her tea and forget where I am...'

Feng tried her hardest not to swallow and as soon as he laid her back down, she opened her mouth a fraction and let the liquid slip out. She needed to remember, she had to avenge her family, she had to make her murderer pay!

Darkness. Floating again in a boundless void, neither hot nor cold, neither wet nor dry. There was nothing she could perceive, not even her own body. Perhaps this was all a nightmare? Perhaps she would wake up to the songbirds that had set up a nest in her *wutong* tree, chirping their dawn melodies for her? She fought to hold on to some part of herself, praying that the elixir she could still taste in her mouth would not rob her of her whole self. She began to fade. She was struggling to recall her home and her family. Soon she could barely remember her own face. The last thing she saw was the smiling face of a young man as he clutched at the branches of her very own tree, desperately trying to keep up with her.

Darkness again. Now she was cold and damp. She was earth mixed with ash and charred remains of beauty and life. Shovels prodding and digging, disturbing her rest. Sunlight as parts of her were lifted high in the air only to be tossed again onto the floor of a filthy cart. A short journey, then shovels again, lifting and dumping then shaping and patting. Then silence and darkness and the chill of winter.

Rebirth

The next thing she knew, Feng was waking up on the damp, dewy grass under a *wutong* tree; the scent was unmistakable. Her body was shrouded in layered, thin silk robes, her eyes bound with a scarf. In her hand was an unfamiliar object. Instinctively, she traced its contours. It was a wooden shaft with a handle formed by a stylized carving of a dragon, whilst the top was a superbly cast brass phoenix head.

'Ah, a staff of sorts,' she thought to herself. 'Probably for carrying a processional round incense censer.' She paused, perplexed. 'How did I know that?'

She stood up, cautiously extending her hands in front of her, suddenly aware that she had no sight. But she was soon reassured. All of her other senses were immeasurably sharpened, as if she had been blind her whole life. Straightening, she lifted her face to the sun. She inhaled deeply through her nose. She was somewhere familiar. The smells and sounds that flooded her heightened senses told her the story of a place where she had been happy, perhaps the happiest ever.

After a time, her unexpected sense of well-being gradually gave way to an inexplicable, though powerful, sense of purpose. She found herself walking briskly toward a destination she seemed to know. Arriving at an entrance, she asked to see the head of the household. When he arrived, he assumed she was begging for money or food and started to turn her away, but she swiftly interjected:

'I am here to offer my services as a lantern lighter. This is a large estate with many lanterns, and I am sure that you will be happy with my work.'

Sensing, before he could even speak, that he was about to reject her, she was somehow driven to march past him and into the main hall. Knowing he would be hot on her heels and without being quite sure what she was doing, she lifted her lantern staff into the air. As she did so, she felt a surge of raw power course through her and through the shaft to the phoenix head.

As expected, moments later the head of the household stumbled in behind her, sputtering, but his angry demeanour evaporated immediately when he saw that all the lanterns were lit and blazing. She was hired on the spot. She was given use of a small cabin on the estate that lay on the banks of a small stream. Food and anything she needed she could get from the house.

And so each late afternoon she would set out for the main house swathed in her wide robes and carrying her staff. Her only request was that no one be allowed to watch her work. Very soon she knew her way around every corner of the estate. She was not spoken to very often and herself spoke even less, preferring to offer a simple bow or a smile. Then one day she could feel a sense of excitement in the house and was informed that the master would be arriving soon. Perhaps affected by the contagious atmosphere, she too felt a surge of excitement rising within her. The day the master was due to

arrive she came to the house a little earlier than usual. There was a palpable euphoria in the air. The master must be much loved, she thought.

Over the coming weeks, each day, she would wait eagerly until it was time to go to the house. She would perform her task of lighting the lanterns with her usual mystifying speed and efficiency until she came to the top terrace. Aware that the master would be seated here enjoying the splendours of twilight, she moved slowly and deliberately, ascending her small stepladder to lower each lantern before lighting it and hanging it back up using her elegantly fashioned tool. As she did so, she could feel his eyes following her every move and found that she rather liked it. Each evening, she would perform her ritual in the most elegant and alluring way she could, ending it with a polite bow before striding back through the garden toward the *wutong* tree. And every evening that walk was the saddest moment of her day, and every morning she awoke with a burning desire to get to the evening and relive that magical hour. After several months, she realized that she was happy and content, but had a yearning for more. One evening, she was up on her steps lighting the final lantern of the night, the one nearest to him, when she accidentally dropped a piece of an oil lamp. Like a flash, he was up, retrieving it and holding it out to her.

She reached down to take the fallen piece from his outstretched hand and offered a mumbled 'thank you', embarrassed that she had disturbed him, but also delighted.

'I am sorry to have startled you,' he said, his voice deep and smooth. 'I was just thinking that you come here every day and perform your task in such an exemplary manner and…' There was a pause, as if he were unsure. 'Well, I really just wondered what your name was?'

She was slightly taken aback, she had not expected this at all and was not prepared, but somehow she had the answer to hand.

'My name is Lan, my lord. After the orchid flower,' she said, trying to sound as calm as possible even whilst her heart was trying to burst out of her chest.

'That is a very pretty and graceful name…very…feminine,' he answered awkwardly.

Recovering her composure, she was unsure what to do so she simply offered a warm smile and left. As she walked away toward the *wutong* tree

and her cabin beyond, she thought what an odd compliment that had been. Whilst she was thrilled at the unexpected exchange, somehow, the words he had offered with such clumsy kindness grated on her very soul. That night, she dreamt her favourite recurring dream. In perfect solitude, she was climbing trees and running up hills, scaling rocks and throwing sticks. This must have been when she was at her happiest. This time, however, she had the constant feeling that she was not alone. The next morning, she woke up early to the chorus of the songbirds. Unable to help herself, she walked out into the garden, her feet bare, the cold wet dew soothing on her wrinkled and scorched soles. The smells of the new morning swept over her and she felt a sense of optimistic excitement fill her soul.

—VII—

The Enigmatic Eunuch

wherein appears in our tale a kindly person, neither young nor old, neither sage nor green, who lives amidst secrets and whisperings, & whose brush with certain dark doings attracts the attention of a clandestine company.

Chasing Clouds

FURTHER STRANGE TALES
FROM THE IVORY CRESCENT

Far from home

POLO WAS THE MOST UNUSUAL of all the Palace eunuchs. For a start, there was his name, Polo. This was certainly not the name he was born with; it was rather a nickname the other eunuchs had bestowed on him due to his pale skin and rich, curly locks. Everyone in the Palace knew of the great European traveller Marco Polo, who had been such an important guest at the Yuan dynasty court, and his close relationship with its emperor Kublai Khan. Polo the eunuch was certainly from somewhere in the Mediterranean too but had been taken from his home when he was just an infant. He was also unusual in that he had a very specific job within the Palace, one that had been created by the Emperor and that answered only to him. As such, although there was plenty of envy about his privileged position, he was set somewhat apart from the viper's nest that was the community of Palace eunuchs. Polo was in charge of a harem of young boys. These were brought to the Palace from all over the Empire and beyond, selected for their pure looks and varied talents. The Emperor, it seemed, liked to be surrounded by young boys at times, energized by their playfulness and innocence. There was of course a certain added attraction for the Emperor, as there was for a number of other important officials, but this was another matter.

Polo's job was to look after the boys, make sure they were fed, watered, immaculately groomed and joyfully dressed. He also oversaw their education, something that he had initiated, so that they might be able to carve out happy lives for themselves when they grew too old for their role. But most importantly, Polo was their protector, and this responsibility he accepted with great zeal. Perhaps he had an innate maternal temperament; perhaps it was a result of his own unusual upbringing – to which we will get in a moment. Whatever the reason, he excelled at his tasks and kept all the boys in the harem in line. In time, he even became popular with many of the other eunuchs. His total detachment from the multitude of power struggles, political alliances and petty rivalries that dogged this community made him a rare commodity indeed: a shoulder to cry on, a fair and honest advisor and, more often than not, a pure and simple friend. With the imperial family too, Polo's stock was so high that when the Emperor finally died, he was present at the entombment and entrusted with the great privilege and responsibility of making sure the tomb was perfect before it was sealed.

Polo took the death of his mentor, the Emperor, very hard, and was prepared to leave the Palace. However, following the dramatic events that saw the death of the Emperor's son and the ascendancy of his uncle, the Emperor's brother, to the throne, Polo was persuaded by the new monarch to stay on. His position and the harem were not only of great importance to the new Emperor, but also to a select group of highly important officials and ministers who had been granted access to this special place and these special boys. At one point these included none other than the Minister of War, the Minister of Finance, many members of the judiciary as well as a number of famous artists, scholars and generals. The small harem was not only a playground for certain proclivities, but also a sanctuary, an oasis of simplicity and calm in a world – the Court – so full of treachery and intrigue.

A metamorphic past

Polo's own past was not without its own turbulence and torment. Passed from pillar to post until the age of about eight, Polo ended up in a strange monastery run by an unconventional sect of priests. These priests did not appear to belong to any established religion but instead seemed to be a rather strange cult. Within the monastery, besides the priests and a handful of nuns, lived a large number of orphaned youths, both boys and girls, Chinese and foreign. They were well fed and cared for and their grooming and hygiene were treated as matters of the utmost importance. Their days were spent acquiring the basics of a classical education, exercising, learning skills such as acupuncture, tai chi, dancing and massage, and playing, which was considered key to their development. It was here, of course, that Polo learned the skills that would prove so useful in running the imperial harem.

Every ten days or so there would be parties in the monastery. Large, elaborate, hedonistic parties frequented by a great number of wealthy men who had often travelled long distances to be able to attend. These parties, the children were minded, were secret and never to be spoken of. The guests would eat, drink, sing and dance, whilst the young boys and girls served and sometimes entertained. After the meal, a guest might approach one or more of the youths and disappear with them into a private studio. The details of these trysts were not to be spoken of amongst the youths, that was a firm rule. Polo's encounters were by and large as one would have expected, with one or two men having somewhat shocking desires and a handful turning violent. The young boys and girls were always well nursed after such an encounter and those guests never seemed to return.

Within this community, Polo had a special friend, an elderly priest who had taken a shine to Polo on the first day. He was kind and gentle, and their relations were of a far more tender and delicate nature. Polo stayed in the monastery for a decade or so, knowing no alternative. But one day everything changed. A disgruntled guest who had been barred from entry for abusing two young boys and beating them had spilled the beans to the local magistrate. The town's militia would surely raid them within days. For most of the youths, the fate that awaited them at the hands of the authorities promised to be far worse than what they had already experienced. The elderly priest explained to Polo that he had a very good friend with contacts inside the Imperial Palace in the Capital. The best thing for Polo's future, he suggested, would be to join the imperial household as a eunuch. Polo was terrified but trusted the priest. The next day, Polo sat on the bed as the priest heated a blade over a fiery brazier. The molten wax he had used in preparation hardened on the floor beneath. A few painful minutes later, it was over, the transformation complete. The priest instructed Polo on the best way to dress the area and there followed a tearful farewell. The following day, sore and bandaged, Polo headed off toward the Capital and a new life as a Palace eunuch.

The unsettled tomb

Amongst Polo's duties at the Palace, the one he took most pleasure in was tending to the late Emperor's tomb. Each month, he would travel by carriage to the valley that the Emperor and his ancestors had chosen as their final resting place. This was a huge complex approached by a five-mile-long road, called the Spirit Way, lined with statues of animals and guardian spirits. Great red arches, vast marble columns and more statues adorned the individual stone paths leading to each tomb. Polo would assure himself that his master's tomb was clean and in good repair. He would then lay down fresh offerings from himself and the Emperor's family. He would walk carefully once around the perimeter, then return to his apartment in the Palace and get drunk. Only once a year did he deviate from this ritual. Once a year, on the anniversary of his master's death, he would take a special offering, sometimes a painting or a poem recently composed by a new scholar, a fine bowl of exotic fruits, or just his master's favourite tea. Once a year, on this anniversary, he would bring this offering and enter the late Emperor's grave.

It was common knowledge that whenever an imperial grave was sealed, it remained sealed for ever. Desecration of such a tomb by forced entry and looting was punishable by death on earth and by one's heart being torn out in the underworld. It was less common knowledge that most important tombs were designed with a secret entrance. This was not only so that more direct offerings could be left by the grave but also in case any close family members or friends found themselves in great need. At times like these it was considered permissible for them to enter the tomb to try to raise the spirit of the deceased. In the case of the late Emperor, Polo had been entrusted with knowledge of and keys for this most secret entrance. So, once a year, he would bring any special offerings and place them directly at the Emperor's grave, taking the opportunity to make sure that all was as it should be. On this particular occasion, he had not noticed anything untoward until he was leaving.

Passing the grave of a long-dead empress, Polo noticed fresh footprints in the earth heading toward a thicket of bushes. Unable to ignore this anomaly, he followed the trail round the back of the bushes, where they disappeared into a narrow tunnel only large enough for a slim figure to crawl through. Sighing, he got to his knees. Polo reached the end of the tunnel only to find a locked grate, but he could clearly see that the footsteps continued beyond it, this time in the dust. Perhaps, he told himself, this was simply evidence of the same ritual he himself had just performed. Private offerings at the graveside by a trusted soul who had knowledge and access to the secret entrance.

Part of him felt guilty for assuming the worst. Part of him remained suspicious, but he could not explain why. It was only the following day, feeling the compulsion to assuage his doubts, that he began to make some enquiries.

Strangers in the sanctum

Very discreetly, Polo visited the keeper of the libraries and was soon able to gain some clarity. Not only was it four months until the anniversary of the death of the empress whose tomb had been disturbed, she had also been dead for almost two centuries. It seemed unlikely that someone would be tending her grave. After a few troubled nights, Polo decided it would be injudicious to follow his enquiries any further. He had to think of his position and that of the harem. The well-being of his boys was all that really mattered. Soon he had managed to put the matter out of his mind and he went on with his normal life.

One day, he was walking down a corridor when he passed the door to the office of the Chief Eunuch. Out of the corner of his eye, he caught a glimpse of a cloaked figure as it darted into the shadows across from the door. The next moment, the office door opened and Polo was surprised to see three men exiting, one carrying a small sack. This was quite unusual as it was expressly forbidden for any male persons other than the eunuchs to be in this part of the Palace. The Chief Eunuch was probably conducting some business that he preferred to keep far from prying eyes.

Polo knew the Chief Eunuch well. He was a good man who took the well-being of his colleagues and charges to heart. However, in his advanced years, he had become prone to gambling, which had long worried Polo somewhat. Still, he ran a very tight ship and Polo was confident that he had everything under control.

Some weeks later, Polo was again passing the Chief Eunuch's office when he saw a group approaching. He stood to one side to let them pass. The first man was powerfully built and gruff-looking, cloaked and hooded. Polo noticed his rather large feet. Looking up at the second figure, he was surprised to recognize an old regular of his harem, Shao Xu, the chief of the Palace police. Now, Polo was nothing if not discreet, but when their eyes met,

he was surprised to be faced with a completely blank expression. My word, he must be an excellent actor, Polo thought to himself. A third person walked past, unremarkable, but the fourth twisted away as he passed and sneezed. It was only after this strange procession had disappeared that Polo recalled the cloak of this fourth figure, with its rather distinctive dark green colour, as the same one he had seen weeks before, fading into the shadows just paces from where he now stood.

Polo was quite perturbed by these two incidents, but not enough to investigate further or to seek an explanation from the Chief Eunuch. Then one day he received a visit in the harem from his old patron Shao Xu, who greeted him with his customary good cheer and embraced him warmly. Sitting down with some tea, as was their custom on these occasions, they exchanged gossip and laughed at some of the new fashions seen around the Court of late. Polo then congratulated Shao Xu on his most convincing acting when they had met in the corridor a few weeks earlier.

'You almost had me doubting if we had ever met!' Polo laughed.

But his remark was met with a very different sort of blank stare.

'Whatever do you mean?' asked the chief. 'Last time I was here was a little over a month ago. Surely you remember? We had tea and played chess with that delightful boy from Yunnan.'

'Oh no,' Polo replied, 'I don't mean that time. Of course, I remember that day. That little blighter won a small fortune from me. No, I mean a few weeks ago when we passed each other in the corridor. You were with some colleagues, off to visit the Chief Eunuch.'

Shao Xu appeared totally bemused and explained that during the week in question, not only had he not visited the harem, or the Chief Eunuch, but that some mysterious thefts of highly prized treasures had taken him to the Summer Palace to investigate. They both sat in dumbfounded silence for a moment. Shao Xu knew Polo as a serious and scrupulous man, not one who would make such a blatantly incorrect claim without good reason. So he asked Polo to recount the entire episode to him in the most minute detail while he took notes. Polo did as he was asked and, after seeming to hesitate for a moment, also told him of his discovery at the tomb of the empress. Shao

Xu seemed very interested and said he would investigate. He too thought it strange that unaccompanied men should be roaming the corridors of this highly restricted area.

A most private secret

Polo heard nothing from the chief of police but was comforted by the fact that the right man was now looking into these anomalies. In any case, Polo was far more concerned with another matter. It was the end of the month and, as was his custom, he would leave the Palace and go down to the pleasure district for the evening, a treat that he allowed himself once a month. In the late afternoon, he gathered up some things in a large bag, and after making sure that his boys were fed and happy and that his deputy was in place, he put on an unusually shabby dark cloak, lifted the hood over his head and descended into the hurly-burly of the Capital's busy lanes.

It was a half hour's walk to the pleasure district if one walked fast. Polo knew every short-cut and cut-through on the route and so was mostly able to avoid the jostling crowds. Polo was always nervous on this walk, eyes darting between the oncoming faces, scanning for anyone who might recognize him. He had become quite adept at doubling back and meandering outside shops, pretending he had nowhere in particular to be. But he did. He most certainly did. On this occasion, however, he had the distinct feeling that someone was watching him. Possibly following him. So he took extra precautions, changing his route and stopping in shadowy corners to observe until he was sure that he was simply being paranoid. Perhaps it was the excitement. This time, because of all his careful manoeuvring, it had taken him a little longer to reach his destination. He would just have less time to prepare once inside.

Madame Yao's was the most exclusive and refined of the many establishments in the area. It may not have been as famous as the renowned establishments down south, but it was certainly a place of rare sophistication. Here, gentlemen – for they were the only ones allowed entry – could escape the drudgery of the dusty city and their complex and draining jobs and enjoy the company of elegant, talented courtesans and like-minded fellow patrons.

This was no low-class brothel, or even a high-class one. This was one of a long tradition of sanctuaries where gentlemen could socialize with cultured, artistically gifted ladies, at a price, and discuss art, practise painting, listen to music and have the sort of convivial exchanges that were impossible with their wives and other female family members, governed as both parties were by the strict protocols of a patriarchal and formal society. What these exchanges led to was a private matter and a matter of choice on the part of both participants.

Polo had known Madame Yao since he first arrived in the Capital. She had helped find homes and employment for a number of others who had escaped his unusual community. She was a true friend and always insisted that Polo use her private apartment for his liaisons. Entering by a side door, Polo was greeted by the burly guard whose job it was to deal with any unruly customers. Polo was very fond of him, though he did cut quite a menacing figure. Once inside the private rooms, a beautifully appointed haven of sophisticated taste, Polo headed straight for the Madame's dressing room. Here all the daily grime as well as the expertly applied make-up were washed off, clothes were removed and thrown into a pile in the corner. Polo would also remove his trademark hat, under which his curls were always carefully arranged so that they flowed out from its edges. Finally, the specially designed bodice that bound his torso was removed, as were all his undergarments. The last part of the operation was the careful removal of the artificially scarred wax appliqué that covered the area between his legs. The priest had taught him masterfully. Whilst Polo's lack of male genitalia had only been checked a few times upon his arrival at the Palace, the ritual of applying the wax disguise to this most delicate of areas was one that Polo followed daily.

Rising and shaking loose an unexpected mass of long curls so that they cascaded gently over her shoulders, Polo walked over to the large mirror. Every time was a surprise, a small private miracle. Looking back at Polo through the glass was the naked figure of a beguiling woman. Tall, dark, with strong, angular features and pronounced curves, she was everything that a pretty, demure Chinese courtesan could never be. Perhaps that is why she always had the pick of the crop. The name she went by was Genji, 'valuable as gold', and she was one of the most sought-after, if elusive, courtesans in the

Capital. Now she would dress, deftly apply her subtle make-up and the transformation would be complete. This night, she was to have a new caller, a rich and influential one by all accounts. Hopefully he might be handsome too, she thought, and cultured and kind; for what Genji sought above all else was love. A fleeting love, to be sure, a love with no future, but a love nonetheless. A meeting of minds and souls far beyond a meeting of bodies.

The evening was a great success. Genji relished the discovery, the dance, the flirting, the deep, free-flowing discussion of the beauty of a recent flower painting that Madame Yao had hung in her apartment. He was tall and strong, confident but also somehow vulnerable. As he was about to leave he asked if he could see her again the following night. Feeling both validated and disheartened, she explained that he would have to wait for another month, as she was due to leave on a trip. Reluctantly, he agreed to wait. The end of these soirées was always bittersweet. If the man was dull or worse, there was disappointment at the evening but relief that she would not have to see him again. But if it was promising, like tonight, Genji felt her complex situation encroaching like a dark shadow on any chance of a happy and fulfilled love. Then quickly she would remember her boys. Soon after the man would leave, she would be Polo again and back home with her most precious boys.

On this occasion, the parting lasted a little longer than unusual, as she rewarded her admirer with a few last stolen moments by the open door. A final squeeze of the hand, he turned to leave and Genji, out of habit, peered out into the corridor to watch him walk away. And then she spotted it: the hem of a dark green cloak, protruding ever so slightly from a shadowy recess. She quickly closed the door, turned and leant against it for a moment, catching her breath. It's just a coincidence, she told herself. It could have been a cloak left hanging by one of the patrons. Slowly, the terror of being discovered subsided enough for her to change, pack up her things and prepare to leave. She wrote the Madame a brief note of thanks and left it on the table together with a fine embroidered silk square she had found in a market the week before. She composed herself, made her way down the stairs and, as the burly guard opened the door for her, Polo emerged once again into the busy nightlife of the city.

A terrifying turn

It was a full week later that Polo received a note delivered by messenger from police chief Shao Xu. It asked if Polo would kindly present himself at the office of Chu Lai in the Ministry of War the following day at noon. There was an added note that it was about the strange goings-on they had recently discussed. Polo was intrigued, though his nocturnal experience at Madame Yao's had left a certain residue of apprehension. Nonetheless, the next day, dressed in his most official-looking garb, he presented himself as instructed. A servant let him in, and Polo was relieved to see that his friend the police chief was there. He was introduced to Chu Lai, whom he had seen around Court many times but had never met. He seemed like a highly competent and trustworthy soul. Next he was introduced to a handsome man with a strange circular marking on his forehead.

'This is Du Yun,' explained Chu Lai, 'he is in charge of the Imperial Collection.'

Next to Chu Lai was a tall man in military uniform. He too was very handsome and exuded a quiet authority.

'This is the Captain,' said Chu Lai. 'Just that, no name, just the Captain. He is my right arm...and sometimes my left, too.' He chuckled at his own joke.

The introductions, casual as they were, had settled Polo's initial nerves and he allowed himself to survey each of the people in the office once more. Just then, Chu Lai's hand seemed to motion toward a further figure, slightly behind Polo. Turning to follow his gesture, Polo was horrified to come face to face with a man in a green cloak.

'And this...' began Chu Lai.

Shock had taken hold and before he could finish Polo inadvertently blurted, 'What is he doing here.'

Time seemed to stop as Polo and Genji's worlds prepared to crumble about them. Their secret was discovered. Their life, their career, their boys...what would become of their boys? Slightly surprised by the interruption, Chu Lai paused for a brief moment, then continued with his introduction.

'This is the Palace Detective.'

The man in the cloak was young, with a bright aura about him. He was

nothing at all as Polo had imagined him. He had bowed politely at the introduction and greeted Polo's terrified gaze with a rather sweet and reassuring
smile. Polo and Genji were fighting back raw panic. How could it all end like
this? Resolving to take the honourable route, Polo turned to Chu Lai and
was about to begin a full and impassioned confession when the Palace
Detective interrupted.

'I have been investigating certain nefarious activities involving some very
precious stolen treasures, and we believe that you could be of great help to
us.' He paused, looking steadily at Polo as if to allay his fears. 'The chief has
told me that you two are friends and that you brought certain anomalies to
his attention.' Polo was motionless as well as speechless. 'I am sorry if my
presence has concerned you over the past few weeks, but I have been working
undercover as a servant, trying to get some answers. By the way,' he added,
clearly seeking to end on a friendly note, 'I hope you enjoyed the opera last
evening, I heard it was quite good.'

A wave of relief began to flow over Polo. This mysterious young man either
did not know his secret or was biding his time. In any case, it seemed that it
would be safe for a little while longer. Polo was invited to sit, which he did gratefully. Regaining some form of composure, he listened with increasing attention
to the discussion of the strange events that had been taking place. As each
of the experts gave his report, what unfolded was an intrepid and dastardly
scheme that it was hard to believe could be happening right under their noses.

Desecration and larceny

The reports concluded, Chu Lai began to lay out the scheme as he understood it. It appeared that a group of ingenious criminals, some clearly in
powerful positions, had embarked on a scheme to pilfer rare and sacred
treasures from the graves of deceased members of the imperial family. They
had somehow managed to elicit the unknowing collaboration of several very
highly ranked officials, like the Chief Eunuch and the keeper of the tombs.
This it appeared they had done by somehow being able to impersonate key
figures in the Palace hierarchy so convincingly as to fool even those who

knew them well, Polo's encounter with Shao Xu in the corridor being one such example. Initially, the Captain and Du Yun protested that this was impossible, but Shao Xu assured them that it must be so, and that these impersonators had somehow managed to persuade the Chief Eunuch to part with some rare Palace treasures. Perhaps the Chief Eunuch's gambling had become more than an innocent pastime.

'But how can this be!' they protested.

Blank faces all around until the young man in the green cloak chipped in.

'I'm afraid I believe I know how they did it, but before I can reveal it I must make sure. I will continue my investigations and hopefully confirm my fears to you.'

All Polo had heard so far would of course explain the disturbed tomb of the empress as well as the unusual presence of strangers in the eunuchs' quarters in the Palace. But something had gone wrong and the perpetrators had to risk exposure to get the pieces back from the Chief Eunuch. The Detective explained that he believed this web of theft and deceit extended far beyond this plot to loot imperial tombs. There had been reports of pieces gone missing from the imperial warehouses, Du Yun confirmed, as well as newly ordered treasures of great expense never reaching the Palace.

Chu Lai had been sitting in silence for a while, gently thumbing a favoured brushrest as he thought.

'I fear that this goes further even than theft,' he now said. 'This fits into a pattern we have been investigating for some time now that points to a very powerful group with far-reaching tentacles. It is why I have put this secret department together. We must expose this coven and find out their goals. But we must do this in the most discreet way possible. We cannot show them our hand before we have them cornered.'

Turning briefly to look out of the window, he sighed and turned back to the room.

'I need not stress how important it is that what you have all heard today does not leave this room. We shall meet again soon when we have more information and can plan our next move. In the meantime, I am grateful...the Emperor is grateful...for your vital and loyal help.'

—VIII—

The Bloodied Brush

wherein a key member of our cast, a seasoned soldier, is witness to a gruesome tableau & entrusted with a priceless token, only to become hounded by dreams churned with disquiet, leading him, by a detour, to a most startling encounter.

Chasing Clouds

FURTHER STRANGE TALES FROM THE IVORY CRESCENT

The bloodied brush

IT WAS A BITTER NIGHT as the Captain made his way secretly out of the fallen capital of the Kun. The wind had picked up and was blowing east, bringing with it the stench of carnage and charred flesh. It had seemed a miracle of good fortune that he had been in the Kingdom of Kun just as the An had attacked, and whilst his small coterie of men could have done little to stop them, the chance to deliver the queen of the Kun to the safety of the Emperor, as was her husband's wish, seemed truly heaven sent. Unconsciously caressing the bundle in his pocket, he thought about how that had been the end of the good fortune. For now he was riding back toward the Capital, the Kun fallen to a barbaric neighbour, Queen Hong dead like her beloved husband and nothing to show for his fortuitous presence other than a bloodied brush.

The Captain had been on a expedition on behalf of Chu Lai and the Emperor, gathering information on the growing threat from the Kingdom of Tibet. His mission had ascertained that a Chinese nobleman, Lord Jiu, once an imperial governor, was now in the employ of the king of Tibet as a military advisor. Such information was certainly a cause for heightened vigilance, if not outright alarm. On his return, a stop in the Kingdom of Kun was a treat that he simply could not pass up. This strange small kingdom had been a paragon of culture, diplomacy and benevolence for so long that it almost felt as if one was visiting the base of heaven itself. The Captain had first visited during a military campaign in a neighbouring state and had longed to return ever since.

He had been with the captain of the guard when the invasion started. They had just settled down to a sumptuous dinner. At once they charged to the ramparts to assess the situation, but as the Captain prepared to call his men to action, his host stopped him, explaining that he was needed for a far more important task. The Captain was told of a secret protocol, written by the king, which said that in the event of danger – fully knowing that the Kun could offer little in the way of defence – the primary task would be to get his wife, Queen Hong, to the safety of the Imperial Capital where the Emperor would personally ensure her future protection. Together, they sped through a labyrinth of secret tunnels and staircases toward the main gates, where they were soon joined by the distraught queen. The two captains explained the protocol to her and were ready to commence their escape when she turned on her heel and fled from whence she came, slamming doors and dislodging torches as she ran. Taken by surprise and not sure how to proceed, they hesitated but eventually gave chase.

They had almost caught up with Queen Hong when she reached her husband's studio and swiftly shut the heavy door, bolting it firmly from the inside. The captain of the guard implored her to open it, but was greeted first with silence, then, after some moments, with the sound of gentle singing from within. On the insistence of the Captain, they began to try to force the door open, but it had been well designed and installed to protect those inside. It took them some time to prise the hinges loose and break it open.

Inside, the scene was one of macabre beauty. The body of the king, who had taken his own life, lay in the centre of the room, covered with fine silks, his head on a pillow taken from the daybed in the corner. Draped over him was Queen Hong, her hand on his cheek, the other clutching something by her side.

None of the Kun guards seemed willing to enter this sanctuary, so the Captain stepped into the room. Inside, he could see that on the far wall, not visible from the doorway, the words 'Heaven to Hell' had been written in beautiful calligraphy on the whitewashed walls, in blood. Already dry, this had presumably been the work of the king as he waited for his life to drain from his body. However, around the calligraphy a great swathe of wall had been painted with fresh blood, the queen's, creating a haunting canvas of vermilion richness. The Captain moved to the queen's side and realized she was still living. He turned her to face him and she briefly opened her eyes. Staring at him, she smiled and closed them again.

'Find it someone deserving,' she whispered, trying with her little remaining strength to move her hand, still clutched around something. Then she was gone.

Reaching for her hand, the Captain saw that the item it was holding was a finely carved brush. The dragons that danced along its wooden shaft were gleaming with blood, its fine horsehair bristles stained red to the core and stiffened with the drying blood. Instinctively, he took the brush and slipped it into his cloak, hoping nobody had seen. Clearly this was an object of great importance to the Kun, but the Captain was now bound by the wishes of a dying queen and he would fulfil these whatever the personal cost.

The next moments were a melee of frantic activity as he was led back through corridors and tunnels to a secret exit on the edge of the city where his men had gathered. Before he mounted his horse, he invited the Kun captain to join him.

'There is nothing you can do here,' he said. 'Come with me and live to fight back.'

But this fell on deaf ears, as he would have expected from a man of virtue. As he turned to mount, the Kun captain grabbed his arm.

'Honour her wishes,' he said. 'She was the beacon of our people.'

A melancholy mist

For months after his return to the Capital, the Captain was plagued by a recurring dream that would wake him up many nights. A bloodied room, red walls of an impossible richness and the smile of a dying queen, her last act on earth, a gesture of arresting warmth. Why this event should have affected him so much, above all the other scenes of grief and carnage he had witnessed in his time, he could not fathom. Perhaps he was struck by the futility of a perfect love and uncommonly virtuous lives, seemingly counting for little in fate's cruel eyes. But affect him it most certainly did.

The first to notice was Chu Lai, when they were on a trip to the market together with their friend Du Yun. As they were rummaging through some scrolls, Du Yun trying to point out the finer points of a particularly ingenious fake, the Captain suddenly rushed off after a woman who had brushed past them and stopped her, only to have to apologize to her and explain that he thought her someone else. When Chu Lai asked him whom he thought he had recognized, he simply replied 'no one in particular', an answer that seemed totally out of character.

Chu Lai had also lately noticed the Captain's mind wandering, his usual sharpness blurred by what seemed to be a fog surrounding him. He even

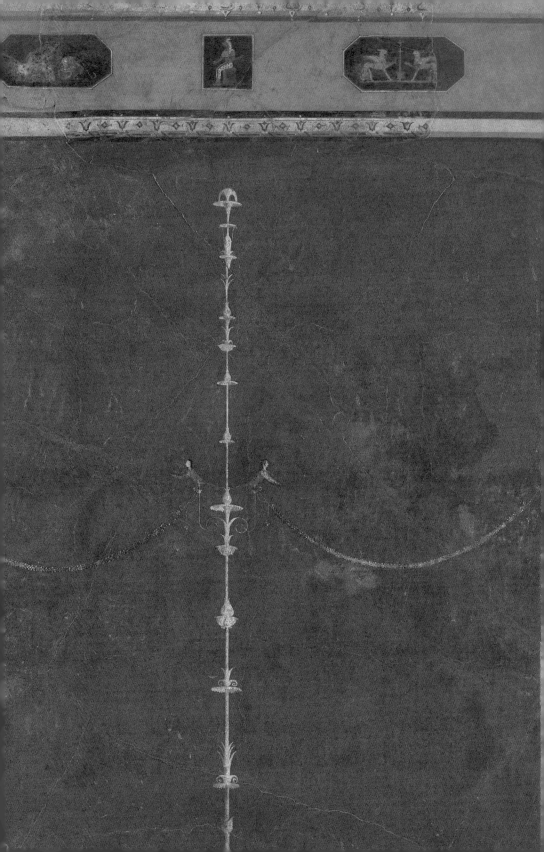

seemed reluctant to offer suggestions when discussing strategy, as though he had somehow lost confidence in his abilities. The final straw for Chu Lai came when they were having a meeting regarding some strange anomalies and thefts that had been reported within the Palace. The week before, they had decided to set up a loose department to look into this and the possibility of a wider conspiracy, and Chu Lai had put forward some names as possible candidates to join this new group. One of Chu Lai's recommendations was a loyal spy named Shy whom they had used on several occassions. The Captain asked some further questions about him, taking careful notes. Nothing strange in that – except that he knew Shy; he had been the agent who had worked closely with his brother Gang on the mission during which Gang was killed. Such a lapse was simply unthinkable.

Chu Lai's answer was to take the Captain out for a feast and drinking binge to see if he could get his mind off, or on, whatever was disturbing him. He needed his Captain on point. But what was intended as a raucous distraction turned instead into a rather melancholy journey of nostalgic introspection. The two colleagues probably both regretted many of the innermost thoughts they shared that night, but nevertheless it was a moment that cemented their relationship into something greater, if unspoken: a true friendship. Amongst other things, Chu Lai learned that the Captain had once been engaged to a young artist called Na, but that he had been forced to abandon her to answer his call to arms. Last he had heard, the Captain had mumbled, she had moved to the Capital to serve as apprentice to a famous artist, but what was the use – even that was a decade ago.

To a man like Chu Lai, life presented an endless number of complex puzzles to which his instinct was to try and find solutions. This is what made him so very good at his job as Minister of War. However, he was not well versed in solving problems like the one that had befallen his friend – a malaise that resided primarily in the mind but was beginning to affect his physical being too. Perhaps a few more drunken nights out or some further nostalgic meandering would have helped, but Chu Lai was a practical man, and practical men almost always seek practical solutions.

The portrait

Some weeks later, the Captain was in Chu Lai's office going over some unusual events that seemed to form an uncomfortable pattern. As they were reviewing one such case, Chu Lai unexpectedly changed the subject.

'The Emperor has suggested – and you know what that means! – that we all have our portraits painted.'

'Really?' asked the Captain. 'I feel for you. It sounds very tedious.'

'I am sure that it will be, but that is his wish and I am to find the appropriate artists to perform the task.'

They returned to their papers until Chu Lai piped up once more, as if he had just remembered.

'I have found an excellent artist to do yours,' he said nonchalantly. 'I will arrange for your first sitting.'

'Mine?' said the Captain, taken aback. 'What do you mean, mine? I thought this was a ministerial thing.'

'No, dullard!' Chu Lai replied teasingly. 'For some reason, the Emperor thinks you are deserving of such an honour. I tried to put him right, but he was adamant. Old age, I say.'

The Captain shot him a scowl.

Sure enough, the day came and the Captain reluctantly made his way to the address Chu Lai had given him. It was a small complex, but very central. Above the entrance, a sign read 'Studio of Elegance and Learning', which he thought an interesting name. Inside he was greeted by a servant who took his cloak and showed him into the main studio. An assistant welcomed him and invited him to sit on a very fine chair whilst he prepared some tea.

'The master will be along momentarily,' he said. He was a handsome young man, no older than 20.

As the Captain looked around the studio, his eyes rested on a particularly fine, partially finished portrait of an elderly scholar. The skill of the artist was evident. The confident lines, the brushwork – but what struck him most was the expression the artist had managed to capture. In the sitter's half-smile there was pride, whilst in his eyes there was a sadness that touched the Captain deeply. Well, at least Chu Lai had not chosen a novice to do his portrait. He was shaken from his reverie by sounds in the corridor and he composed himself and stood up to greet the incoming master.

It is a strange thing when time stops. When all around seems still and silent, the only noise the thundering beat of one's own heart. For as the artist entered the studio, the Captain was rather surprised to see that it was a woman. Not only that, but in front of him was a woman of uncommon beauty and grace, with eyes that pierced his defences with ease. In fact, in front of him was the most beautiful and beguiling woman he had ever seen. In front of him, as if the last decades had never happened, stood Na Wen, his one true love.

—IX—

Fated Fusion

wherein love progresses, step by cautious step; a figure from the past, armed with inglorious schemes, darkens the doorway once more; & a dire secret comes to light, culminating in a frightful blaze which leaves new life in its wake.

Chasing Clouds

FURTHER STRANGE TALES
FROM THE IVORY CRESCENT

Scintilla

EVERY EVENING, FOR SEVERAL WEEKS, Prince Kai and the lantern lighter, Lan, performed the same dance with slight variations. She would light the lanterns in his vicinity with her usual elegance, always taking her time, always subtly altering her performance. Kai on the other hand would try to balance an air of disinterested nonchalance with an inability to keep his eyes off her for very long. Following their first exchange, he was desperate to initiate another, but struggled to find the right path. The atmosphere when they were near each other was palpably electric, yet it remained shrouded in a tense silence. Finally, one day, he could stand it no longer.

'How is the water in the pond near your hut?' he blurted, surprising her as well as himself. 'I was just wondering if it might be warm enough to swim in?' He tried to recover from what he was already convinced was a pathetically transparent ploy for her attention.

'Oh, it is very pleasant, my lord, very pleasant indeed. You should surely bathe there whilst it is so pleasant.' Immediately, she was reviewing every word and intonation, berating herself for her clumsy language. Surely he would think her a bumpkin.

'Perhaps I will,' he replied with passably feigned confidence.

That night, Kai was in a deep slumber, dreaming of her movements and flowing robes, when he was woken by the sound of soft footsteps approaching him. He sat up in alarm, but was greeted with a firm, soft hand on his bare chest and a slender finger pressing against his lips. Her smell was intoxicating, her touch sublime, her breath sweet and cool like the breeze caressing their bodies from the open window. That night, Kai ascended to heaven in the folds of her smooth, silken skin and the cascades of her long fine hair on his limbs. No words were uttered, for none were needed. At one point in their lovemaking, he flung out a hand, accidentally knocking his water flask off the table. He could hear it smash into a thousand shards; it sounded like the gods applauding.

In the morning, Kai awoke feeling as he had never felt before; energized, emboldened and alive. As he lay there, eyes closed, listening to the chirping of his choir of birds, he resolved that he would indeed go for a swim today.

The prospect of the cool rippling water gave him a sudden thirst and he reached for his flask and took several long gulps before it hit him. It had been a dream, just a puerile, fanciful and wonderful dream. Now his feelings turned to embarrassment and guilt that he should think of her in that way. Suddenly he had no desire to go for a swim after all.

That evening, as she approached, Kai could feel his body stiffen with discomfort. The ritual passed in silence, and for Kai at least, it was tortured and uncomfortable. That night, he lay in bed chastising himself for having ruined the brightest part of his day with a sordid carnal fantasy. He fell into an uneasy sleep, tossing and turning as if he were involved in a fierce wrestling match. Hot sweat rolled down his brow as his convulsions brought on a feverish heat. Then abruptly it stopped and his whole being was overcome with a sense of calm, as if he had just dived into the soothing waters of Lan's pond. He recognized her touch, then her scent and soon he was ascending to a mystical peak. As this pattern recurred, so his guilt grew, but he was powerless to stop these dreams fuelled by his deepest desires. Thankfully she seemed unaware of his discomfort; in fact, she seemed in high spirits, walking more lightly, moving effortlessly. Her charms were impossible to ignore and soon enough he found he was able to resume their habitual dance, even asking the odd question from time to time.

Something wicked this way comes

In the middle of one sunny morning, a servant came to Prince Kai with a letter. It had been delivered by hand by a private runner. He was slightly shocked to learn that the letter was from Lady Jiu, wife of the former governor and previous owner of the estate which now belonged to Kai. Nothing had been heard of the Jiu clan since the invasion by the southern barbarian state and it was presumed that they had either perished or were in hiding because of their dubious and felonious past. Whilst they had never been officially charged, probably because of their disappearance, it was widely held at Court that Lord Jiu was greatly responsible for the events leading up to the invasion. It was thus with quite some surprise that he read that

Lady Jiu would be passing through, with her daughter, on the way to visit her ailing mother. She would of course not intrude on the prince's privacy but wondered if they may have use of one of the pavilions that stood on the edge of the estate, so that they may avoid the 'complications' of staying at a local inn. Kai replied that he would be delighted to receive her and that she was welcome to use his guest pavilion. Given her current predilection for privacy and discretion, he added that he would not prepare a banquet in their honour, but perhaps they could call on him at their convenience.

The day came and, as was their custom, Lan made her way up to the terrace just before twilight, expecting to find Kai in his usual seat. Instead, she could hear that he was entertaining guests in his studio. As she hurried past discreetly, she was stopped in her tracks by one of the voices emanating from the studio.

'Well, you know how people will talk!' said the lady's voice, laden with a superior tone. 'In fact, we had nothing to do with that awful business. We are now honoured guests of the king of Tibet.'

Lan was frozen still where she stood outside the open window. That voice, so piercing, so familiar.

'Well,' it continued, 'Lord Jiu is actually a most trusted adviser of the king.'

Lan was still unable to move as she began to perspire with trepidation. Where had she heard that voice?

'Oh yes, I have also been very well, thank you,' said a second familiar voice, full of airs and graces. 'There is even talk of my marrying the prince and heir.'

Lan took three deep breaths and dragged herself back the way she came. That evening, she lit the lanterns on the terrace as quickly as possible before hurrying home in a state of agitation that she could not explain to herself. Was she simply disappointed that she had been robbed of her treasured evening pleasure? Was she jealous, hearing Kai entertaining women in his studio? Who were they? Where did they come from? He never received social calls. She ate a small meal and tried to settle down to sleep but found it impossible. After an hour of tossing and turning, she decided that perhaps a walk in the cool night air would calm her down. Once outside, having no particular plan, she decided to take a path she had never taken before. The smells of early night were a symphony of sweetness on her senses and she began to feel a calm drift over her. Suddenly she smelled the distant aroma of burning wood and quite without thought started to head toward it. As she drew near, she could hear voices on the path ahead, moving toward what she assumed was one of the estate's guest pavilions. She darted into the bushes by the side of the path and crouched down low.

Dispatch from the past

Having seen his guests off, Kai was disappointed to return to the terrace to find the lanterns already lit, and no sign of Lan. At a loss for what to do, he sat down to witness once more the spectacle of nature unfolding before him, but that evening it seemed dull and insipid, lacking the spirit and spark of all the previous times. After a simple dinner accompanied by copious amounts of wine, Kai retired to his studio. He lit some incense and called for some fresh wine to be brought. The servant brought it with his favourite cup, a generous one of *huanghuali* with carvings of pine, bamboo and prunus, set on a gracefully shaped foliate tray of the same timber. Also on the tray was a letter, stained and creased.

'We were clearing out the last of the pavilions in the west wing when we came across this, hidden in a book,' said the servant, gesturing to the letter. 'It's how we found it, the seal was like that.'

Kai thanked him and picked up the letter to examine it, though he knew almost at once what it was. On the front, in his handwriting, were his parents' names. It was the letter he had given to Lady Jiu's servant to send home; obviously, it had never been sent. Turning it over, he could see that the seal had indeed come away from one side of the paper. Had it been opened with a sharp knife? Or had time just taken its toll on the wax? His mood was such that he simply tossed it on his painting table and returned to his newly replenished wine.

Lying in bed later, he could not settle vague visions of dark clouds and agitated seas that kept creeping into his mind. No chance of any good dreams tonight. He turned this way and that but try as he might he could not get comfortable. How could he feel like this just because he missed one of his 'special' evenings? But there was something else too that was agitating him. In his mind's eye he could see the figure of Lady Jiu, head flung back with laughter. She was holding something, but he could not make out what. Then he saw it was the letter. Why hadn't she sent it? Was it just the oversight of a busy social lady of the house? But it was addressed to the Emperor. How had it survived for so long and why had it been hidden? Suddenly, he had a plan. Night-time is often a very poor counsel. But his mind was set and he sprung out of bed, dressed, grabbed the letter and stormed out of his studio, heading straight for the guest pavilion. He was determined to seek an explanation from Lady Jiu.

Yet as he walked, the fresh night air restoring calmer thoughts, he wondered if he was going mad. How could a host burst into a guest's pavilion in the middle of the night? Had he lost his sense of propriety altogether? He was approaching the pavilion, his pace already slowed by the return of rational thought, when he was stopped in his tracks. Up ahead a shaft of light streaked across the darkness. The pavilion door had opened and a group of cloaked and hooded men was being ushered inside.

Nocturnal japes

Kai stood motionless for a moment, taking in the perplexing sight in front of him. His instinct to march to the door and demand an explanation quickly resurging, he watched as the last hooded man began to close the door, whilst remaining on the outside, presumably to act as guard. Yet still Kai seemed rooted to the spot. Suddenly, a hand was on him, yanking him into a nearby bush. As he regained his balance, ready to fight, a finger pressed against his lips. The soft touch was followed by a subtle, beguiling scent and his aggression deserted him.

'What are you doing here?' she said softly.

'I was,' he stuttered, 'I was going to question Lady Jiu about something.'

'In the middle of the night?' she asked.

'I couldn't sleep,' he replied, suddenly feeling rather foolish.

'Me neither,' she said. 'So I came out for a walk and stumbled on this place. Then I heard men, four or five of them, so I hid. Do you know who they are?'

'No,' said Kai, who at this stage had almost forgotten why he was there.

'Well, perhaps' – she paused for effect – 'perhaps we should take a closer look?'

There was a mischievous tone in her voice that he had not heard before in their brief exchanges. And it was infectious. He nodded and somehow she seemed to sense his approval. She grabbed his hand and began to lead him silently through the bushes. They were both giddy with juvenile excitement.

'What an adventure!' he whispered.

Lan squeezed his hand either in agreement or to mind him to be silent. When they had almost reached the pavilion, Lan released his hand and pressed herself up against a tree. Through a window, he could see Lady Jiu standing at a table with a couple of men at her side. They seemed to be looking at some papers. Lan was straining to listen to the distant voices, which Kai could hardly even hear. Instinctively, he took a few careful steps forward in order to get a better view. Crack. A twig snapped underfoot. In the deafening silence of the night, it sounded to them like an explosion. The guard turned toward the noise. Kai froze and began to move backwards very slowly. Just as the guard started toward the source of the noise to investigate, the cloud cover broke enough to allow a shaft of majestic moonlight to illuminate the scene.

Lan grabbed his hand and yanked him away. The force of her prise astonished him. Now they were moving impossibly swiftly through the undergrowth. The darkness was blinding, but Lan did not break pace and he followed. She guided him at full sprint through, over and under all the obstacles that he could not even see. After several minutes she abruptly stopped, taking shelter behind the large trunk of a long-deceased tree. Her back against its scorched husk, she pulled him to her and again pressed her finger gently to his lips. They stood there in perfect, motionless silence, listening for any signs of pursuit. Pressed up so close to her he could feel her chest undulating in time with his as they tried to control their heavy breathing. Adrenaline was coursing through their veins. Danger had ignited their survival instincts. Safety appeared to have been reached, but could they be sure? Then the most unexpected thing happened. She started giggling. It was an instinctive expression of relief and it was infectious. Soon they were laughing out loud in unison. It was a free, guttural laughter, innocent and true like that of excited children who had just escaped punishment or performed a prank. There in the shade of the burnt-out trunk, it was as though they were suspended in a dreamlike vignette in which the outside world seemed to fade away into insignificance.

They stopped to catch their breath and a shaft of moonlight fell across her mouth. Her smile was as captivating as it was large. Kai was instantly back in his dreams, happiness and desire engulfing him completely. Throwing caution to the wind, he leant forward and kissed her. Suddenly acutely conscious of his action, he began to panic. But lo, calamity averted – she was kissing him back. Her hands found their way tenderly to the back of his neck. He cupped her face with both hands and drew her closer. He was intoxicated with her. But this was not the smooth, supple skin of his fantasies. This was scarred and riveted. As his fingers moved down to caress her neck, it felt as if they were tracing the contours of an exceptionally textured scholar's stone. His hand moved to gently cradle the back of her head. No hair. Just an infinitely varied landscape of undulating and creviced scar tissue.

She broke away and looked at him sternly. Panic flooded back. Then a burst of laughter and they were off again running, at a far more gentle pace, toward the main house. By the time they were approaching the fork in the path, they were walking. She let his hand fall from hers. He was aware of her stiffening, as naive embarrassment seemed to take hold. They reached the point where they would have to separate to return to their own homes and stopped.

'I suppose we should try and get some sleep,' she said tentatively.

'Yes…yes, of course,' he stammered.

As he wished her a good night and turned to leave, a sense of despair rose up inside her. Silly girl! She had allowed herself to be swept up by emotion. He had touched her; he had uncovered her secret. Now Kai was vividly aware of her disfiguration. He was disgusted and waiting for the chance to flee. She had traded her whole future, the promise of many more twilights full of joy and quiet longing, for a moment of pure unguarded ecstasy. She had just begun to try to utter some form of apologetic plea when he put a finger gently to her lips. Then he drew her to him and kissed her as if he were trying to fuse their souls into one. It may have been a few seconds or an hour, but he released her and started to turn for home.

'I can't imagine I will get much sleep tonight,' he said with a confidence that surprised him. 'I will be counting the hours until I see you again...please don't make me wait until twilight.'

She stood there open-mouthed as his footsteps receded, swathed in the darkness of the early morning mists. Then she fell to her knees and wept in sheer relief. He did not forsake her. He was not repulsed by the secret of her charred skin. How could he not be? But it didn't matter – her soul had already ascended to the dancing clouds, as the birds began their dawn chorus.

Morning has broken

Kai and Lan were both awakened by a warm ray of sunlight falling across their faces. He rose and dressed, hoping against hope that it had not been another dream. The morning held some errands that he had to deal with regarding both the estate and the province. But though he was there in the various meetings with his staff, he was not present, such was his sense of continued ecstasy. His life had a true meaning now. After his meetings, he headed toward the terrace to take tea in the hope that he might see her walking across the grass to join him. However, as he neared his destination he was disturbed by a servant who claimed that there had been an incident in town that night and that the chief of police was in the house with a man in his custody. The surprise shook Kai out of his stupor and he followed the servant to the main hall to discover what had taken place. There he found the chief of police seated on a bench, with two burly officers standing next to him. Seated beside him, his hands bound, was a scrawny middle-aged labourer with bright orange hair.

'Your Excellence!' said the chief, rising swiftly whilst yanking his prisoner to his feet.

'Please sit,' Prince Kai replied, gesturing with his hand. 'Please tell me what this is all about.'

The chief of police explained that there had been a disturbance in the tavern late last night. The orange-haired man, who went by the name of Chak, had become inebriated and was bouncing about the place in a panic, claiming that 'they had found him' and 'they were going to kill him'. Kai looked quizzically at the chief. This hardly seemed a matter of great urgency. Sensing his displeasure, the chief quickly went on: 'This sort of thing is not uncommon, of course, so we dragged him away and locked him in a cell overnight to sleep it off.'

Again, Kai seemed unimpressed.

'It was the story he told us this morning when he had sobered up that had us worried.' The chief paused. 'But perhaps I should let him tell you himself.'

Kai agreed and turned to the bedraggled Chak, who begged for a glass of water before he began.

Dark secret

Lan had waited as long as she could. She had bathed in the pond, cleaned her hut and washed all of her clothes. She felt like she might burst any minute, so despite the fact that it was only late morning, she started to make her way up to the main house. As she approached, she was greeted with the welcome sight of Kai walking toward his – 'their' – favourite spot. Then a servant appeared, and after a brief exchange Kai turned and followed him back toward the main hall. Lan was unsure what to do. It would not be proper for her to be lingering about the house so far in advance of her nightly chores. If Kai was not free, her presence might arouse disapproval or even suspicion. She about-turned several times before curiosity and longing got the better of her and she headed toward the main hall. Once there, she felt even more unsure what to do. Peering through the lattice window, she could see Kai sitting with two other men, one in uniform and the other, bound, with orange hair. Behind them were two guards. The orange-haired man had just been handed a cup of water. Looking about her, she saw a lantern nearby, knelt down next to it and began to take it apart to clean it. All the while she was keenly listening to the conversation inside. The orange-haired man, she supposed, had finished his water and was beginning to tell a tale from many years back.

Inside, Chak had drunk his water, cleared his throat and begun his tale, which started many, many years prior. Chak was a local man whose father had worked in the kitchens of the estate during the tenure of Lord and Lady Jiu. A strong young man, Chak had been employed doing various odd jobs around the estate and had eventually been put to work in the stables and as a cart driver, moving goods around the premises. One summer, the Lord and Lady were due to receive a most distinguished visitor for an extended sojourn. New servants were employed to impress the illustrious guest, a prince of the realm. Chak was deemed to be too scruffy and common to serve and be seen. He was allowed to work in the stables, but only at night when there was no chance of an embarrassing encounter.

Chak paused to gulp down some more water and Kai looked at him and then the chief, intrigued that this story appeared to be set during his teenage visit. At the same time, he could not help wondering why he was listening to this.

Chak resumed, his voice now more serious. It was late one night when Chak was disturbed at his work by four large men whom he knew to be in the employ of the estate. The leader ordered him to prepare a cart and place a comfortable chair on it. Lady Jiu needed to make a trip to the village. Surprised but delighted, Chak prepared the cart, tethered a horse to it and stood ridiculously to attention beside it, holding the steed until he was needed. A few minutes later, Lady Jiu appeared, her head cloaked, and without saying a word climbed aboard the cart. The heavily armed thugs signalled for Chak to mount the driver's block. When the cart began to move, they began to run alongside it, their lit torches rising and falling with every stride.

'She was hardly pleased to be riding in a filthy cart,' Chak chuckled. 'I had just moved a load of dirty straw out of it.'

He was directed to drive to a house on the edge of the village which he knew to be the doctor's home. Once arrived, he was told to turn the cart around and wait. He watched as the thugs banged on the door and pushed their way in. A few minutes later, Lady Jiu herself entered. There was shouting and wailing and sounds of a struggle, followed by Lady Jiu shouting menacingly. Then there was a blood-curdling shriek followed by more wails and sobs.

Outside the lattice window, Lan was listening in utter astonishment. With every word a new wave of painful consciousness swept over her. Inside, Chak had paused for yet another drink as Kai sat opposite him as if in an incredulous trance. Chak continued his story.

It was some minutes after the bone-chilling scream that Lady Jiu left the house followed by her chief henchman and one of the other brutes. She turned to her henchman and said something, then headed back toward Chak and the cart.

'As she approached,' Chak recalled, 'she turned back to the brute and said something I will never forget.' He paused as if the memory was painful for him. 'She just said – as if it was a normal domestic request – she said: "And tomorrow make sure to send for another physician." And then the bastards burned the place to the ground with that family inside.'

After a heavy pause, Chak went on, saying that the fire had raged all night and threatened to spread through the village before finally being controlled. The next day, he told his father what had happened. Upon hearing his tale, his father immediately had him pack his things, sending him to stay with relatives in another province. As things turned out, it was only after the war that he returned home. All had seemed well until a few days ago, when he spotted the leader of the henchmen and one of the other thugs in the tavern. Though he had done his best to hide, he was sure they had spotted him and that they were now going to silence him for ever.

'I wouldn't have said anything, ever…but they are going to kill me.'

Kai stared at him, realization mingling with raw fury in his thoughts. Lady Jiu had murdered the doctor and his family in cold blood. She had murdered Feng. She had shattered a beautiful young life and by consequence his own heart. Revenge would be his and it would be swift, decisive and bloody.

Righteous inferno

Before Chak had even finished his story Lan was up and charging across the garden toward the pavilion where Lady Jiu was temporarily residing. There were no lucid thoughts in her mind. All the joy and optimism of minutes before had evaporated and been replaced with a searing rage. Her thoughts would not, could not, stray from her task. Even as the pieces of her fractured past came together in her head, a force far stronger than her was driving her toward the pavilion. Vengeance and fire. Fire and vengeance. As Lan approached the pavilion, she could feel herself burning with fury, burning with fever.

She was fifty feet from the front door when she instinctively grasped her dragon-handled shaft with the phoenix head and pointed it at the house. A beam of white light struck the roof and it erupted into flames. Then another and another. Soon the whole pavilion was ablaze and Lan stood in front of the entrance, no emotion at all inside her. But remembered words began swirling around in her head:

'Perhaps I will send her back as a ghost...to seek vengeance on her murderer...I am not sure, there may be another way.'

Screams from inside the pavilion shook her from her trance. As she faced the appalling spectacle before her, she was no longer in the here and now; the cries emanating from the burning building were those of her dying mother, father and brother. Without hesitating for a second more she charged into the house and began to drag out the victims inside. Some had already been overcome by the fumes; others she directed to the door. Breaking through the door of the master chamber she found Lady Jiu and her daughter cowering in a corner, trapped by a screen of fire. Lan charged straight through the flames, covered the women with their cloaks and, in a feat of other-worldly strength, swept them both up in her arms, crashing through the burning carcass of the building until they were safely outside. Letting go of the women and lifting her head, she could sense her beloved Kai charging toward her. She stayed upright for as long as she could, her charred body visible to all, the chasms where her eyes had been staring hopefully in his direction. Then she fell.

Kai arrived in time to catch her body before it hit the ground. He held her in his arms, looking down at the charred and bloodied face he had held so fondly just the night before. He wept, his tears caressing her ashen skin. With all of her strength she managed to squeeze his hand and as he looked at her in amazement she was able to utter a single phrase:

'My name is Feng, my love...Feng!'

Fire & light

Darkness. Floating again in a void, neither hot nor cold, neither wet nor dry. There was nothing she could perceive, not even her own body. She was desperately trying to hold on to an image, a beautiful young face looking at up her through the branches of the *wutong* tree. Suddenly, she was there, sitting on an upper branch of her very own tree. Perched on the branch a few feet away was a white monkey.

'What! It was not my idea to appear to you as a stupid monkey!' The voice crackly and aged. 'We just wanted you to be at ease.'

'Then show yourself!' Feng said, surprising herself with how calm she sounded.

The monkey nodded and in an instant transformed itself into a bent and craggy figure of an old monk, his long wispy beard drifting gently in the breeze. He almost lost his balance and she grabbed his sleeve.

'Bah...stupid tree. Stupid monkeys with their stupid balance. I don't know why this had to be done in a tree!'

Regaining his balance and his composure, he cleared his throat, spat and introduced himself.

'My name is Bo and I have lived for far too long.'

Feng peered at him quizzically.

'It's not important,' he said, waving his gnarled fly whisk dismissively. 'You have suffered too much for a soul so precious, but the great Lord Yama' – he paused and spat again as he uttered the name – 'was unable to decide what to do.'

There was another pause. Feng looked at him, urging him to continue.

'Yes...well. He decided...in his infinite wisdom...' He spat again but this time it landed on his leg. He cursed and wiped it with his sleeve. 'It doesn't matter what he decided, how he decided, why he decided, he is an ass and the place is run like a zoo!'

Feng glared at him with growing impatience.

'Suffice it to say,' the monk continued, taking his sweet time, 'that you were given a choice...fire or light...and you chose light.' He paused to find the right words. 'You chose the light of life over the fire of revenge. You have proved Yama wrong and like me you have beaten their system.'

'But I did nothing,' Feng said, 'I started the fire.'

'Yama pushed you toward revenge…stubborn ox. He was sure you would act on it. Bah…but you showed him! Maybe now they will stop making stupid mistakes!' Again he spat, this time avoiding himself.

'But what does this mean? Where am I now? What will happen to me? I want to go back…back to…' She stopped herself.

'Questions and details, always questions and details…' This was not a monk with much in the way of patience. 'You have unwittingly beaten the system, so your reward, like mine, is the great honour' – he pulled a sarcastic grimace – 'of serving him on earth when needed.'

'So I will go back?' Feng asked excitedly.

'Let's just say that when you awaken you will have back some of what was stolen from you.' He tried to muster a smile. 'And you shall see your prince once more.'

Bud to bloom

It had been several weeks since the fire and Kai was taking a well-deserved stroll through the estate. Every day he spent like the previous one, by her bedside. At first Feng's chances looked hopeless. Kai had called in all of the best physicians, apothecaries and even alchemists, but all of them merely shook their heads sadly and said she should already be dead. After a few days, however, when Kai had all but given up hope, a strange monk arrived at the estate, claiming he had heard of Feng's plight and thought he could help. He was a scruffy old man who carried a strange folding chair on his back and was more than a little partial to wine. He insisted that whilst he tended to her no one else could be present and handed Kai an exhaustive list of herbs, bandages, medicines and flowers that he needed…and wine. The monk spent three full days and nights locked up in Feng's hut. On the morning of the fourth day, he emerged, set up his folding chair on the grass outside and sat in it, flask of wine in hand, basking in the morning sun.

'Well?' demanded Kai.

The monk looked up and squinted at Kai. 'Not bad…'

'What do you mean, not bad?' pressed Kai.

'The wine is not bad,' the monk replied quizzically.

'What about Feng?' Kai was quickly losing his temper with the insolent old man.

'Patience, patience…did no one ever teach you that?'

Kai lunged at the monk, grabbing his robe by the neck. The monk, not expecting this assault, immediately shouted, 'Alright, alright…I was just trying to build a little drama!'

Kai released his grip.

'Tomorrow, at twilight' – he paused and smiled at Kai ironically – 'Feng will wake up.'

Kai fell to his knees.

'You must carefully remove all her bandages and bury them under that *wutong* tree over there.' He pointed without looking. 'Then you will have your prize.'

His cryptic irony would normally have sent Kai into a rage, but he was so overwhelmed with relief and joy that he hardly flinched. He thanked the monk and asked if he might now pay him: 'Any amount…anything.'

The monk spat on the ground and turned toward Kai. For once his expression was serious and stern.

'Just look after her and make her happy. It is the best revenge.'

Kai nodded and placed his palms together in a sign of heartfelt gratitude.

The following morning, the monk was gone. Kai entered the hut and found Feng bound in bandages that had somehow been blended with leaves, herbs and flowers. She looked like a spring bud ready to blossom. Just before twilight she started to come to and Kai began to remove her bandages with great care. As he unwrapped her arms, he was amazed to find that the skin beneath was soft and supple like that of a young woman. When he got to her neck, he found no trace of the rippled scar tissue that had so enticed him that magical night. When he finished gently unwrapping her head, so only her eye mask was left, he was amazed at the full head of long, lustrous hair that cascaded down to her shoulders.

'Kai,' she asked, 'is that you?'

'Yes, my love,' he said, squeezing her hand reassuringly, 'but don't strain yourself, I am just removing the bandages as the monk instructed.'

Feng smiled. An image of Bo up in her tree flitted across her mind. She waited in silent anticipation until he had finished, so that all that was left was the bandage covering her eyes. Then she took his hands in hers and pulled him toward her, and they embraced with all the longing and gentle passion of those who could never have dreamed of such a moment. After a blissful eternity, Feng rose and went to bathe her body in the cooling waters of the pond. Kai watched, incredulous at the lithe beauty of the woman in front of him. When she was finished, she kissed him once more and dressed herself in a simple loose-fitting robe.

'Take me there,' she asked him, 'take me back to our magical place.'

Without speaking, Kai rose to his feet, lifted her effortlessly in his arms and made his way across the garden to the terrace from which they had so often enjoyed the spectacle of twilight together. He settled her gently on the chair and she inhaled the scents of the early evening like a heady elixir. In silence Kai gazed out at the spectacle unfolding before them and held her hand tightly. Suddenly she withdrew her hand and Kai turned to face her. Feng smiled and unexpectedly started to untie the bandage that covered her gauged eye sockets. As the last knot melted away and the bandage fell, Kai found himself staring into the infinite beauty of the eyes that had so captivated him as a teenage boy. Feng in turn gazed for the very first time upon her love's aged and furrowed face. This was the man who had brought her back to life. This was the woman who had sparked his first passions and had now re-ignited them. But now Kai faced a difficult choice...which natural, heaven-crafted spectacle to lose himself in.

Epilogue

Later that year, around the time of the Mid-Autumn Moon Festival, Prince Kai and Feng were married in a twilight ceremony followed by a great feast to which the whole village was invited. It was an evening of unparalleled joy and rejoicing. On their wedding night, Kai gifted Feng a small golden egg that the monk Bo had given him. The instructions were for her to swallow it before they made love. Six weeks later, Feng announced that she was pregnant and the following year, in the height of summer, she gave birth to a baby boy. They named him Huang, meaning yellow, but he soon became known as Long, or dragon, on account of his indomitable, if slightly mischievous, personality.

Finally, the southern quadrant of the Empire could rely on foundations as strong as the highest peaks. From these foundations, the province flourished and Prince Kai saw to the needs of his populace to the best of his abilities, ably assisted by his formidable wife. After the fire, an investigation found that Lady Jiu had been gathering military information with the aid of a network of spies. Orders direct from the Emperor decreed that Lady Jiu, her daughter and all of her accomplices be executed, their heads sent back to the Capital to be displayed on pikes. Prince Kai had to inform his uncle the Emperor that Lady Jiu and her daughter had died of their injuries, though he did send back the heads of her spies. In fact, on the insistence of Feng, Lady Jiu and her daughter had been returned to Lord Jiu in Tibet.

'After all,' Feng said to Kai, 'is she not the very source of our current happiness?'

No more was seen of the old monk Bo, nor the orange-haired informer.

Mad Monk Bo

wherein our troupe is joined by a cantankerous spirit, outwardly crude, inwardly affable, whose tired tilt through the centuries is leavened by a novel quest: to help track down an escapee of most uncommon stealth and stamina.

Chasing Clouds

FURTHER STRANGE TALES
FROM THE IVORY CRESCENT

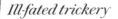

Ill-fated trickery

IMAGINE YOU ARE BORN, an unremarkable boy, to an unremarkable family, in an unremarkable place. Your early life is a constant struggle for survival coupled with moments of unadulterated joy, your mother's warmth, exhilaration, your first adventures, the deepest despair, your first love. Then, you are a young adult; having managed to temper many of your core emotions, you become a far more useful member of society, sensible and pragmatic. Survival, yours and your family's, is again at the forefront of your existence. Then, with age and experience, you perhaps add a certain competence, even a modicum of success.

For some, ploughing through middle age, pragmatism and success start to give way to cynicism. You might start to ponder the why's and what for's; perhaps you begin to seek a greater purpose or truth. Maybe you had always pondered these issues, or it is possible that your parents instilled in you the answers of a religious upbringing. Nonetheless, as you head toward your twilight years – if you are humble and reflective enough not to be obsessed by what you have achieved or what you have accumulated – these larger and more complex questions begin to reside more and more at the forefront of your mind. Then your lifespan runs its course and you find yourself being processed in the underworld kingdom of Diyu based on the piety of your life. Pretty soon, your soul has been 'cleansed' and you are sipping Old Lady Meng's Tea of Forgetfulness to prepare you to cross the Nai He bridge for another turn of the wheel of life. And another and another and another.

All this was almost certainly the case for Bo, and it is impossible to know how many lives he had lived before something quite extraordinary happened. Soul newly cleansed, he was next in turn to see Old Lady Meng when everyone around him seemed to freeze.

Turning, Bo felt his blood chill in his veins as none other than an angry Lord Yama, King of Diyu, stormed into the room flanked by two fearsome guardians. Old Meng rose to her feet to greet him and, wishing to clear the area, handed Bo his cup and ushered him on. Bo obediently put the cup to his lips and was moved on toward the bridge. Still befuddled from coming face to face with the terrible Yama, it took him a moment to realize that there was no tea in the cup. One thing was certain, however: he wasn't about to turn back.

And so it was that Bo was born again an unremarkable baby, to an unremarkable family, in an unremarkable place. But this time, he was born with all of the knowledge and experience of his previous life.

Possesed of this latent knowledge, which seeped gradually into his consciousness as he grew and matured, he was naturally drawn to the philosophical questions of life and the universe. He examined many roads until he seemed to settle on the Way, a path set out by Taoist doctrine, which seemed to afford him the greatest sense of comfort and purpose. He began to take greater notice of everything and everyone around him, realizing in time how all was connected by a powerful life force. Bo lived this life following the Way to the best of his abilities. As he was growing old, he began to feel great regret that soon the knowledge and experience of his rich life would be washed away by Old Lady Meng's magical tea. So, he hatched a plan.

When he could feel his days on earth coming to an end, Bo took a section of a sheep's stomach and swallowed it whilst tying the open end to his remaining back teeth. After he crossed the threshold to the under-world, his soul underwent the usual cleansing and was cleared to return to earth in a new body. Reaching Old Meng, he was handed a cup – this time full – whose contents he dutifully swallowed. Just as he was preparing to cross the Nai He bridge, however, he reached into his mouth and pulled out the sheep's stomach that contained the unabsorbed tea.

In Bo's third life, enriched with the knowledge and experience of two previous ones, he continued to follow the Way and study the deep questions of the universe, using his accumulated wisdom as a platform. Bo repeated this pattern over many lifetimes. Each time he could count on starting where he had left off in his previous life. In his fifth life he turned his attention to alchemy and in his eighth to discovering an elixir of immortality. By his tenth he had experimented with Tantric Buddhism, Zoroastrianism, mystical Judaism and almost every other religion, belief system and cult he could find. And yet, with all of his extraordinary knowledge and experience, he could not find any meaningful happiness or inner peace.

It was at the end of his twelfth life that, in despair at the spiral he had tricked his way into, he decided to come clean to Old Lady Meng. He could have just drunk her tea and started again, but he felt he had to unburden his soul of the death-defying scheme he had employed all these years.

'Old Lady Meng,' he began, 'we have met so many times before, I think of you as my actual mother.'

Startled, she shot him a quizzical look.

'I must tell you that for twelve or more lifetimes, I forget, I have cheated you with a rather ingenious contraption made of a sheep's stomach and returned to life with all the accumulated knowledge of my previous existences.'

Bo apologized profusely, begging for mercy and forgiveness and promising that he would no longer try and trick her. He was ready for a real rebirth. A blank slate. A return to innocence. His confession made, the relief he felt was unimaginable and he was reaching out in all serenity to receive his magic tea when he felt two strong hands on his shoulders. A horse-faced guardian had grabbed him and was soon marching him to the throne room of the fearsome Yama. He had barely crossed the threshold when he threw himself to the floor and pleaded for forgiveness. All he now desired was to be reborn again as a clean slate. But Yama was furious and Bo quaked with terror, fearing a lifetime of torture in the eighteen layers of hell. Then Yama bellowed out a tremendous burst of laughter.

'Oh no…no, no, no. What a terrible waste of your accumulated knowledge that would be!'

Only slightly unnerved that Yama could apparently read his thoughts, Bo was able to muster a grateful smile.

'No, my cunning friend,' Yama continued, 'the earth needs a man of your considerable talents. No, what I have in mind is a punishment that fits the crime.'

Bo was once again shaking with fear. What terrible hell on earth was he to be consigned to?

'I think it best if instead of a rebirth, I sentenced you to a term on earth in my service, helping those with both mundane and more exceptional problems,' Yama announced, with a chuckle reminiscent of a roll of thunder.

Well, Bo was quite relieved. A life helping others sounded far better than torture at the hands of the demons of hell.

'To start with, let's say a period of 500 years, shall we?' Yama proclaimed in an amused tone, cracking a gavel with a loud bang. 'With an initial review at 200?' he mused. 'No, let's say 300 years!'

And with that, Bo's future was sealed.

Bucolic inferno

For several generations, Bo set about his task of helping people and guiding them as he had done in his previous lives. He was sure that this path was the one that would lead Yama to look upon him with pity and perhaps even a little respect. Sometimes he was a travelling monk; other times he would set himself up in some village or town and try to make a true impact on the entire town with his counsel and wisdom. He was content in his work and could often see the long-term benefits of his guidance. He was greatly liked and made friends with young and old alike. Having no great concern for himself, he was able to enjoy the life he had created for himself in the gratifying knowledge that he was doing good work. To him, this did not seem like much of a punishment at all.

However, there is an interesting thing that happens when you remove any of the cornerstones of a man's life. No fear of death makes one complacent about life and all it has to offer. A lack of concern for the 'future unknown' creates a mental lethargy that soon becomes ingrained. A lack of personal ambition removes from a soul that spark that ignites passion and creativity. Moreover, living life through the problems of others, however commendable, over time robs a man of any sense of self and, in the end, of self-worth. Then came the deaths: friends he had made who were dear to him passed on. Then he noticed that he was burying their children and grandchildren. And there were tragedies, wars, famines and floods. All of their devastating power multiplied by the endlessness of his life cycle. For Bo, life came to resemble one interminable season and sadly it looked a lot like winter.

From time to time, Yama would send agents to Bo to instruct him to perform some unusual task or give him a delicate mission. This was his only respite. This was when he truly came alive, when his two worlds came together as one and he felt the *qi* surging once more through his veins. He relished these missions and undertook them with enthusiasm and gusto, but they remained few and far between.

So, with time, what had begun as a state of serene contentment had soured into impatience, depression and a sense of irritable helplessness. His perfect life had turned into a private hell, just as Yama had planned, he presumed.

'How is it possible that they never learn?' he complained at his first review in front of the Great Yama, as if he were no longer a part of humanity. 'I help a father through a terrible crisis, guide him, nurture him and put him back on a true path, only to realize that his mistakes have been repeated by his son and I am going through the entire cycle again!

'And how can I love if the only thing I am sure of is that those I love will abandon me in the blink of an eye?

'What good is helping people if it doesn't change anything in the future? What is the point?'

Such an endless cycle coupled with these worries and deliberations can wreak havoc on a man's psyche and soul. Even one as gifted and resilient as Bo.

Enchanted forest

For some time, the Empire had been experiencing a period of great uncertainty. Floods and weak harvests had caused great unrest and the imperial granaries were running low. Moreover, China's neighbours to the north and west seemed to be growing stronger and more daring, with cross-border raids becoming ever more frequent. In times like these, it was not uncommon for people to seek answers and guidance from a variety of sometimes rather unorthodox sources. Alchemists, Taoist and Buddhist priests, sages, shamans and the like were all in high demand. About half a day's ride from the Capital lay a small forest that had become a haven for such spiritualists and clairvoyants.

Local innkeepers had built retreats to house the multitude of visitors and were only too happy to keep their star attractions, these holy men, well fed and watered. In a small but beautiful clearing in this forest, surrounded by ancient moss-covered stones, was a tree with a hollow chasm in its trunk. Nailed above the chasm was a sign in elegant calligraphy that simply read:

MASTER BO – SPIRITUAL GUIDE

The chasm in the tree was well appointed with cloths and furs lining the walls and floor. There was a portable hand warmer, carved with petals on rippling water, and a lantern that emitted a warm glow. In the centre of the chasm, seated cross-legged and draped in a most elegant monk's robe, was as fine a figure of celestial sagacity as one could imagine. Elderly but still handsome, with clear, piercing eyes, a warm smile and impossibly elegant fingers, here was a holy man of some repute. Outside, an orderly queue had formed despite the early hour, for people of every background travelled from far and wide for an audience with Master Bo. A young boy, fresh and bright, tended to the queue, offering water, tea and simple treats, all in exchange for a fittingly generous donation. He was followed by a poor unfortunate carrying a cage full of songbirds, their chirping intended to entertain the growing line. Eventually, each visitor would be shown into the chasm, where they would extend their greetings, along with a further donation, and air the problems or grievances for which they were seeking guidance.

After listening intently, the elegant monk would bow deeply and explain that he would meditate briefly on the matter. He would then turn and retire to a tiny nook behind a curtain at the back of the chasm. Here he would commune with the spirits and gods in order to return, some moments later, with a solution, a prayer or an instruction, thinly veiled in metaphor or parable. Often, the delighted pilgrims would offer a parting gift – coin, of course – as a way of thanking the sage for bestowing his vast wisdom on them. Though to the cynical observer this set-up may have had all the signs of a common scam, the advice given was in fact more often than not insightful, comforting and extremely helpful indeed. Certainly worth the long journey as well as the loss of coin.

A familiar stranger

Autumn days were often the busiest in the enchanted forest. The weather was not yet cold and with the Mid-Autumn Festival approaching it was a time of resolution, consideration and also strife. One particularly warm and sunny day a stranger approached the clearing in the forest. Inside, the monk was dispensing wisdom, whilst outside a generous line of generous pilgrims had begun to form. The stranger was a large man with a big square head and round, bulging eyes. His hair flowed about his head in a wild frenzy that

seemed to have a life of its own. As he approached, many who happened to glimpse him recognized his features, but were soon convinced that he was just another traveller, familiar only because they had passed so many like him on the road, and within a short time they had forgotten all about him.

Paying little attention to the queue or its young attendant, the large man made his way around the trunk, where a dishevelled old man, sitting on an unusual folding chair with a large flask of wine at its side, was facing the gnarled trunk, seemingly arguing with a small fissure in its bark.

'Tell the idiot to go back and apologize to his wife. Tell him...in your own kind way...that it is a miracle a woman would come within a mile of him in the first place and that he should thank his lucky stars. The fact that she is reluctant to lie with him might have something to do with the awful stench that emanates from him, which I can smell from over here. So perhaps one of your special herbal baths might help!'

Cursing under his breath and spitting on the ground, the scruffy man turned in his chair and appeared somewhat shocked to see the huge frame of the cloaked stranger looming over him.

'For pity's sake, Zhong Kui!' he hissed. 'Must you sneak up on people like that? You nearly made me soil my trousers.'

'And how would you be able to tell?' replied the stranger, his voice deep and gravelly. 'Looks like you haven't changed them in over a decade!'

'Pah...' spurted the old lush, taking a swig from his flask. 'What difference does it make?'

'Just courtesy, to all those who have a functioning nose.'

'What do you want, anyway?'

'Tell you what, Mad Monk Bo, let's get you to a tavern and I will tell you all about it.'

Excited by the prospect of fresh wine, hot food and pretty girls, Bo grinned broadly. Turning back to the fissure, he bleated:

'You'll have to make it up for a while, you useless lump. You must have learned something by now! I'm off to the tavern with this mysterious stranger! By the way, the next one is easy, I saw him in the queue when I went for a piss. Tell him he is a gambler with an unlucky aura, he will never win!'

As the unlikely pair started toward the tavern, they glanced back to note, with great amusement, the look of abject terror on the face of the elegant sage inside the chasm.

Brief & debrief

The tavern was bustling with thirsty travellers, many of whom had covered long distances for an audience with one of the sages of the forest. Bo was happily feasting on a sumptuous meal washed down with enough wine to lay out an ox.

'Tell me about your trip down south,' Zhong Kui asked. 'How was your patient?'

'She was quite an exceptional creature and as instructed I restored her to her former self,' Bo replied. 'By the way, do you have any more of that concoction you gave me from Yama? It really did the trick. I was thinking some of my customers would pay handsomely for it. Who knows, I may even try some myself.'

'No...I was just the courier. Even if I had some, I wouldn't give it to you.' Zhong Kui's tone was playful. 'What on earth do you want more money for, anyway?'

'You don't understand,' grumbled Bo.

'Try me,' teased Zhong Kui.

Bo grimaced, clearly reluctant to engage in this discussion, but Zhong Kui shot him an unimpressed look that seemed to loosen his tongue.

'Two things,' Bo began. 'Firstly, if they don't pay good money for guidance or remedies, these peasants don't value them!'

Zhong Kui nodded before insisting, 'But you already make a good living. Why do you need more money?'

'I don't!' Bo spurted, 'and I do.'

There was a short reflective pause before he continued.

'It's the human game! Get more money, get more fame, get more power, do more stuff!' He sat back in his seat and crossed his arms as if in a sulk.

'But what need have you to play such a game?' Zhong Kui prodded.

Bo shrugged his shoulders and looked at the floor.

'Well?'

'I'm bored! I'm bored, I'm bored, I'm bored!' he shouted. 'And Yama doesn't use me enough. I loved my mission down south. I made a difference. I changed lives. I met an extraordinary being! Here, what do I have? I am surrounded by mind-numbing mundanity! Do you understand?'

Zhong Kui laughed. They had this same conversation every time they met, and every time he was able to get a rise out of Bo.

'Well, lucky for you, I have need of you for something very important.'

Bo's face lit up and he leaned forward, full of eager attention.

'You remember the woman you told me of? Who visits you regularly and talks of beings from beyond and if it is wrong to fall in love with them?' Zhong Kui waited a moment for Bo to recall. Such quantities of wine could not help but have some effect on his mind.

'Oh yes…she is totally off her rocker, comes back at least once a month telling me of dreams she has about a handsome demon and wondering if that means she's evil or doomed! Bonkers! Why, what of her?'

Zhong Kui ignored this question and continued. 'So, she must be quite local to come so regularly?'

'Yes, lives two valleys over, she says, but why are you asking about her? She's a poor deluded soul who fabricates crazy fantasies to fill the empty numbness of her peasant life!'

'I ask,' Zhong Kui paused, knowing full well that the suspense was eating Bo up inside, 'I ask because I fear she might be telling the truth!'

There was a stunned silence before Zhong Kui took pity on Bo and explained that he had been tracking a most valuable target, a highly evolved demon who had been visiting this area regularly.

'Can't you catch him?' Bo asked.

'Yes, but I think this demon has something far more valuable to offer me: a secret I can exploit,' said Zhong Kui. 'I think it has something to do with this woman of yours and I want you to find out for sure.'

'Yes, yes, of course!' Bo was delighted by his new mission. 'Anything to help catch the evil bastard creature!'

Zhong Kui's hand shot across the table and seized Bo's wrist. There was a rather terrifying flash of anger in his eyes.

'Demons are not evil,' he hissed. 'They do terrible things because they were created to do so.'

He let go of Bo's arm and sat back, then continued more calmly.

'Even the most evolved of demons struggle with the concept of choice. Of good and evil. Of consequence. They are a most effective tool or weapon and have been contaminated by the worst of human weakness. But it is only those who do harm by choice that are evil.'

Bo nodded, suddenly sorry that he had said such an infantile thing. He had been on this earth for many centuries and still had much to learn. He returned to his food in a more pensive state, but also full of zeal for his new mission. At last something worthwhile, something different, something that would make him feel alive and not just living. After the meal, Zhong Kui said he would send word and that Bo should report his findings in the usual way. They walked back down the forest path together until Zhong Kui forked off to the left, joining a crowd of travellers heading back to the Capital. Bo returned to his tree and resumed his task of dishing out lashings of advice and wisdom to simple minds. Sitting on his aptly named 'Drunken Lord's Chair', he thought again of Feng and Kai from his adventure down south and of his upcoming task. The air smelled all the sweeter for these warming thoughts.

—XI—

Self-righteous Suicide

wherein a miserable young wretch must endure a cascade of indignities at the hands of his superiors before finding himself suddenly, godforsaken, at the heart of a state tragedy – and at the mouth of the loneliest path of all.

Chasing Clouds

FURTHER STRANGE TALES
FROM THE IVORY CRESCENT

Mischievous jape

'IMPOSSIBLE BUFFOONS!' he muttered to himself as he pulled up his leather breeches, having cleaned himself up as best he could with a handful of large leaves. They had been on his back mercilessly since he had been attached to this elite Imperial Guard troop on the dash back to the Capital. He was only a lowly private, but they needed an extra man who could handle horses so he was requisitioned post-haste. The sudden death of the Emperor had forced his son and heir to abandon his military campaign against the northern barbarians in order to take his place on the throne and try to restore order and stability to a highly unsettled Court. The death of an Emperor, always a traumatic event for the national psyche, was also always an opportunity for power grabs, political manoeuvres and even coups. So they had ridden hard for six days and were now within a few days' journey of the Capital.

Chung had been the butt of all the jokes and japes his vastly superior travelling partners could come up with. Frogs in his shoes, a snake in his bed, constant ridicule and name-calling and the rest. But that morning was the worst yet. As he scrambled to grab a quick breakfast before they set off again, someone had handed him a bowl of congee. Unbeknownst to him, it had been laced with yak milk that had soured and a healthy dose of chilli powder at the bottom. How they roared when, having wolfed down most of the bowl, he finally swallowed a huge spoonful of chilli-infused gruel. They laughed and danced as he hissed, spat and ran in search of water, which they had conveniently hidden. By the time he was finally handed a bucket, he was bright red and his lips and mouth were burned from the vicious concoction. They must have stolen the chilli from the apothecary as it was like nothing he had ever experienced before, and he was from Sichuan.

To Chung's great chagrin, but to the absolute delight of his tormentors, this turned out to be the prank that kept on giving. Throughout the day, Chung would have to ask for permission to break ranks and dash off into the woods or high grasses to respond to rather violent calls of nature. His stomach was churning and heaving like a volcano ready to erupt, which it did at least six times throughout the ride that day. Each time he would have to clean himself up as best he could and gallop to catch up with the rest of the expedition. And each time he caught up, the merciless mocking would begin anew. 'Wow, don't ride so close to us!' they shouted, 'you smell like a pig's arsehole!' 'If that whiff hits the royal nostrils, you'll be hanging from a tree in no time!' Whenever his comrades seemed to be quietening down, another bout would whelm up inside him and the whole brutal spectacle would start again. Finally, they pulled into a small valley and the order was given to make camp. All he had to do was survive the night and the next three days. Surely he would be promoted, having been part of such an illustrious imperial force. But his stomach was not going to give him an easy ride and as everyone else was settling down to sleep, he was forced to trudge off once more in search of a private place to relieve himself.

It was a clear night and strangely mild, so he walked up a nearby hillock until he saw a small wood, which he thought would be perfect. He had brought his blanket with him, thinking that he might wait for his stomach to calm down before returning rather than continuously running back and forth. Crouched in a clearing several hundred feet from camp, he stared up at the magnificent moon, illuminating the whole sky and bathing the landscape around him in an enigmatic blue hue. Then another unannounced eruption shattered his moment of calm.

Vile treachery

After about an hour and several more violent bowel movements, he had just cleaned himself up when he heard unexpected sounds. At first they were muffled, but soon they became louder, with shouts and groans and the unmistakable sound of clashing steel. He began running back toward the camp. As he got closer, he knew that something was terribly wrong. The camp was shrouded in darkness, every fire, torch and lantern extinguished. He dropped to his knees and began to crawl forward as silently as he could, using the long grass for cover. Soon he reached a knoll on the edges of the camp. Now flat on his stomach, he cautiously raised his head for a better view.

Directly below him, a chilling spectacle was unfolding. A large number of cloaked figures were darting back and forth across the camp, swords and

pikes clearly outlined against the eerily bright sky. Tents had been ripped open; before them, amid a tangle of armour and bedding, lay ominous dark lumps. He scampered twenty feet to his left. Here he had a perfect view of the imperial tent and the muffled activity that was building around it.

A figure was being dragged out of the tent and hauled toward the centre of the camp, where a fire was being rekindled. In the moonlight, Chung could see that it was the prince. As his captors flung him onto a small pile of fallen guards, keeping two swords firmly at his throat, a mounted figure approached, cloaked and hooded. In the light of the fire, Chung could see the terror etched on the prince's face. The prince was a leader renowned for his bravery. It was clear to Chung that it was not his obvious impending death that terrified him so, but rather the face of the menacing figure in front of him.

Chung watched, transfixed, as the figure dismounted and sauntered toward his victim. As he did so, he tossed back his hood and drew his sword as if in a single, fluid motion. When he reached the prince, there was a brief, heated exchange that Chung could not make out. Then the figure took a purposeful stride forward and plunged his sword deep into the prince's chest. More indecipherable words were exchanged as the prince lay dying, then the man abruptly swung around to head back to his mount. At this very moment, a shaft of moonlight struck his face, as if choreographed on a stage. Chung stopped breathing. No member of the imperial forces, even one as insignificant as he, could have failed to recognize the man who was now spurring on his horse below. It was none other than General Wu, a highly feared and powerful member of the Wu clan and a man who at that moment was supposed to be leading his forces through Mongolia to outflank the barbarian army threatening the Empire.

Aftermath

Terrified, Chung buried his head in the long grass and prayed that he would not be discovered. He could hear muffled orders and a great deal of movement as the attackers readied to depart as quickly and silently as they had arrived.

He must have stayed in the same spot for more than an hour after he heard the final signs of their departure. At last, he pushed himself up on his elbows to survey the situation. Morning was beginning to break and the fire was now just a pile of glowing embers. After a few minutes, satisfied that it was safe, Chung raised himself to his knees and finally to his feet. Slowly he began to make his way down the hillside toward the camp. At every turn, he was greeted by a gruesome vision of death and carnage. This had not been a fight, it had been a well-orchestrated mass execution. Finally, Chung found himself standing above the lifeless body of his would-be emperor. So shocked was he by this ghastly sight and the contorted visage of his leader that he dropped to his knees and wept.

After a while, Chung was able to compose himself somewhat and began to search the camp, tent after tent, for any possible survivors. He found none; the attackers had been clinical. This was an act of treachery that he found hard to fully comprehend. He was just a simple private who had a way with horses. He was not even supposed to be here. Were it not for the prank they had pulled on him, he too would be but a crumpled corpse.

Making his way gingerly across the destroyed camp, he began to feel that something was unusual. Strewn about the scene were signs of the assailants; a scimitar here, a snapped pike there. A helmet, some pieces of torn uniform. As Chung examined these more closely, he could see that they were all weapons and armour used by one of the fearsome nomadic tribes that had recently unified under a new khan and attacked the north-western border. The scene was supposed to look like an attack by the Empire's enemies. Only Chung knew that it was actually a vile act of treason by General Wu and a force of his most skilled henchmen.

All of a sudden, Chung was even more terrified, if that were possible. He was just a humble private, a soldier of no significance. He was not supposed to be here. He was not supposed to see. But he was and he had and in his mind he resolved that he would ride to the Capital and seek an audience with the high command of the Imperial Guard and tell of all that he had seen. Fate had placed him at this scene and had spared him so that he might witness this terrible act. It was his duty to reveal this perfidy, this heinous crime against the entire Empire. He would right this wrong as he alone could, and his loyalty would be greatly valued. He would be rewarded, he might even be a hero.

Chung's mind began racing. This hideous event might be the greatest stroke of fortune of his entire life. Great rewards and honours lay in store. His rank and status would rise immeasurably and he would bring unthought-of honour to his family and his descendants. Who would ever have believed that poor, hapless Chung could bring such glory to his humble family line? He began to fantasize about the upcoming days and weeks. His arrival at the Capital, his revelation, the shock, the implications, the gratitude, the rewards. The new Emperor might want to hear his account first-hand. Perhaps he would even honour Chung with some small holding or minor title. Lost in his giddy daydream, he was standing in a hall bedecked with gold, face to face with the new Emperor.

The new Emperor. Suddenly, the walls of his fantasy began to crumble around him. He felt weak in the knees. The new Emperor! Who might that be? One of the dead prince's brothers? Perhaps in cahoots with the Wu clan? Perhaps this was all a coup and he would arrive at the Capital to find Lord Wu himself installed on the throne. They would not want to hear his story nor would they want it heard. He would not survive the first hour.

His very bones shuddered at the thought. Even if the new Emperor had nothing to do with the massacre, who would believe him? Who would take his word against that of a general from one of the most powerful families in the land? Again, he would not make it through the day. Perhaps he should just return to his unit and say nothing? But his commanders were well aware that he was posted to the imperial retinue for this journey. Why was he back? How come he was the sole survivor? Was he the traitor who gave the nomads inside knowledge of the camp? He might survive a week before being court-martialled and having his body ripped apart by four horses or fed to rabid hounds or hungry pigs. No, the gravity of his situation was suddenly terribly apparent to Chung. He was doomed. He sank to his knees and wept once more. Long gone were his dreams of fame and fortune.

Self-righteous suicide

Chung must have stayed kneeling at the feet of the dead prince for hours as the next thing he knew the sun was blazing directly overhead, warming the chilled winter air. As the warm glow thawed his frozen bones, a new path opened up to him in his mind. There was a way. A way to be a hero, a way to bring honour to his family name and even wealth to his young wife and his parents. But first, he had to try and make sure that someone would be able to work out what had truly happened here. Rummaging through the prince's tent, he came across a fine box sitting next to an unfinished letter the prince had obviously abandoned to get some much-needed rest.

The box was very small, fitting comfortably in the palm of his hand. It was the most extraordinary thing he had ever held. It was square with a raised cartouche on top and rounded, indented corners. The body was carved all over with billowing clouds and the top inlaid with silver wire in a thunder and lightning pattern. Chung wondered how long it might have taken someone to craft such a treasure. He sat at the table and cut a piece of paper to fit the inside of the lid. Then he wrote on it as best he could, for his calligraphy was rudimentary at best.

> There were no barbarian warriors here on this day.
> Just a serpent named General Wu and his assassins.
> I pray for a righteous justice for this vile traitor.
>
> *Your Invisible Witness*

He skimmed over his work, deciding that it would do, then placed the note inside the lid with the ink facing the timber and covered the other side with a layer of seal wax he had just warmed. He was not sure who, if anyone, would read his note, but he had to release himself from the burden of this knowledge somehow.

Now he was ready and feeling strangely calm. He placed the box in the pocket of the dead prince's robe. Surely, no one would search such a hallowed corpse until it had been brought back to the Palace. Then he walked over to where he had seen a discarded scimitar, picked it up and returned to the prince's side. Carefully, he laid his body across that of the dead prince.

This was how they would find him, a lowly foot soldier laying down his life in a vain attempt to save his prince, heir to the imperial throne. His family name would be showered with honour. His wife and parents would receive a hitherto unthinkable pension, fit for a hero of the realm. This would be his sacrifice for his living relatives and dead ancestors. Using both hands, he thrust the scimitar into his abdomen so forcefully that it passed through him and into the prince's limp corpse. A strange calm fell over him as his hands released the handle and his arms fell away to either side. Had he not been gasping through his final breaths, his consciousness fading fast, he would have been proud of the scene he had engineered, his dying body draped, arms wide, chest proud, over his master's corpse as a barbarian blade fused the two together in a macabre union.

—XII—

The Portrait

wherein an undreamt reunion
engenders joy and agony before
taking an astonishing turn;
a commission is subject to myriad
delays; & a new keeper is found for a
precious heirloom.

Chasing Clouds

FURTHER STRANGE TALES
FROM THE IVORY CRESCENT

The first sitting

INSIDE THE STUDIO OF ELEGANCE AND LEARNING, the atmosphere was electric. Both the Captain and Na had clearly suffered a monumental shock at finding themselves face to face after so many years. The pause seemed to last for ever, the silence echoing. Despite the Captain's rigorous training and his extraordinary experiences in the field, it was Na who recovered first.

'Please sit down,' she said, her voice slightly shaky. 'Have you been offered tea?' She gestured to her assistant. Perhaps he had not recognized her? Perhaps he did not remember her? Propelled by her feisty spirit, she decided to opt for a more direct approach. It was a risk, but she was not one to play it safe.

'You look well, Chonglin,' she said with a casualness that belied the chaos in her mind. 'The years have been good to you.'

A muted 'thank you' was about all he could muster, clearly still somewhat dazed. Unsure how to react to his silence, Na decided to continue down the path she had chosen and took full control.

'Let's get started, then,' she said, busying herself gathering her tools as her assistant laid out a sheet of silk on her painting table. 'No point wasting time with idle chat.'

Again, it was all Chonglin could do to nod in passive agreement. Inside, though, he was bursting. He had a hundred questions, a thousand stories and a million apologies to make, but right now, a nod was the best he could manage.

The next hour passed with almost no conversation, but for the odd 'turn this way' from Na and some unintelligible sighs and sounds from him. But as the day progressed, guided by the steady hand of Na, who was growing in confidence from moment to moment, they began to talk. It was small talk at first. The weather, the blossoms, the state of the Court, but soon she was asking him about his life. His family, the army, his experiences. And Chonglin was now able to reply in a reasonably erudite manner. His answers were short and lacking in any great detail, but the ice had definitely been broken.

'How about you?' he asked, finally having found some sure footing. 'This studio is very impressive.'

'Yes, I moved to the Capital many years ago to apprentice under a great master. After his death, I was going to return home, but suddenly could see no reason why I could not follow in his footsteps and take over the studio. After all,' she added playfully, 'my family name is not entirely unknown in the world of art and culture. And I have never looked back.'

Chonglin asked about her family. Her father had sadly passed, but her mother was well and enjoying her garden. Chonglin felt a sadness at the thought of the death of her father. He was transported back to the day he had asked him for Na's hand in marriage. He remembered him saying that it was pointless for him to have an opinion as Na seemed to have already decided. His only condition was that he continue his studies and pass his final exam to become a *jinshi* scholar. This, he said, would secure the future of the young couple. Driven by these thoughts, Chonglin asked the question he had wanted to ask since she had entered the room.

'And did you marry? Do you have a family?'

Na blushed alarmingly for a moment, but quickly recovered her aplomb.

'Oh yes,' she said. 'I married a highly respected judge and we have been blessed with three wonderful children. Two boys and a little girl, who has them and her father wrapped around her finger.'

Chonglin could feel the blood drain from his face and prayed it was not noticeable. What did he expect? He had abandoned her as a young girl to answer his call of duty. They were young. She was extremely beautiful, intelligent and talented too. He remembered his joy and surprise that she had chosen him in the first place. As if reading his mind, and with a slightly mischievous tone in her voice, Na exclaimed:

'Well, I couldn't very well wait for you to return, could I?'

A chill ran down his spine.

'The letters were lovely, though. Thank you. I was sad when they ceased.' Her tone was now full of nostalgic warmth.

The day came to an end and Na asked if he might be available to sit again in two days. Chonglin agreed, trying to mask his enthusiasm. That night, he slept a deep sleep, the likes of which he had not known for many years.

A protracted process

A portrait, even a very elaborate imperial work, could normally be completed in half a dozen sittings, or perhaps a couple of weeks. This portrait, on the other hand, was clearly proving to be very difficult to get right, for Na required Chonglin to sit every two or three days and so far this had been going on for over a month. She had finally settled on a standing portrait, to accentuate his impressive frame, but also wanted to highlight the scholarly aspect of his character by having him read a book. During the many hours they spent together, they chatted about many different things. At first, each day would begin with a period of awkwardness, but soon they fell back into a familiar pattern of talking and teasing that had made their courtship so exhilarating all those years ago.

'Will you be going to the pleasure district tonight?' she would tease. 'Seeing as you have never taken a wife, you must be quite the regular.'

Chonglin would inevitably blush and this would only encourage her. Yes, he did indeed visit the pleasure district and had done so throughout his life. Like any man he sometimes craved female company. But a wife? There had only ever been one candidate in that contest.

On occasion, he would retaliate.

'Don't you have to get home to your domestic bliss?' he would jape, though the mere thought of it was like a dagger piercing his flesh.

The two months of sitting for his portrait were as happy a time as Chonglin could remember having. On the days he was due at the studio he awoke with a vigour and sense of expectation he had not thought possible. It was such a pleasure, he thought, to have someone with whom he shared a past. To have an friend from his past life. As he sat and she painted, he found himself gazing at her for hours, hoping that the day would never end.

So nice to have an old friend, he kept telling himself. But, in truth, every half-smile, every accidental touch, every tease and every look were now a drug he could not live without. What would he do when she finally finished the portrait? Would it be inappropriate to have a second one done? Perhaps in full military regalia? Or in scholar's robes? What of a third and a fourth?

But his nights were filled not only with anticipation but also with guilt and remorse. He was plagued by thoughts of what could have been. Could he have come back for her? Would she have waited for him if he had asked? These questions began to preoccupy him so much that he started thinking of them during his precious sittings. Finally, reluctant to taint the pure joy of these sessions, he summoned up the courage to bring up the subject in conversation.

'I am so sorry, Na,' he said one day out of the blue.

'About what?' she answered. 'Have you accidentally broken something?'

'No,' he replied. 'I am sorry about abandoning you and not returning.'

'Don't give it a second thought,' she replied jovially. 'As you can see, I managed to land on my feet.'

Chonglin knew that she was making light for his benefit, but he was so desperate to unburden himself that he pressed the matter.

'At first, once I had finished my training and been promoted, I thought of coming back.' She listened silently. 'For years, I told myself that I didn't because I could not subject you to the nomadic life of a military man. Not you who had so much talent and sophistication. You who were born to thrive surrounded by culture and art.'

'It might have been nice for me to have had a say in that,' she retorted, a hint of resentment creeping into her voice. 'And now what do you think?'

'Now I think it was fear. Fear of getting my hopes up, only to be rejected. Fear of trying to win you back and losing you all over again,' he said with uncommon candour.

Na was taken aback by this honest confession but once again decided to err on the side of lightness.

'You're probably right,' she said mockingly, 'I did have so very many suitors after you left.'

They both laughed, but it was a nervous laugh, as if they both needed a relief from the tension. Then, taking her opportunity, she asked him the question she had been longing to ask all these years.

'Did you ever think of asking to be reassigned to the garrison near me? It's one of the most important and prestigious in the country.'

Embarrassed, Chonglin did not want to admit that he had never considered

this option. He had assumed his fate, after the death of his brother, with passive stoicism. He had chosen the path of the martyr without considering that he was not the only one affected. Indeed, in his years of service he had followed orders and accepted posts and missions without question, as if this was the punishment due to him for surviving his brother, father and fallen comrades. Sitting there under her steady gaze, he felt unable to answer her straightforward question.

'Well, no.' Again she had beat him to it. 'Not Chonglin. You would not have asked for anything for yourself. You would not have challenged the hand that fate dealt you or challenged a superior for the sake of your own happiness.' Noticing that her tone had turned rather bitter, she changed tack and returned to jest. 'No, I'm afraid that you, Chonglin, are cursed with being the world's most dutiful and responsible man.'

That night, Chonglin was tormented by her words. Was it so wrong to put duty above personal happiness? Could she really resent him for upholding the good name of his fallen brother and family? Could she really blame him for not doing more to fight for the future they had dreamt of? Surely not. But then again, why not, he thought. Deep down he resented himself for all of those things.

Crossing lines

That was the last time their conversations touched on their past together. The atmosphere returned to a cheerful mix of wit and superficiality. But a further ingredient seemed to have been added. There was now flirting. It was subtle at first, but both Na and Chonglin became prone to delicate teasing and thinly veiled innuendo.

'My goodness, it is beyond me how a man such as yourself can't find himself a wife,' she would joke. 'I tell you, if women were afforded the same privileges as men, I would think about taking you as a second husband.'

'No need,' he would reply, 'I could simply add you to my roster of regular dalliances. Best to keep it from your husband, of course.'

There was also more physical contact, as if they were both seeking a glimpse of the impossible. They would now embrace when meeting or parting and she became given to straightening his clothes. He in turn might bring a beautiful flower that he had 'stumbled across' on his way to the studio. They would stop to take tea and sometimes stroll in the garden as Na would claim her creative spirit was in dire need of air and sunlight.

Then, one late afternoon, when it was nearing time for him to leave, she quite unexpectedly asked if he might want to stay for dinner.

'My husband has taken the children to visit his parents,' she explained. 'It's his father's 80th birthday. I should have gone with them, but I have too many things that need to be finished this week. It will just be a simple meal here, if you don't mind.' With a touch of drama, she added: 'I cannot bear going back to an empty house. I miss them all already.'

That night they had a very pleasant dinner together and she suggested that they do the same again after their next sitting in two days' time. As they were parting, Chonglin quite naturally took her hand in his. She did not pull away and they stood there facing each other for a moment before she warned him mockingly: 'Careful, Captain. People might talk.' And she smiled one of her smiles, turned and went back inside.

That night, Chonglin found it impossible to settle down to sleep. Her final words had struck him like a mallet hitting a giant bell, calling his conscience back to its rightful place. 'Careful, Captain. People might talk.' He had been so careless, blinded as he was by a happiness he had long forgotten. What was he thinking? What was he playing at? He had ruined this woman's life once, how could he put her reputation at risk in this way? She was a married woman, with an eminent husband and a family. How could he play with these lives with such frivolity, simply for his own fleeting happiness? On the other hand, was she not playing the same game? Perhaps for her it was a simple distraction, an amusing way to pass the time? Or was she toying with his emotions in retribution for his youthful decisions? Regardless, he had let his imagination run wild. The Captain had built his life on certain immovable principles of honour, dignity and uprightness. They were the bedrock of his character, but he could feel them crumbling beneath his very feet.

At their next sitting, Chonglin was resolved to act with the reserve and decorum he knew the situation demanded. That morning, the atmosphere was decidedly frosty as he politely declined to engage in any of her teasing games. Na was slightly bemused, but reacted with great composure, retreating behind a far more professional and detached mask. At first, Chonglin was relieved that he no longer had to parry her jests. But nary an hour had passed when he found himself longing again for their witty exchanges, for their stolen glances and nostalgic meanderings. Suddenly, he was racked with doubt. Had he offended her? Had he overcompensated for his earlier behaviour by withdrawing too far? Had he once again ruined the only thing that had ever brought him true joy?

At the end of that session, Na announced, quite matter-of-factly, that the portrait was practically finished and that the next session was due to be their last.

'I just want to finish some of the details and have one last opportunity to compare the work to real life…if it is not too much bother for you?' She paused lightly. 'It is perhaps an indulgence on my part. Maybe it's not even necessary…'

'It's no bother at all!' interrupted Chonglin, his tone laced with apprehension.

Finished? Over? Chonglin suddenly felt cold and hollow. So soon? It was probably for the best, he thought, but immediately admonished himself. How could not seeing Na possibly be better than seeing her? He had never before felt such conflict within himself.

The day of their final sitting, Chonglin brought with him some delicacies as well as two flasks of very fine wine. He also brought the carved *huang-huali* brush given to him by the dying Queen Hong, for surely there could be no more deserving custodian of this precious heirloom than Na. He resolved to give it to her at the end of the session. A parting gift, if you will. He had reconciled himself to the fact that this dreamy interlude was to end, but at least it should end with a celebratory atmosphere rather than the cool detachment he had regrettably created. In the late afternoon, Na presented Chonglin with the finished portrait and he was almost moved to tears. It

was a masterful representation that somehow melded the Captain's dignity and success with the final traces of Chonglin's innocence and potential. He masked his moment of emotion by opening the first flask of wine and raising a toast to Na's talent. A wave of melancholy swept over him. Noticing his brow darken, she quickly raised her glass to offer a toast to his patience as a sitter, then another to whatever fate or happenstance had caused their paths to cross again after so many years.

Soon, mostly thanks to Na's ability to subtly change the mood, and helped along by the wine, they had returned to their usual playful, witty and flirty tones. They sat on two chairs by the fireplace polishing off the second bottle of wine, Na idly slicing a fine pear with a small knife. Suddenly she grabbed his hand and dug the point of the knife into his wrist, almost piercing the skin.

'Tell me, Captain!' she said, putting on a menacing voice. 'Tell me, on pain of death…or at least pain of pain…' They laughed heartily before she continued her charade. 'Yes…in absolute honesty and for the prosperity of the whole Empire and the honour of his Imperial Greatness…' She paused as if now thinking of a suitable question. 'Tell me, if the Jade Emperor burst into this room and offered you any wish because of a service you had rendered in a previous life' – she paused, catching his gaze – 'what is it that you would wish for?'

'I think…' Chonglin began, 'I think I should like that knife for fear that you might end me with it!'

And as they laughed he took the knife from her with his left hand, leaving his right still firmly in her grasp.

'Seriously, Chonglin,' she said, sobering somewhat, 'it seems like you have never placed your ambitions first. What would you wish for?'

Chonglin sensed he was at an epochal moment. He was aware that an opportunity like this might never present itself again. Loosened by the wine and the emotion, he decided to allow himself a final chance at redemption.

'I would wish for…' He paused; this was the point of no return. 'I would wish for the impossible. I would wish to go back in time and make things right between us.'

'What, and rob me of the life and family I have built for myself?' she chastised. 'Come on. Think again. No time travel.' She drained her glass.

Of course, you fool, he thought to himself. She is married with a family, she is happy and fulfilled! What are you saying? Suddenly, a voice inside his head whispered, 'You're losing her!'

'Yes, of course,' he managed to stammer.

'Come on, Chonglin!' she said. 'Even you can't change the past! No need to right the wrongs of the world…there must be something you want.'

'You're losing her!' the voice hissed again. His head swirling with wine, hope and fear, Chonglin knew that time was running out. Fate would not wait much longer. From deep within himself he dredged up a moment of pure clarity accompanied by an unexpected surge of courage.

'In that case, I would wish that you would suddenly decide to leave your husband and run away with me.'

There was a moment of silence, then Na burst into laughter.

'Seriously, the great Chonglin would want me to leave my husband, destroying both of our reputations and bringing shame on the names of our families. I don't believe you. You are too proper, too deferential, too uptight to take such a risk. Anyway, what of the children?'

'Well, of course they could come with us,' he joked and they both laughed again. Chonglin's gambit had not worked, she had not taken him seriously. He had totally misread the situation. Thank goodness she had chosen humour as a response, at least giving him the chance of an honourable retreat.

'She will be lost forever,' the voice sighed, as if it too had all but given up on him. At that moment, it was as if Chonglin was elbowed out of the way as the Captain stepped in. If this was a battle then he would do anything to win. This was not a time for bumbling self-doubt. This was not a time for cowardice in the name of duty and propriety. This was a time for courage and action.

'But what if I am serious, Na?' he said quietly, no trace of jest in his tone.

Na withdrew her hands from his and sat back in the chair, looking forward, avoiding his gaze. Chonglin could feel the life force draining from his soul.

'What if you were serious?' she repeated. 'Leaving aside the arrogance of the idea that I would be willing to throw away everything that is important to me – could you really risk your position, your standing, your reputation and all that you have become, for love?'

He paused. The fatalist in him saw despair, but the strategist saw hope for one final opening. A chink in the armour. If there ever was a time to unleash the big guns, it was now.

'Not for love,' he replied, and she looked at him quizzically. 'But for your love.' There was a silence. 'For your love I would risk all those things and more. I would give up most of my life for even a year of your love. What eats at me daily is that I should have done this years ago. I should have fought for our love and our future. It is my great regret, only it took our meeting again to admit it to myself.'

'Hmmm…' was all she replied as she sat back in her chair with a smug little grin on her face.

'But could you really suffer all of this loss together with the ignominy of bringing up another man's children?' she finally asked.

Still unsure if this conversation was real, imagined or simply a joke gone too far, he now had no option but to see it through.

'It would be an honour to bring up any child of yours,' he replied.

'In that case,' Na began, the mirth back in her voice, 'if the Jade Emperor appeared and offered you a wish and that is what you chose, I would have to take it under serious consideration. But first I would have to check one thing.'

Still not sure if she was playing with him, such was the confident mischief in her tone, he simply replied: 'Check what?'

Na rose from her chair, straightening her clothes as she did. Slowly and with an almost feline litheness, she took the two steps over to where he was sitting and unexpectedly placed herself in his lap. Then, sliding one hand behind his neck, she drew him to her for a passionate embrace. Chonglin was now sure he was dreaming, for never could he have imagined such a passionate and prolonged kiss. After a few minutes, Na broke off and, still in his lap, leaned away from him a little.

'Yes,' she said. 'That all seems fine.' She smiled. 'But before you truly consider taking such a momentous decision, there is something you need to know. A dark secret that I have not yet told you.'

Chonglin was confused. Caught between hope and despair, between heaven and hell.

'What is it?' he asked.

'I never married!' she replied.

Chasing Clouds

wherein a dark confederacy is lured into the open by an irresistible treasure, an elusive emissary leads our heroes in a dizzying chase, and familiar faces appear in a most unexpected constellation, before dispersing once more, mercurial, like threads of cloud racking past the moon.

Chasing Clouds

FURTHER STRANGE TALES
FROM THE IVORY CRESCENT

Dark clouds

DU YUN'S FINGERS were inadvertently tracing the contours of the silk bag he held on his lap under the table. Crisp recessed beadings framed the contours of clouds, bulging with life as they wafted elegantly toward a central valley before billowing up to another crescendo at the opposite end. They were sitting at a large table in a nondescript and rather damp and gloomy room lit by a single lantern. They had all followed the detailed instructions on how to get to this secret location and had all taken great lengths to be sure they had not been followed. Absolute secrecy was key for this plan to work. Chu Lai was speaking, explaining how they planned to lure out their targets by using a fabulous treasure as bait. Around the table, in addition to Du Yun and Chu Lai, Minister of War as well as leader of this secret group, were four others, all wearing dark cloaks as instructed.

To Du Yun's left was his friend Zhu Chonglin, known to all simply as the Captain. He was Chu Lai's right-hand man, strategist and man of action. Next to him was Ying, a fresh-faced young man who held the unofficial and secretive position of Palace Detective. Directly across from Du Yun was Polo, the exotic-looking eunuch who was in charge of the 'Palace boys' and who was to be the one to set their planned trap. Next to Polo was a swarthy man with deep, dark eyes, introduced simply as Shy. Chu Lai had explained that Shy had been an invaluable asset to him in the north for some years, a spy of great skill able to blend in effortlessly amongst the locals.

What he failed to add was that he was also the last man to have seen the Captain's brother, Gang, alive.

Chu Lai was summarizing what he had learned since their last meeting about the strange thefts that had been happening in and around the Palace. In the meantime, these had been joined by a number of further strange and unsettling events. Corpses discovered in back alleys, mauled and stripped clean of their most tender flesh as if attacked by a beast with a particularly refined palate. There had also been some sinister and rather dramatic examples of political intimidation, such as the chief justice coming home to find his wife, children and servants all tied up in the courtyard, their foreheads marked with the name of a man whom he was due to try the following week.

The politically motivated events, Chu Lai explained, appeared to be the work of a mysterious secret organization that had been wielding influence for centuries. Whether by nature of their nefarious activities or through some actual intelligence, they were often referred to as the 'league', 'society' or 'brotherhood' of shadows. They had often been dismissed as a myth, but of late, Chu Lai had become convinced of their existence and their hand in any number of dark affairs. Then, some weeks ago, Ying's attempts to identify and infiltrate the group had finally begun to bear fruit. Soon after, another mauled body was discovered, dumped in an alley like the others. This time, Chu Lai was able to identify the body as belonging to one of his agents who had been charged with keeping a discreet eye on the Wu clan at Court. A second body was discovered a few days later. This time, Ying identified the mangled remains as belonging to a member of the group he had infiltrated.

Now that a number of these events, the maulings and the thefts, seemed to be intertwined, Chu Lai saw an opportunity. The plan, he announced, was to let it be known that Polo was in possession of a great rarity that he was unable to sell on the open market and would prefer to sell in a more discreet manner. Given Polo's station as well as his access to the Emperor, it would not take a genius to work out that he had managed to pilfer something from the royal collection. The problem was that the piece needed to be exceptional enough for the buyers to risk coming out of the shadows, but also something that would not be too obviously missed. This was where Du Yun came in: as keeper of the Imperial Collection, he was perfectly positioned to choose the right piece. Chu Lai had charged him with making his choice and bringing the object to this very meeting. When he removed the piece from his bag, it was one that none of them had ever seen before.

Cloud pillow

No, old friend. This is a pillow fit for an emperor or a deity. Not for the likes of you, or me for that matter.

As Du Yun placed the loosely wrapped treasure on the table, the words he had uttered to his former mentor's corpse echoed in his head. Slowly he unwrapped the silk package, revealing a *zitan* pillow carved all over with animated clouds. He had imagined this piece in his isolated paradise and drawn it in his notebook before seeing it magically appear as a 'real' object in one of the Red Slayer's famous hoards of loot. How it had come into being, he could never explain, but that it was fit for an emperor or a god was apparent to him from the first moment.

'I took this from the corpse of District Magistrate Yang,' Du Yun began, piercing the expectant silence around the room. 'He had misappropriated it in some way, as he had done with so many treasures before. But I knew this piece was destined for a more exalted head.' His gaze fell on Chu Lai, whose eyes he could feel on him. 'It was always my intention to present it to the Emperor, but something held me back. Perhaps its tainted provenance? Perhaps some silly bond I imagined? I know it was wrong to keep it.'

'Thank goodness you did!' exclaimed Chu Lai. 'The Emperor might have had your head if you offered him a pillow that had been used before. More so by a scoundrel! Doubly more so by a dead scoundrel!'

Du Yun could feel the blood returning to his face. A great weight lifted from his soul. They all took turns handling this rare wonder, mostly in silence, sometimes with an accompanying superlative.

'Yes, my dear Du Yun,' said Chu Lai, 'you have done well in keeping this until now. I think it is just the piece for our intended purpose.'

'Agreed,' the Captain declared, partially in support of his friend Du Yun.

'It is exquisite,' Polo whispered almost unwittingly. 'Who could ever have conceived such a thing.'

'This will certainly get their pulses racing,' said Ying. 'A piece of this quality and importance makes our job much easier. Besides, it could very plausibly have been pilfered by Polo from the late Emperor's tomb, to which he has sole access. So our backstory fits perfectly.' The detective's mind always saw things in interconnected webs.

'Then it is agreed!' said Chu Lai. 'We will set a trap with this rare pillow as bait. And with luck, we will get one step closer to whatever dark powers have been at work here.'

They all voiced their agreement and arranged to reconvene in two or three days' time. There was no time to waste if this audacious plan was to work.

A well-laid trap

It was the Palace Detective and the Captain who drew up the detailed plans for the proposed trap. Ying, in his role as infiltrated servant, would let slip some conversation he had supposedly overheard the last time he had visited the Chief Eunuch's office. Then, if they bit, and after agreeing on a suitable fee – no self-respecting servant would part with this information for free – he would spin them a most alluring tale. Then a meeting would be set for the exchange. This would be the easy part. It would be foolish to expect the exchange to go smoothly; they were after all dealing with a group which had shown its willingness to do almost anything to protect its secrecy. This was where the Captain and the Detective came in. This was the closest they had got to uncovering this shadowy group and they would do all in their power to put an end to it, spending sleepless nights hunched together over maps and papers, developing ploys, bluffs and contingencies.

The evening of the exchange came. Polo sitting outside the tavern in the market square, pillow carefully wrapped but visible on the table. It was half an hour before the meeting, and Polo could already feel the adrenaline surging. How had it come to this, he thought somewhat frantically. What would become of his boys should anything go wrong? Before Polo walked over to the square, Shy had rubbed the underside of the pillow with a distinctive scent. It was not strong, but very particular and a favourite of his tracking hound, a huge beast with long, wispy fur. This was but one of their safeguards. Polo scanned the market square, trying to appear calm and nonchalant. Who were his allies? He had been told the square would be full of them, but all he could see were market traders, stall minders, loafers and luggers, bent-over women trying to scrape together enough morsels for the family's evening meal. Where were the soldiers, where were the strongmen?

'Just try to be calm,' the Captain had said in his warm, caring manner. 'You may not see us, but trust that we will be there. Just try to be yourself and stick to the plan.'

The waiting seemed endless. Polo's eyes were getting tired from scouring every passing figure, every face, every pair of hands, every shoe, for any possible clue. In the end, the moment arrived. From across the square Polo spotted the intended target, strolling toward him with no attempt at subterfuge or evasion. Dressed in a rather striking maroon cloak, hood raised, the figure approached, an abundant sack of coin safely secured to its belt. Polo remembered to breathe and placed a firm hand on the wrapped pillow on the table. The seconds before the mysterious apparition finally reached the table were interminable. Polo mustered his courage. In a moment the complex dance of negotiation and subtle trickery would begin and he would have to try to remember all he had been taught and instructed to say and do. The figure reached the table, a short, stocky man with slightly unusual features and a pallid complexion.

Polo took a deep breath and looked the man in the eye.

One final assignment

Ji Ren was tired as he approached the square. It was a clear night and warm, but still he wore his maroon cloak with the hood pulled up. They are expecting a villain, he thought to himself, best to dress the part. He was prepared, he knew his brief and he would not fail, but he was tired. It had been too long and he had sacrificed too much for his masters. He had so much to live for, he just wanted a clean break and to live his own life. A life that had taken on a whole new meaning after he had met her. Met them. His new family. He couldn't believe how lucky he had been, a chance meeting, a helping hand, an unexpected connection and an hitherto undreamt-of love.

He had guarded them jealously, but he was desperate for them and tired, so tired. And they had promised. One last mission and he would be free. Not like last time. This was different, they said. And all he could do was believe them, for without that glimmer of hope, he couldn't go on. He couldn't keep putting them through this. He just wanted a normal life. They deserved it, and so did he. Thinking of her now, with the little ones clinging to her skirt, he was almost brought to tears. Concentrate, he berated himself. Just one more and you are out.

As soon as he entered the square, he knew it was a trap. Of course, he had expected it, they all had. That's why they sent him. He could not make them out amongst the growing evening crowd, but he knew they were there. He could sense it on his skin and in his nostrils, like he always could. For Ji Ren was no ordinary demon. He was one of the last survivors of an ancient, highly specialized lineage: the hunter-hunted.

Hunter – hunted

The hunter-hunted were highly unusual demons who were designed to punish those who in life had terrorized and hunted others, who had derived pleasure from the fear and desperation of their prey and often from their final torment and pain. These demons were specialized both in evasion when hunted and in hunting their targets. Their powers were the widest-ranging of all demons, but purely instinctive. Thus, when fleeing, these demons could leap farther, run faster and smash through almost anything in order to avoid capture. If in real danger, they could pass through walls and spontaneously camouflage so skilfully they were undetectable from even a few feet away. They had no control of these powers, which simply kicked in when needed. This made them unpredictable prey, which was even more infuriating for their hunters.

At some point in the chase, when the soul of the hunter was at its most exasperated, frustrated and fatigued, the demon would turn into the hunter. Now the hunter became the prey as the demon turned the tables on the bewildered soul and set about giving chase. And although the demons' skill was so prodigious that each quarry could be caught within minutes, they were equally adept at drawing the process out, much like a cat might do with a terrified mouse. This was the fate of those who had been cruel and voracious predators in life: an endless cycle of futile hunting and terror-stricken flight. Although Ji Ren had been born on earth and had never visited Diyu, he had inherited these skills from his ancestors. This made him a most effective weapon and tool for all manner of tasks. It was no wonder his masters were reluctant to let him go.

Snatch & bolt

As Ji Ren approached the table, he could see the terror in his counterpart's eyes. A shame – they seemed such warm and kind eyes, too. Normally, he would make contact and begin the sensitive process of examination and negotiation, but he was tired and fed up. Everyone involved knew how this would play out, so he decided to save them all some time and without uttering a single word he snatched the silk bundle from under his adversary's protecting hand, turned tail and ran.

The first to try and intercept him was a brawny fishmonger who had a stall a few feet away, but Ji Ren simply palmed him off, sending him flying into his stall. As he sped forward a terrified woman threw a bucket of water in his direction, soaking his back. Next was a group of four who blocked his passage with well-drilled movements obviously designed to steer him down a specific alley. Clever, he mused to himself as he vaulted straight over them with a single giant leap. He kept running, confusing his pursuers by heading toward a large wall. Within seconds he was up and over it like an winged monkey. Down the other side and through another market, he ploughed on without even looking back. He smashed though a series of thick wooden doors and into a rather refined garden that he would have liked to have taken a better look at. Then down into a deep drain and out the other side, now beyond the walls of the citadel. Taking a circuitous route, he was heading for a wooded area to the north-west of the Capital, and then he would be gone.

The chase

Polo shrieked as the stranger grabbed the silk bundle and stood bolt upright watching him flee, making short work of all the attempts to intercept him. Had it not been such a failure, it would have been quite the spectacle. There were many more failed attempts to apprehend the thief than the thief had even noticed. They had planned for every possible escape route, but no one could have been prepared for this. No one, that is, except the Captain and the Palace Detective. Far outside the city walls, they waited on horseback with Shy and his hound at the ready. Night was beginning to fall. If the thief escaped, as they assumed he would, he would undoubtedly head north-west to the woods. They may not spot him, but if they were correct, the hound would soon pick up the scent.

They had only been in position for about ten minutes when the hound leapt up and was off, the three riders following closely on its heels. Heavily armed mounted soldiers had been stationed on all the roads to help intercept their quarry; there was no escape. The three men continued their chase at breakneck speed until they reached one of their mounted patrols on a peripheral road. However, they had seen nothing. The hound continued to pull and was off again, heading west this time. Shy's idea to douse the silk wrapping in scent was paying off. They rode hard for a further thirty minutes until they reached a fast-moving stream. The hound was over in one leap and was soon wrestling with something on the other side. When they reached him, their mounts snorting with exertion, they saw that the dog had a lifeless hare between its jaws. Tied around its neck was the square of silk.

'Crafty,' uttered the Captain. 'So now onto our next trick.'

On his command, the Palace Detective released a hawk. This was their backup plan. The liquid that had been thrown over the demon in the market square was not just dirty water. It was in fact a chemical mixture that emitted a very distinctive glow that the trained hawk was highly sensitive to.

As the majestic bird lifted off, its powerful wings propelling it ever higher into the moonlit sky, they readied themselves and set off once more in pursuit.

An unexpected encounter

Ji Ren stopped running and chose a gnarled trunk to sit against as he afforded himself a drink of water and a short rest. His hare trick had worked a treat. He had been able to smell the stench of that silk wrapping from across the square. Who did they think they were dealing with? The clouds were starting to gather above him. Good, he thought. A nice storm would make his escape even easier. As he rested, he reached inside his cloak and drew out the *zitan* pillow. He was not much for fine things, but even he could see the brilliance of the carved clouds. A lone shaft of light made the surfaces of this rare treasure gleam as the clouds above began to part again. Oh well, he thought, maybe he would still have to work a little to escape. As he rose, his highly sensitive ears picked up horses and a hound in the far distance. I'm impressed, he thought to himself as he set off again. Speeding over a large hill, he noted that the moonlight had got brighter, seeming to illuminate everything around him.

As he reached the brow of the hill he sensed danger and upped his speed, but somehow instead of accelerating he seemed to be slowing down. Soon he was hardly moving at all, despite his most strenuous efforts. As he turned to look behind him, he was brought up short by a sight to his right. In the neighbouring field stood a group of people. They were silhouettes he would have recognized anywhere: his love and her two children. His treasures. His life. Behind them and at a slight remove was the silhouette of a wiry old monk who seemed to be sitting on a strange reclining chair, tipping back a flask as if he had no worries in the world. Something caught Ji Ren's eye and he turned his gaze back to the road ahead. Just a few feet in front of him loomed a giant figure with a large square head and huge, bulging eyes of flaming red. He wore the robes of a scholar and in his right hand held a carved brush that he was pointing at Ji Ren, seemingly holding him in place by some magic.

Now, Ji Ren had never been to Diyu and, for a demon, he was quite young. He had spent his entire life amongst men and was not very learned in the ways of demons, gods and wizards. But even he instinctively knew who was bearing down on him on that country road. Stories of this mythical figure had been handed down through the generations. In front of him was none other than Zhong Kui, the legendary Demon Queller and the scourge of all demons throughout the ages. Ji Ren was desperate. His day of judgement had come and he knew what lay in store for him. All the stories were quite explicit. The Demon Queller loved to inflict pain and misery before consigning a demon to oblivion. All of a sudden, it was as if they were all enclosed in a calm bubble, a warm glow surrounding him. He could now see the faces of his loved ones. Zhong Kui's eyes turned a passive grey colour as a small dog emerged from his cloak.

Destroyer of demons

'There is no point in fighting.' Zhong Kui's booming voice reverberated through Ji Ren's whole body. 'But you already know that, don't you.'

Ji Ren nodded.

'And I suspect you also know what is in store for you, demon!'

The emphasis on this last word tore through him like a shard of glass. Again, all he could do was nod.

Zhong Kui waved his brush and Ji Ren was lifted off the ground and wafted through the night sky until he was hovering over the incredulous faces of his human family. A loud belch from the reclined monk broke the silence.

'Pardon,' the monk said, followed by a guttural laugh.

'And these humans here,' Zhong Kui continued, 'what are they to you?'

'They are my family, my life,' Ji Ren stammered. 'I would give anything, I beg you, don't hurt them, they are innoc...' And he could not continue as the tears began flooding out.

Zhong Kui sighed and lowered his brush, returning Ji Ren to the ground with surprising gentleness.

'It is a good thing Bo here ran into your dear woman as she sought advice about demons and the like,' he said. 'Most would have labelled her insane, but Bo is quite the sage, despite his appalling manners.'

The monk smirked and emitted another enormous belch.

'Had we not found her, we may never have known what a gentle and loving demon you are.'

Ji Ren was confused. Was this just a callous game to cause him even greater pain?

'You see, Ji Ren,' Zhong Kui continued in a calm but gravelly voice, 'you are a demon by heritage, but a human by heart. Your ancestors were not good or evil, they were designed for a particular purpose. It is not your fault the two worlds collided. Your instincts are to serve and obey. It is not you who are evil, but those who wield your power.'

The Demon Queller paused to let his words sink in. Ji Ren was born a demon and had always considered himself a doer of evil deeds. This was what he had been told. Evil deeds were what he was instructed to carry out. Only his chance meeting with his one true love had cast all of his beliefs into total confusion. Now he stood in front of her, shaken, desperate and confused, but all the same calmed and warmed by her gentle smile.

'You have a choice to make, demon.' This time Zhong Kui's tone had a jovial tinge. 'You can return to Diyu with me and suffer the destiny of all captured demons. Or…' He paused for effect. Ji Ren's world was suddenly illuminated by a gleam of hope. 'Or', Zhong Kui continued, 'you can remain here and live your life to its full and most natural conclusion.'

'But how?' implored Ji Ren. 'I am a demon!' Tears again began to stream down his cheeks.

Zhong Kui sighed as he looked for the right words.

'You are not only a demon, though,' he finally said. 'You are also a husband and a father. Let those things define you.'

'But how!' Ji Ren beseeched. 'My masters, they will hunt me down.'

'Nonsense,' said Zhong Kui. 'There will be no need for them to hunt you down. You will return to them willingly and hand them their bounty.'

'I don't understand,' said Ji Ren.

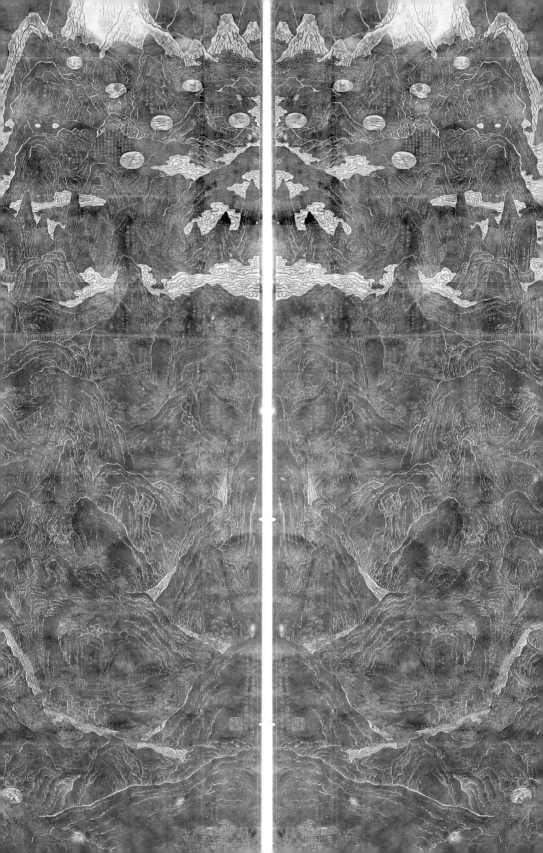

'In a few moments, over that hill will come your pursuers. They are good men, with good hearts. Help them in their quest and you will go a long way toward making up for your previous earthly sins.'

At that moment the hawk swooped over the hill and started circling above the group. Close behind it followed the three riders. Emerging over the crest of the hill, they were greeted with a most unexpected scene. The demon, now without his cloak, was clasped in a loving embrace with a fulsome woman and two young children. Behind them, seemingly blind drunk and singing rude songs, was an old monk in a reclining chair. Directly in front of them was a strange cloaked traveller of rather unfortunate looks, with a small dog yapping around his heels. As they dismounted, the Captain was the first to draw his sword.

'There is no need for that,' Ji Ren said gently. 'You will have no trouble from me. I surrender myself peacefully.'

The Captain and his comrades had dismounted ready for action but were somewhat dumbfounded by the scene before them. There was an awkward silence, as if nobody knew what to do next. After what seemed like an eternity, it was Zhong Kui, now returned to a normal size, who spoke.

'Well, I am just a weary traveller who really must get to an inn soon. It was a pleasure to bump into to you and your family.' He nodded toward Ji Ren. 'But I fear it is time for my companion and me to leave.' He straightened his robe and gave a lopsided smile. Then, turning, he said, 'Coming, Monk?'

'No, I fear I'd better stay here and help Ji Ren explain a few things,' Bo replied.

'Very well,' said Zhong Kui as he began to leave. 'I will see you at the inn.'

Then, with a curt 'gentlemen', he bowed politely to the heavily armed party. They returned the greeting, all but Ying, who stood motionless with his mouth agape. As Zhong Kui strode past him, tugging his little palace dog behind him, he shot him a playful look.

'Boy!' he uttered in a warm tone. 'You look well.'

And with that he trundled off.

Index

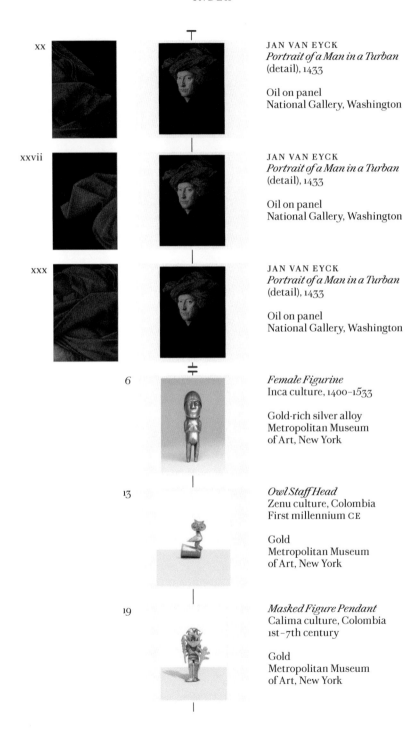

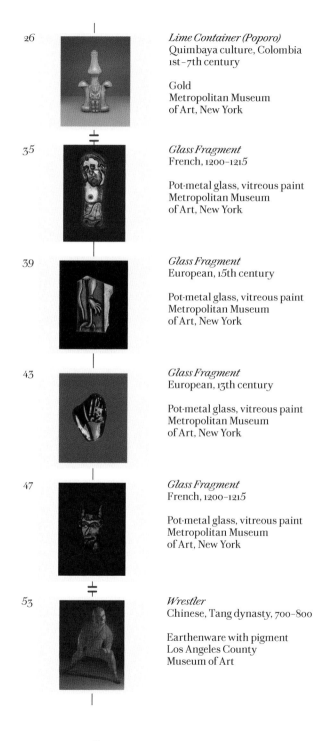

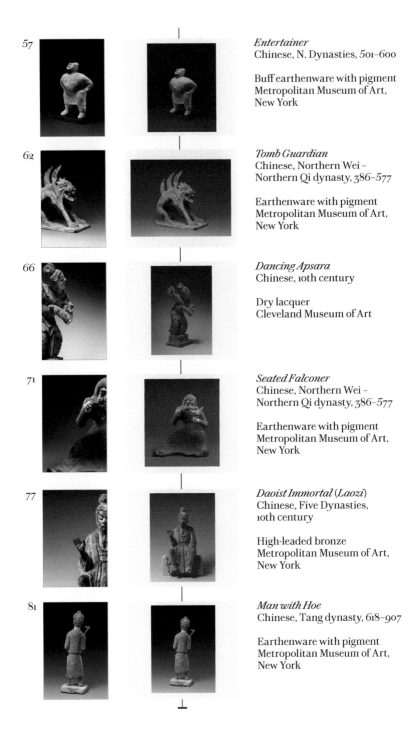

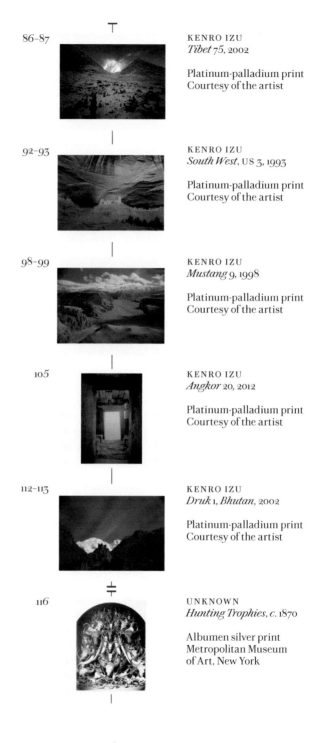

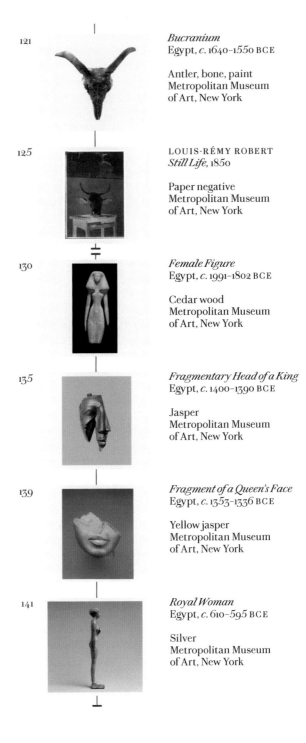

121 *Bucranium*
Egypt, *c.* 1640–1550 BCE

Antler, bone, paint
Metropolitan Museum
of Art, New York

125 LOUIS-RÉMY ROBERT
Still Life, 1850

Paper negative
Metropolitan Museum
of Art, New York

130 *Female Figure*
Egypt, *c.* 1991–1802 BCE

Cedar wood
Metropolitan Museum
of Art, New York

135 *Fragmentary Head of a King*
Egypt, *c.* 1400–1390 BCE

Jasper
Metropolitan Museum
of Art, New York

139 *Fragment of a Queen's Face*
Egypt, *c.* 1353–1336 BCE

Yellow jasper
Metropolitan Museum
of Art, New York

141 *Royal Woman*
Egypt, *c.* 610–595 BCE

Silver
Metropolitan Museum
of Art, New York

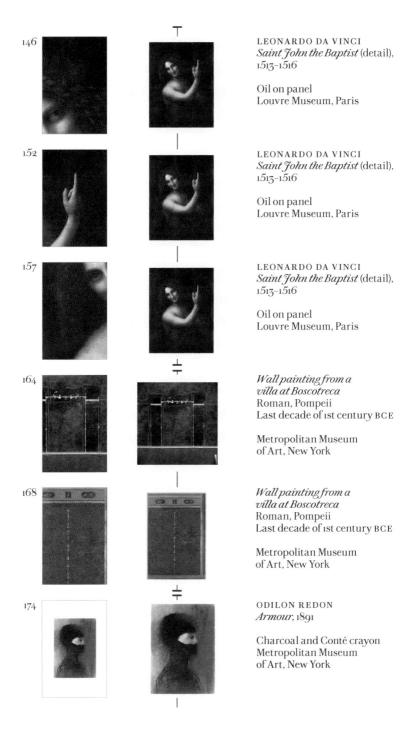

146 LEONARDO DA VINCI
Saint John the Baptist (detail),
1513–1516

Oil on panel
Louvre Museum, Paris

152 LEONARDO DA VINCI
Saint John the Baptist (detail),
1513–1516

Oil on panel
Louvre Museum, Paris

157 LEONARDO DA VINCI
Saint John the Baptist (detail),
1513–1516

Oil on panel
Louvre Museum, Paris

164 *Wall painting from a
villa at Boscotreca*
Roman, Pompeii
Last decade of 1st century BCE

Metropolitan Museum
of Art, New York

168 *Wall painting from a
villa at Boscotreca*
Roman, Pompeii
Last decade of 1st century BCE

Metropolitan Museum
of Art, New York

174 ODILON REDON
Armour, 1891

Charcoal and Conté crayon
Metropolitan Museum
of Art, New York

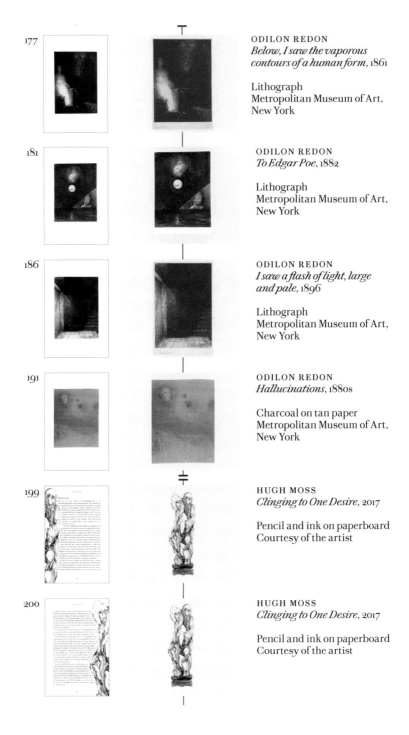

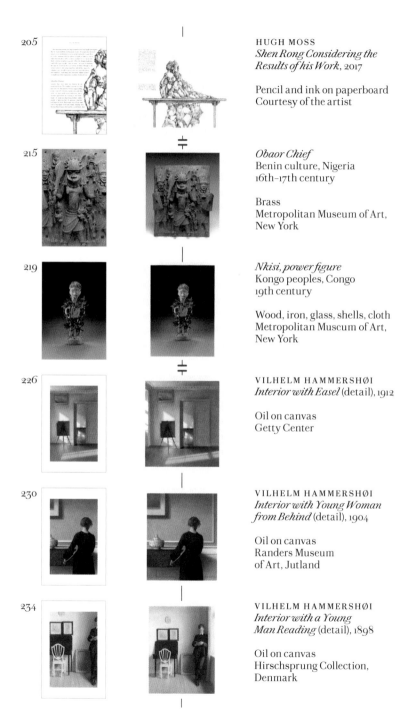

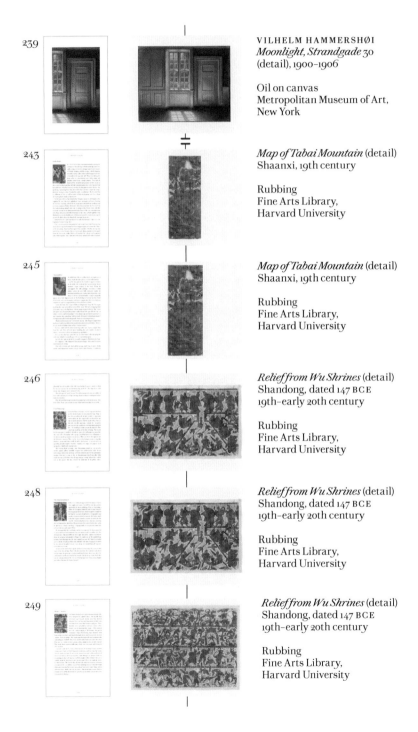

239 VILHELM HAMMERSHØI
Moonlight, Strandgade 30
(detail), 1900–1906

Oil on canvas
Metropolitan Museum of Art,
New York

243 *Map of Tabai Mountain* (detail)
Shaanxi, 19th century

Rubbing
Fine Arts Library,
Harvard University

245 *Map of Tabai Mountain* (detail)
Shaanxi, 19th century

Rubbing
Fine Arts Library,
Harvard University

246 *Relief from Wu Shrines* (detail)
Shandong, dated 147 BCE
19th–early 20th century

Rubbing
Fine Arts Library,
Harvard University

248 *Relief from Wu Shrines* (detail)
Shandong, dated 147 BCE
19th–early 20th century

Rubbing
Fine Arts Library,
Harvard University

249 *Relief from Wu Shrines* (detail)
Shandong, dated 147 BCE
19th–early 20th century

Rubbing
Fine Arts Library,
Harvard University

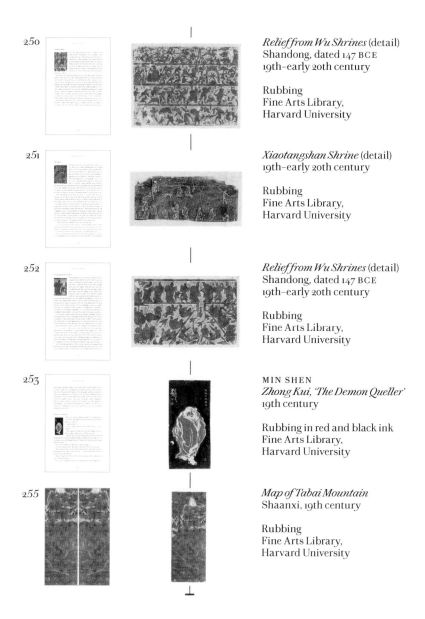

250

Relief from Wu Shrines (detail)
Shandong, dated 147 BCE
19th–early 20th century

Rubbing
Fine Arts Library,
Harvard University

251

Xiaotangshan Shrine (detail)
19th–early 20th century

Rubbing
Fine Arts Library,
Harvard University

252

Relief from Wu Shrines (detail)
Shandong, dated 147 BCE
19th–early 20th century

Rubbing
Fine Arts Library,
Harvard University

253

MIN SHEN
Zhong Kui, 'The Demon Queller'
19th century

Rubbing in red and black ink
Fine Arts Library,
Harvard University

255

Map of Tabai Mountain
Shaanxi, 19th century

Rubbing
Fine Arts Library,
Harvard University

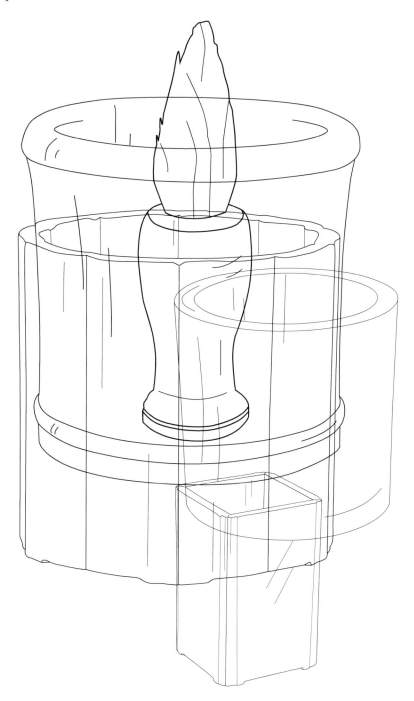

IT IS HARD TO PINPOINT all of the inspirations that lead one to create an entire world and its multitude of characters. Of course, any book of this kind, with its fable-like qualities, relies heavily on the stories one read as a child, be they by Hans Christian Andersen, Dr Seuss or numerous others. My first memory of the East was watching television series like *The Water Margin* and *Monkey*. In terms of more modern inspirations, the worlds crafted by P. G. Wodehouse in *Jeeves and Wooster*, William Goldman in *The Princess Bride* and Wes Anderson in most of his films, but most particularly in *The Grand Budapest Hotel*, have inspired me to create a time and a space that are slightly outside reality; close enough to be under-stood but separate enough to possess a sort of timeless stillness.

The most linear literary inspiration for the creation of this series of short stories is the work called *Strange Tales from a Chinese Studio* by the 17th-century Chinese writer Pu Songling. However, the most direct inspiration has been the exceptional 'scholars' objects' that I have had the privilege to handle and spend time with. For those with a further interest in these, I wrote a book in 2014 entitled *Custodians of the Scholar's Way: Chinese Scholars' Objects in Precious Woods* that not only introduces this field and celebrates these great artworks but also contains a number of the pieces that inhabit these stories.

Although the objects described in this book are open to the interpretation of the reader, their inspirations can be found in the dramatis personæ at the beginning of this book.

To further investigate the objects mentioned in these stories please visit: www.sylpheditions.com/cloudcollector

Colophon

EDITORIAL: Mona Gainer-Salim
DESIGN: Ornan Rotem

Set in Chiswick Text, a contemporary seriffed
typeface designed by Paul Barnes, influenced
by the British lettering tradition that began in
the 18th century.

Printed and bound in the UK by Zone Graphics,
on Mohawk Everyday and cover in Favini Lunar.

SYLPH EDITIONS · LONDON | 2021
ISBN 978-1-909631-39-7
www.sylpheditions.com